Ignition

Unknown Criminal

Written by: A.K. Patten

Legal Notice

Ignition: Unknown Criminal

"Anywho, you ready for your first raid Mr. Lons?"
-Dusk

Austin Patten
Acknowledgments

Wow. I'm finally here. A (self) published author. Not gonna lie it's pretty weird. Though pretty awesome to finally breathe and say "I'm done." Well, at least this one book. I have many plans for the future of the Ignition universe.

First things first, I want to thank YOU! The reader, who decided to buy this book. I really hope you find enjoyment from my first attempt in diving into my Sci-Fi universe!

However, I wouldn't be here if it weren't for some amazing people. My mom, besides the fact that I wouldn't be able to create this book without her bringing me to life. She had always been caring and supportive of my life decisions and I could never thank her enough for that. Life, yes, I have a friend named Life. That is not a nickname. Anyway, Life has been with me since the beginning of this writing journey and has always been willing to kick me in the butt to write or help destroy writers' block, even when bringing up random ideas out of nowhere. Just wanted to say thanks Life. Corbin, another great friend and also my roommate. He has always seemed to see the potential in my story telling, even when I don't. Though it may not seem like much to some, hearing those words always gave me some confidence to keep going. Thank you Corbin. Bec, a wonderful friend and a fellow indie author. She has been a great source of help, whether it was being inspired by her own works or even just talking about writing in general. Thank you Bec. Jordy, thank you for also being there to support me when I doubted myself, Especially when we play video games (Which I know we need to play more.). Thank you Jordy. Josh, hearing this man talk about the many, many, MANY stories he's read, it's been a blast using them as inspiration to help my own writing (Plus I know I need to play games with you as well.) Thank you Josh.

And to those I didn't mention here, you still helped me, even in small ways and I still want to thank you. Give yourself a pat on the back and I truly hope you all enjoy this story.

CHAPTER ONE

It was the late nights that hit Kane the hardest.

His dry, sore eyes soon forced themselves open. Within a few seconds, his eyes were blinded by the shining cyan lights above his bunk.

"Ah-" He grunted, clamping his eyes shut, trying to use a hand to rub them. Keeping them closed, Kane then sat up. With his head staying down, he reopened his eyes. Letting them adjust more comfortably on the floor. A few moments passed when he heard the electronic sounds of his companion soon booting up.

"Morning Helix."

The little sphere-shaped bot, known as a cybel soon floated down. The little screen that was his "face" was blank. Though after it landed on his owner's shoulders. A little smiley face " :) " appeared on the screen. Which Kane couldn't help but give a little chuckle to. "It's good to see you too buddy." Standing up, Kane ignored the tingling under his feet as they landed on the cool metal floor since he was more than used to it.

Spitting the toothpaste out of his mouth, he finished his normal morning routine. Little Helix being there to over-watch, as per usual. After a quick check in the mirror, Kane shrugged at the short mess of his hair.

"Good enough for me," he said before turning to leave the bathroom. Though he was halted by Helix, who didn't think twice before showing a " >:(" on his screen.

"What?" Kane asked, shrugging his shoulders at being suddenly stopped. To which Helix responded by baping his forehead.

"H-hey!" Helix then floated down back to his eye level. The image changed, this time showing a " :(". Then played a little animation of a tear rolling down the little face. Now he's just being dramatic.

"Ok! I'll comb it!" Kane then conceded, turning back to the mirror. Taking his comb, which was waiting patiently by the toothbrush he began to softly comb his hair. While doing so, Helix soon swooped in to nuzzle Kane's cheek easily breaking the originally annoyed look on his face. As he felt the almost soft touch as his little buddy nuzzled him another chuckle escaped from Kane.

"Alright alright. I love ya too bud."

It wasn't long before Kane made his way to the bridge with a nice hot cup of coffee in his hand, soon seeing they were still in hyperspace. The muffled hum of the engines doing their work. Autopilot doing its job while the consoles along the bridge were bright with life. The screens flashing, showing off the status of different functions within the ship while the room echoed with the sounds of computing. Taking a seat in his chair, he observed his bridge. Even though it was rather small and he had no crew to his name, well except for Helix of course. He smiled, enjoying the surprising amount of speed coming from his basic AI installed on his ship.

"Heh, guess waiting for you to go on sale really paid off." Kane mumbled to himself, taking a sip of his coffee before picking up the small datapad resting on the chairs armrest. With the quick press of the power button, the hologram soon projected on the pad. Showing the inventory list of the cargo he was carrying. Nothing too special, just some supplies for one of the outer colonies. *Gwars*, Kane read on the address on the file.

"Not the first time we've been to this little planet huh, Helix?" He asked, though not actually expecting an answer as he saw Helix on his shoulder display a " ;) ". Kane was about to enjoy another drink of his coffee but stopped himself when he felt the ship slow down. He held the top of his cup to avoid splashing, not worrying if any landed on his hand since it wouldn't be the first time and probably not the last. The ship vibrated for a few seconds before the planet zoomed into view. Kane's eyes widened.

Ignition: Unknown Criminal

"Whoa! A little close don't you think?" He asked, looking up as if he was expecting the ship to reply. Hearing a beep from his holo-watch. A message from the shipboard AI, Gwen. He opened it.

My bad, a minor miscalculation. It read.

With a light sigh, he placed the datapad down and rubbed his forehead.

"It's alright, we didn't crash into the damn place." He then heard the beep on the communication console. The flashing red light indicated it was urgent. Probably the union's station wondering why the hell they stopped so close to the planet. Without wasting another second he answered the call. The screen soon showed a union officer who began to speak the moment the connection was secure.

"This is the union station orbiting over the outsider's colony of Gwars. Identify yourself and your sudden business here." He ordered. His face seemed more...stern at the sight of Kane. Another beep came from his watch. Quickly darting his eyes down to read, he noticed it was another message from Gwen.

I advise caution, Union's weapons are currently locked onto us.

Well, guess he can't exactly blame them, his ship was quite close to the station in fact. Wouldn't be surprised if that officer pissed his pants at the sight of his ship jumping right in front of him. The station wasn't too big, although Gwars didn't exactly house a massive rebel presence. So, the union placed a smaller station to simply watch over the planet, to be able to deploy small arms infantry to subdue the populace if required. Though, they may have a few vehicles stored if needed. Possibly, a handful of fighters too, alongside with the weapons already trailing him. However, he soon also noticed the handful of beacons near the station. Which made more sense. If either triggered or destroyed. The beacons would immediately send a signal to the nearest union fleet or station.

"I'm Kane Lons, I apologize for the abrupt jump. I'm here to simply deliver supplies for the colony." He said calmly, sending his clearance along with the list of the supplies he was delivering. After soon receiving both, the officer began to view them. Taking a good few minutes to check them.

"Mhm..." His eyes squinted. As he read, a brow soon rose.

"Seems like a lot of equipment for a farming colony." He commented, looking up at Kane from the files. To which he simply shrugged.

"None of my business sir. I'm just the delivery boy." There was a slight chuckle coming from the background of the call who then quickly grunted as the officer glared at them. A few more seconds of silence passed before he finally closed the file.

"Alright, you seem to check out. So you're clear to enter." There was a slight sigh of relief coming from Kane.

"Thank you I-" He was then suddenly cut off as the call was discontented.

"Oh..." Kane sighed again, his arms then relaxing.

"Well, at least that's over with," he said walking to the front of the bridge.

"Bring us in Gwen," he ordered, watching the ship descend towards the colony's coordinates. For a brief moment, the ship began to rumble. Entering the planet's atmosphere. Watching the ship push its way down, seeing nothing but grey covering the view. A beep came onto the watch and again, Kane looked and read Gwen's message.

Entering the colony in two minutes, they seem to be expecting us, they have set up a ring of flares along one of the fields. A handful of colonists are waiting. Should I land us there?

Flares? A little old school, but it's their supplies. Where they want them to be sent is up to them. Kane thought to himself.

"Yes, Gwen," he simply replied. Helix soon floated next to Kane's face. A " ? " on his screen.

"I know bud, it's strange. But I'd rather not piss off a group of farmers. Especially since they are willing to pay well for this shipment." He said, giving the little bot a pet.

"So, let's make this quick so we can go home. Maybe finally take that break?" He asked, giving a soft laugh as he saw Helix spin with a " :D " on his screen. Soon slowing down to nuzzles the side of Kane's cheek. Seeming to be very excited about the idea to be home.

Light soon shined into the bridge, and the colony was now in view. The colours of orange and pink covered the inside of the ship, trying to mix with the blue lights already inside. It must be morning...or evening. After doing this for a while, it became quite hard to tell the difference. Not that it mattered. The ring of flares that Gwen mentioned also came into view. It was in a field roughly a kilometre or two away from the colony. Kane tried not to think about it as the ship took them there. The people working below, a pretty even mix of humans and gwarians. Gwarians, a lizard-like race which were normally much less powerful in terms of technology but had almost next level abilities when it came to agriculture and farming. It was thanks to that they became rather great allies with the United Galactic Government or known as the U.G.G.

11

Ignition: Unknown Criminal

Trading their skills and farmers for the union's technology and protection.

The ship then softly landed in the field, Gwen making sure they landed within the circle of flares. The ramp of the ship soon came down with Kane walking down the moment it finished, Helix perched on his shoulder. He was greeted with a male gwarian, who easily towered over him. Standing a good seven feet tall.

"Kane Lonssssss?" He asked. The two behind him, humans, had *S7-SMGs* in their hands. Though, like with the officer, Kane stayed calm. Even offered a casual smile.

"That's correct. And you are..." He then pulled out the datapad checking for the name for the order.

"Ahhh, here it is. Eng Wares?" He asked, looking back up at him. With a firm nod, Eng waved the guards to come to unload the ship. Though it bothered Kane seeing strangers enter his ship, he would rather take the help. Since it was a large order.

"Thank you for accepting thisssss. We are in need of extra suppliessssss." He explained, watching the guards carry out the various crates.

"Of course, with how much you were offering for the delivery. Seems like it would've been a crime to decline." He said with a chuckle. It seemed the Eng didn't exactly get the joke and just watched him blankly, making Kane's chuckle a little awkward.

"U-um, so why did you need all of the supplies? I mean it seems like quite a lot. If you don't mind me asking." Kane quickly added the last part, not wanting to get onto bad terms. Eng then turned back to the crates being unloaded. Seeing the larger ones being moved now.

"Things may be changing here. I just wish to be prepared." He replied, eyeing the larger crates being placed down carefully. This answer definitely kept Kane's attention.

"Changing? What do you mean by that?" He questioned with his arms crossed. Eng, however, squinted his eyes, staying quiet for a moment.

"You will find out in time..." was all he said. Kane couldn't help but roll his eyes at this. "Alright, well your men should be done soon. So just sign here..." He handed the pad to him.

"And pay the agreed fee and I shall be on my way," he said rather professionally. Wanting this to be over with at this point. Without further question, Eng signed the pad and grabbed his space credit card.

After the payment was complete Kane shook Eng's hand before heading back to his ship.

"I'll see you around." Kane ended with a quick wave, closing the ramp behind him and made his way back to the bridge.

"Gwen, we're done here. Take us home." The ship then began to launch. Feeling the slight vibration as the ship booted up, Kane looked down as more people came in to help move the crates into the colony. He then saw Eng, staring right at him. Taking him off guard, he just looked back at him. W-what is he doing? He was still confused when he said that things may be changing. But this time he was starting to get disturbed. It was Helix that got him to snap out of his thoughts. Bumping into the side of his head.

"Huh? Oh sorry." He apologized with a nervous smile. Helix tilted himself displaying a " :(? ". Kane then smiled more brightly and gently patted his little friend.

"Don't worry about him. Who knows what he was talking about. Besides, we're done. So let's be happy ok?" Then the old image was gone and was replaced with a " :) ".

"There we are." He smiled himself, leaving the bridge to enjoy his cold coffee.

Seeing Kane's ship leave the planet soon jumping back into hyperspace, the union officer began to make a call. To which an unknown user answered.

"Sir, Kane has left the planet. Orders?" The other was quiet for a moment before replying.

"I'm sending a team of *Specters* to the planet. Have whichever forces you may have at the ready." The officer's eyes widened at that.

"*Specters,* sir? Are you sure that's necessary? Surely I can-" He was then interrupted by a rather booming,

"**YES!!**" The officer nearly jumped from his spot. Sweat forming on his forehead.

"They will arrive shortly, give them the colony's coordinates and send in reinforcements if required. Understood?" The officer took a moment to swallow. Taking hold of his shaking hand.

"Y-yes sir. Understood. And what about Kane?" he then dared to ask. There was a muffled chuckle in the background of the unknown user's call.

"Don't worry about him, a team should be already waiting for him. I should be getting a report soon. I'll expect one from you as well." The officer nodded, unsure if the other actually could see his face or not. Though he got his answer when the other replied.

"Good, I'll be in touch with you soon." With that, the call was disconnected.

CHAPTER TWO

Harmony, one of the U.G.G's most prosperous worlds,
rested nearly dead center within the core worlds. Besides
Earth, at least what Earth used to be, many seem to see it as
the capital of the U.G.G. Being that it was just as plentiful
with resources alongside managing to keep its beauty. Its
almost artificially bright green lights shining throughout the
dark corners of space. Spread along the whole perimeter of
Harmony was an array of U.G.G stations, most were the
heavy-duty defense platforms. Packed with fighters and
even Z-21 Bombers. Tons of turrets varying from rail guns,
missile launchers, and laser defense points planted along
each one of these behemoths. Ships, most of which
consisted more of the medium-sized frigates and cruisers,
sat alongside these stations, creating only a few entry points
to the planet.

On the surface, massive megacities lay along the
land. Along the few untouched areas of the planet peaked
the largest skyscrapers. The purple lighting definitely made
it stick out among the rest of the cities, which stayed
usually within a grey or green color scheme. This city was

known as New Flon. Home to the wealthiest and most powerful people of all races within the U.G.G. Among these people were the galactic leader of the U.G.G or G.L for short.

Alan Dokes is a very interesting and special candidate for the position. What was twice as surprising for most was his high popularity followed by the extensive number of votes he accumulated to eventually earn the title.

"Ah, I see you've finished eating sir," his butler, Hans noticed. Stepping into the rather larger dining area. His footsteps echoing lightly throughout the room. Walking past the medium-sized, rectangular table. Much smaller then one would expect from someone as powerful as Alan. Various paintings of retro-styled robots and other science fiction rested on the walls. A style that most found unpleasant or even insulting, though Alan seemed to have a different perspective on the art. Hans then brought his attention back to Alan, who had a smile on his face as he placed his fork and knife on the plate neatly.

"Yes, it was quite delicious," he commented as he stood up from his seat. "Thank you Hans. We should get ready, wouldn't want to keep United Galactic Government officials waiting now do we?" Handing over the already organized plate to him. To which Hans greatly appreciated bringing out his hands to take the plate. However before he could reply, Hans soon found himself needing to suddenly duck down to quickly save the nearly fallen dishes! Alan gasped before taking hold of his arm, the mechanical one as the hand had a light spasm. He took a few steps back from his butler in case it may not only be his hand that will decide to move out of his control. Especially since nearly his whole left side was no longer organic. Hans then stood up, giving a sigh that nothing was broken.

"Good catch Hans," Alan said, not even thinking of releasing his arm until the hand calmed down. Which thankfully only took a minute or so. Meanwhile Hans was already at work with putting the dishes in the automatic sink that began to clean the dishes the second he dropped them in. Then pressed the holographic button labeled on the wall "Doc.".

"Sir, Doc has been called. It should be only minutes before he arrives." Hans assured him as he came back to the dining area to check on his master. Seeing he was now sitting down, with a sturdy grip on his arm. Alan's eyes didn't dare to move as he kept an ear out for the door.

"Thank you Hans." He said sharply, breathing deeply in hopes of calming the immense pain shooting throughout his arm. He couldn't help but clench his jaw and wince at even the smallest movements his robotic arm would make. Trying his hardest to stop the movements only to find himself not helping the situation.

It was a few more agonizing minutes later before the doc came in. Quickly opening the door.

"Alan! How bad is it?" he asked, already more than aware of the problem. Seeing Alan holding the other arm as hard as he could. Hans then got to work clearing the table. Moving everything off and out of the way. The doctor wasted no time placing his case on the table. Hans cringed a little at the surprisingly loud THUMP from the doctor's case. Though it seemed the table was able to handle it. Using a free hand the doctor then waved Hans over, opening his case. Showing the various tools at his disposal. Hesitant at first, Hans turned to Alan, who nodded.

"It's okay, go help him." After a shaky nod, Hans brought his eyes back on the doc. Who didn't wait any longer to get his tools out.

"Come! We must hurry. Thankfully it seems the surges this time are only light. But if we don't handle this now..." The doctor didn't even need to finish to get Hans moving. Soon stopping beside him, the doctor moved swiftly to get his tools in place. Sliding his skinny form past the butler.

"Alright, Alan. Please rest on the table." He started. Alan sighed before standing up and gently placing himself on the table, facing the ceiling as he laid on his back. Hans then took in a breath at the sight of Alan's arm. The unnatural twitchy flexes the fingers and hand would make was enough to disturb Hans.

"Alright." He looked at the doctor, who tapped his fingers along the table in front of his tools. As if trying to decide which one to use. Though, he turned to face Hans who then asked,

"How can I help?"

——

Within a few hours, Kane's ship began exiting the jump, looming over his home-world of Para V. The dark blue hues shining lightly into the bridge. Kane then stood up and walked closer to the glass. No matter how many times he's returned home, the sight of Para V was always beautiful, swearing he could feel the warmth of his home already. Though Para V was mainly a military world, on the edge of the inner colonies, call it his human attachments but he still found the planet special. His attention was then diverted to the large fleet of union defenses surrounding the border world. As if on cue, Kane received a message on the holo-watch and read from gwen.

Austin Patten

Incoming transmission...

Kane didn't even bother to finish reading and just waved his hand,

"Patch them through." He said, A union officer then appeared on his screen, though this one was far more familiar with Kane.

"Back from another job, Kane?" The officer asked casually.

"Of course, Admiral Scone. Just some deliveries in the outer worlds," Kane replied, "More than happy to be finally home." A light chuckle could be heard in the video feed from the high ranking officer.

"I bet, glad to see you came back in one piece. I've been getting reports of an increase of rebel activity recently. Haven't managed to run into any have you?" He asked, this time sounding more serious. Kane didn't blame him, from the odd reports Kane would listen to on the news the rebels have been becoming bolder in their attacks. Some groups even being able to challenge the U.G.G directly in the outer worlds.

"No sir, It's been clear deliveries for me thankfully. Most if not all of my work has been away from rebel areas," Kane replied. Though before he could ask if he was clear for entry, it seemed like the admiral wasn't done just yet.

"Has there been any suspicious activity with any of your clients? Any unusual requests perhaps?" He asked more sternly. Though, he kept his face to seem casual. Kane tried to keep himself calm, but the questions took him by surprise. Was Scone trying to interrogate him? Even with the increased activity from the rebels, Kane didn't expect this so soon.

"No sir, all of my clients are people of the U.G.G. Nothing else." The admiral then looked down and Kane heard the light scratching of a pencil before scone's eyes rose up to meet Kane.

"Thank you, Kane, I apologize for the sudden questioning but the Union wants to make sure nothing hostile enters the inner colonies. The border worlds are no exception." Kane gave a nod,

"It's more than alright admiral. I wish the U.G.G the best of luck with handling them. The recent news reports have been devastating, " he added sincerely.

"Indeed they have," the admiral replied before giving kane the green light. "You're free to enter, welcome home Kane." With that, the connection ended. Kane was able to let out a reliving breath of recycled air. Helix moved in to lightly nuzzle Kane's chest. Petting the little cybel, Kane felt Gwen take the ship to his apartment docking port.

"It's all good Helix, let's just get home, huh?" He said with a soft smile. To which Helix replied with a " :D " before twirling around in excitement.

It was a few minutes later that Gwen would begin the docking procedure at the apartment docking port. Kane took a seat as he felt the gentle rumble of the ship, soon hearing the muffled thumps of the docking clamps securing the ship in place before the engines would shut down.

"Good landing Gwen," Kane said before standing back up, now aware the ship has safely docked. Helix landed on Kane's shoulder displaying a little " ^w^ " On his screen which made Kane smile himself.

"Another happy landing, let's head home." He said walking out of his ship. Being on only the second floor, Kane just used the stairs once he entered the apartment. Taking out his ID to the scanner by his door, he waited for a second or two before hearing a beep, followed by the red light turning green as he heard the lock click. Kane opened the door and was hit with a potent but sweet aroma. He coughed a little trying to fan the scent away,

"Wow, I didn't expect the air fresheners to still be that strong." He coughed. In response, he heard a handful of beeps that sounded like a giggle on his shoulder. He then had the urge to facepalm at the sight of the closed windows. However, he opted to just sigh as he kicked off his shoes and tossed his coat on the arms of his couch. Opening the windows before stretching out his arms, now being in the privacy of his home he looked around the small suite. Enjoying the simple layout he called home. With Helix still resting on his shoulder, he opened the pantry and grabbed himself a bag of chocolate dips, bite sized chocolate covered biscuits. A treat specially reserved for a job well done. Which Kane definitely felt he deserved tonight, hearing the soft crinkle from the bag when he transferred it from the dark corners of the pantry to the light of his kitchen. After a light pry with his hands followed by a squeaky pop, Kane opened the bag of his chocolate dips before taking a seat on his couch. The moment he sat down his holo-TV turned on from the motion sensors. Automatically starting the U.G.G News channel. Normally, Kane would switch the channels. Not wanting to have some depressing story ruin his good mood.

But it was too late…

Before Kane was able to order to go to another channel, he heard the reporter bringing up Gwars with a handful of photos appearing beside her on the screen.

"W-what the-?" He choked, forcing himself to painfully swallow the dip before leaning in to listen.

"TV, turn up the volume to nine." Kane ordered. Hearing the volume gradually increase.

"A Gwars colony was assaulted by U.G.G forces after it was suspected to be a new holding ground for supplying the rebel forces within the outer worlds..." She started. Showing more clear images of the remains of the colony. Collapsed and burning buildings alongside dead corpses, both humans and gwarians littered the place. Kane gulped down. This was the very same colony he just delivered too! The one he saw outside the field he performed the delivery! A platoon of union security forces was scattered along the colony in the pictures. Though Kane squinted his eyes. Noticing most of them carrying very light weapons, SMG's at the worst. Seeing there was no way they managed to do so much damage.

"...In fact, the rebel presence was strong enough that *specters* were soon involved..." She continued, this time showing a video from what looked like it was filmed from a drone. It showed drop pods suddenly plunging onto the battlefield. Right in front of a large firefight between rebels and the security forces. The doors quickly ejected as the cybernetic soldiers came into view. From there it was all a blur. Rebels were being swiftly taken down. Some quite literally as a few of those rebels were being tackled. While other *specters* led the charge with the security forces right behind them. Kane watched in horror as the rebels were then all shot down. Even those who ran or even went to their knees were practically executed. Though muffled and distorted, Kane heard the begging and screaming from the rebels before being silenced by gunfire. There were no exceptions. Kane didn't even notice his hands shaking until Helix lightly bumped into his head.

"W-who...W-wh-" He was shocked. Trying to breathe as he placed his hands on his lap, wiping his hands on his pants in an attempt to remove the sweat.

"...Thankfully the U.G.G had a successful operation an-" Kane stood up and the tv was turned off. He couldn't watch anymore of that. The knots in the stomach forced him to bring a hand on his belly.

"O-oh god...T-that..I don't.." He stumbled across his words. Still processing everything he just witnessed. The slaughter of that colony, those rebels and on top of all he had unintentionally just supplied them. Then he remembered the questions from the admiral.

Did he know?

The very question twisted his guts even more. He groaned in pain as his breathing began to increase. Thoughts becoming more and more erratic. Helix soon floated down, softly nuzzling his owner's chest, making almost a robotic whine in worry. Kane brought an arm around him.

"T-thank you, Helix. I'm...okay.." He lied, though knowing he had to be.

"I'm glad to hear Mr. Lons..."

At that moment, Kane could have sworn his heart skipped a beat. It was as if he felt the laser sights on his back as he then slowly turned around to meet his intruders. Four Spec-Ops union soldiers all in black uniforms, helmets covering their faces appeared from different areas within the living room, deactivating their cloak. The sergeant, who was distinguished by the green glowing strips lined along the shoulders on his uniform holstered his rifle on his back as he approached Kane. Pulling out a pair of cuffs. The other three then circled him, Helix whimpered and backed into Kane's chest.

"H-hold on...w-were you wai-"

The sergeant who was closing in cut him off,

"Kane Lons, you are under arrest for supplying and possibly conspiring with rebel forces. You are a threat to the safety of the inner colonies and its citizens." He said professionally, stepping even closer. To which Kane instinctively stepped back. Helix looked at the other soldiers that also moved in on them. One of which brought out a Stun Gun and fired at Helix. The electrified shot smacked dead on. Forcing Helix to seize a bit before shutting him down, falling into Kane's hands.

"No! Helix!" Kane shouted, almost missing the sergeant lunging at him! Before the soldier could get a hold of Kane, with Helix cradled in his left arm he clenched his right hand into a fist. Slamming it into the side of the sergeant helmet. There was a light crack heard from his fist, shooting immense pain throughout the whole hand! But it was worth it as the sergeant clearly didn't expect any decent resistance from him. Groaning as he stumbled back a little.

"Oh...You little scumbag." He huffed. To which Kane attempted to use this little time to turn around but quickly felt the butt of a rifle smashing into his face! Collapsing to the ground, his vision blurring he saw the sergeant soon come into view. Taking a firm grip of his hands to place the cuffs on. Then yanked him back to his feet.

"You rebel filth." He spat in disgust before sending a punch into Kane's gut. Making him cough into a wheeze. Grabbing the cuffs that held Kane's hands together the sergeant began to walk to the door.

"Mission complete, let's get the prisoner out of here," he ordered. The rest lowered their weapons, beginning to follow.

Then, there was a sudden shine of light bursting into the apartment.

"What the hell is that?" One of the soldiers asked. Struggling to aim at the windows as the beam began to light up the whole suite.

"We didn't order back up!" Another shouted, soon following the steps of her other. The sergeant kept a tight grip of Kane's cuffs, wiping a pistol out of his holster.

"That's not one of ou-" They all froze as they all heard the hum of an energy weapon charging up.

"Everyone get dow-" The sergeant didn't even get to finish as the entire suite was unloaded with energy projectiles! One of which shredded the sergeant's chest he flew into one of the kitchen walls. Taking Kane with him. Who fell onto the floor beside the dead soldier. Glass and other pieces of furniture shot up and shattered around the place as the soldiers scattered for cover. One getting his head blown off. Gore and brain matter splattering on the floor as he fell on the counter. Dust then covered the rooms as the aircraft kept on firing. Kane forced his eyes closed and turned around on his stomach before opening them again. Soon realizing he lost Helix. He took a moment trying to search for him. Still hearing the other soldiers trying to fire at the craft.

"Where's the sergeant?" One of them shouted through the chaos.

"He's dead! We gotta get out of he-" The voice was then cut off, followed by a thud.

"O-oh God!" She screamed, and Kane turned his head from hiding behind the counter to see her sprinting out of his suite.

After that, the firing soon stopped. The light disappeared as Kane shakily raised his head from the counter. Almost instantly stepping back at the sight of the headless corpse on his counter.

"Ahh! G-god!" He screamed. Soon cursing himself internally for doing so. He looked down to see he was still cuffed. He slowly made his way to the sergeant, trying not to focus on the massive hole which was sizzling in his chest. Taking a second to swallow, Kane knelt down. Searching the pockets for the keys.

"Dammit...come on..." He mumbled under his shaky breath. His search was then halted as he heard a new set of footsteps coming! Was it that soldier coming back? The pilot of the airship? Kane had no idea, though neither sounded good. So he yanked the pistol out of the sergeant's hand and aimed it at the door…

CHAPTER THREE

It was chaos outside his door.

Screams soon filled the apartment after delayed alarms kicked in within the complex. Easily muting the footsteps that were probably still pushing their way to Kane's position. Though after a quick realization, he noticed he was wasting time. Placing the pistol down, he searched for the keys again. Within a few seconds he found them.

"Yes!" He celebrated shakily, hearing the click of the cuffs being removed. He then decided to use this moment to search for Helix. Since there was no way in hell Kane planned on leaving without him. With his eyes darting away from the door, his search began. After a quick look around the kitchen, which is where he was holed up to begin with. The only thing accompanying him was the corpses of the fallen soldiers. Standing up, he thanked himself for being close to the closet. He made his way cautiously to avoid stepping on any glass or scorched marks littered along the floor. With a little leap over a rather large burn on his floor. He quickly flung the closet door open and shoved his shoes on. Now at least feeling slightly more safe, he carefully stumbled his way to the living area. Half tripping over one of the bodies to quickly grab one of the couch's arms for support. There was a handful of crunches under his shoes as held on before regaining his balance. After that he didn't wait another second before scanning his eyes around the shattered mess that was his living room. What was left of the tv splayed in chunks along with the crushed coffee table. While his couch was riddled with the burns marks from the plasma. He didn't even want to notice the...leftovers that lay scattered on the floor. However, through it all he soon spotted Helix. He was pinned under one of the dead soldiers' arms.

"Helix! You alright?" He asked, almost out of instinct. Pushing himself away from the arm before kneeling down by the corpse. Hesitant at first, Kane took in a swallow before lifting the soldier's arm up.

I swear if you move...

A sigh of relief was released as Kane felt no tension from the arm. With his other hand, he scooped Helix from the floor and held him gently in his arm. Back on his feet, Kane began to quickly inspect Helix. The weapon only seemed to have forced Helix to shut down. No actual damage was done to him.

The screams soon began to die down, leaving Kane with the blaring alarms and the possible silenced footsteps. If Kane was lucky whoever was coming was forced to evacuate with the others. Kane soon turned back to Helix and after a press of the button on the top of his head, he watched Helix booting back on. After roughly ten seconds, Helix was back to floating and his screen displayed a " ? ". Alongside a few beeps in confusion. Kane just came in to lightly hug the little bot.

"It's good to have you back bud." He sighed. Though he knew he couldn't make the moment last and soon opened his arms to let Helix look around the apartment. Pistol still in his grip, Kane was ready to leave. His position has already been compromised.

"Alright Helix, I know it's a lot to take in but we have to go. Now." He ordered. Kane bit his tongue, feeling a little bad with how stern he was, and hating to have to order Helix. Helix, of course, did comply. Landing on Kane's shoulder before a little muzzle deployed out of the bottom front of Helix. A stun gun of his own. Seeming like Helix wasn't allowing himself to get caught off guard again. After a slight nod from Kane, he made his way to the sergeant's body one last time. Swiping the few extra magazines he had and stuffed them in his pocket. Before he could stand back up. Helix swooped down by the sergeant's boots displaying an arrow pointing down. Kane raised a brow. "Excuse me?" Kane was aware that Helix had programming to protect him and had an extra tactical advantage thanks to the...experience he's had with being hunted before. Plus Kane's shoes were a wreck thanks to the glass. With a sigh, he took off his shoes and after a light struggle, he managed to get the combat boots on. Which would definitely offer far more protection, alongside a small combat knife was magnetically sheathed to the right boot. Though a little big, Kane tightened them on before finally standing.

"Alright, let's go."

Flashing red and orange lights filled the hall from Kane's suite. Peeking his head out, Helix stayed close behind when Kane stepped out the seemingly empty hall. As they make their way to the stairs, Kane noticed the doors of each unit wide open. Guess Kane couldn't blame them, never in his life had he heard these alarms going off for an actual emergency. So when it came it must have horrified these people. Especially his neighbours, being right beside him when the ship started blasting into his suite. Kane then suddenly bumped into Helix, who seemed to have floated in front of him.

"W-wha-?" Helix then tapped his mouth. Making him shut up. Standing at the edge of the wall, the next turn would lead them to the elevator and across from it, the stairs. Tilting his head ever so carefully to the side Kane tried to see what disturbed Helix. At first, it seemed just as empty as the rest until his eyes came to the door leading to the stairs. A guard was there. Standing at attention, checking at every entrance. His face came towards Kane before he and Helix moved back. Hoping they weren't spotted, they waited a few seconds. Looking back at each other every now and then. Kane began to think.

"Helix, we're fine. Most of the soldiers that attacked us got shot down by that ship." He tried to assure his little bot. Though, he admittedly had a hard time believing the words himself. On the topic of the ship, Kane had wondered for a while what had happened to that ship and why the hell it even saved him.

"Hey! What are you doing here?!"

Kane took another step back by the sudden voice. Kane hid the pistol behind him, shuffling to get it in his pants. Helix floated right beside him as they both saw the guard before them, he didn't go for a weapon as he walked closer. Whipping out a thumb behind him to point to the staircase.

"There's an evacuation, you need to leave sir." He stated calmly. Kane took in a swallow, hands now at his sides.

"R-right sorry." He stammered with a light nod. Trying to walk past the guard he was stopped by an arm blocking him.

"You should've been with the crowd. I'm gonna need to see some identification." Looking back at the soldier's faceplate, only his reflection showed back to him. There was a split-second pause before Kane reached into his pocket, but there was nothing there.

"S-shoot, hold on." He mumbled, holding out his finger for a quick second in case the guard didn't hear him. Shoving his other hand into the pocket as his fingers wiggled within them searching desperately for his wallet. But again there was nothing.

"O-oh no..." He brought his head up to Helix before the guard again. "I-I can't find it...It must b-be in my suite." Kane tried to explain only for a hand to take hold of his wrist.

"What are you doing?" Kane exclaimed, struggling in the tight grip the guard had on him. A pair of cuffs

36

appeared in his other hand. Kane braced his arm to defend himself. Only to hear a screech from the guard after an electrified shock slammed into his back. Lighting up the hall with a series of white and blue for a second till the guard collapsed. Twitching for a few seconds on the floor. Behind where the guard was, Helix was floating closing his weapon back inside.

"W-whoa, thanks Helix," Kane said gratefully, rubbing his wrist. Looking down at the guard, an incoming transmission was coming through his communicator. Both Kane and Helix turned to each other before Kane answered.

"Attention all U.G.G security! A fugitive by the name of Kane Lons has infiltrated Para V! He has been suspected of being with the rebels and must be captured immediately! To any and all personnel who come into contact, use extreme caution! The fugitive has already eliminated security forces and must be taken either dead or alive!"

Kane found his legs shaking a little after the transmission ended. Helix floated down by Kane, A " !?? " In thick bold text on his screen followed by many beeps. Kane nodded shakily,

"Y-yeah, I know I don't have a perfect reputation with the U.G.G but this...this seems a little overkill..." He swallowed as he brought his head to the door. Wondering if

Ignition: Unknown Criminal

it was worth going down. Kane soon noticed the alarms within the complex began to die down. Only the muffled sirens followed by the even more muffled voices outside were heard. From the sounds of it, he and Helix were surrounded. Pistol back in hand, he crept carefully to the nearest suite. From there he peered over slowly to a window to get a view. Dozens of U.G.G security were circling the apartment. Most armed with hand-held firearms, some seemed to have been equipped with heavier firepower! Stepping away from the window Kane turned to leave the suite, noticing Helix was observing the halls.

"Find anything Helix?" He asked, catching up to the floating robot. "It won't be long before the U.G.G bust in here and I'd rather not test my skills at fighting over a dozen soldiers." He said, checking his pistol. Knowing he'd be forced to try to take down a few. However, even with Helix's help they wouldn't stand a chance against them all. Not that he wanted to take a life to begin with. Helix soon finished and came back to face Kane, only shaking himself side to side while presenting a " :(". A sad almost drooping beep was added. Kane sighed before cocking his weapon.

"Then I guess fighting huh?" He said before stepping away from the door. Helix soon deployed his stun gun.

Austin Patten

It took only a few seconds before Kane heard muffled orders being barked from the stairs. Followed a heavy set of footsteps. Kane backed away further, his heart thumping hard into his chest. Knowing he didn't have much time, he took cover in the closest suite. Hearing a faint rattle from the door handle. Within a quick motion, Kane saw a few metallic objects being tossed from the door before it closed again. Before Kane couldn't even process what was even thrown, Helix knew the very second his sensors detected them and blocked Kane's face. An array of flashes filled the halls for a good few seconds before the soldiers began to flood in! Helix didn't hesitate before firing a bolt at the first one in his sights. The bolt smashed right in the soldier's chest! Knocking him back as the electrified intensity forced him to have a seizure.

"Man down! Open fire on the rebels!" The leader of the squad ordered. The rest of the squad swiftly brought up their weapons and fired. Any other orders were soon muffled from the gunshots as Kane took cover with Helix right behind him. Bullets ripped into the walls while zipping past the pair. Kane panted, sweat dripped down his face.

"Oh God, oh God!" He screamed. His arms shook as the gunfire not only continued but seemed to get louder! Helix floated out a little to fire another bolt, another muffled scream would echo in response. He soon floated down to his panicking owner. Pressing lightly into Kane's chest.

"I-I can't Helix." He stuttered. His pistol shook in his hand as he looked at it. Was he actually gonna kill a man today? He's had close calls with the U.G.G in the past. But never once he found himself having to kill. Helix soon looked up at Kane, nothing was displayed this time. The blank screen reflected his face, showing how much of a mess he was. With a sigh, he nodded.

"Alright...Alright." He brought up the pistol with both hands. "I'm ready," he said in a deadly serious tone. To which after a handful of aggressive beeps Helix displayed a " >:(".

With his sweaty palms gripping the pistol tightly, Kane waited a few seconds for the firing to calm down for a few of the soldiers to reload before peeking to fire back. As adrenaline kicked in, he didn't hesitate when to pull the trigger. Firing two then three shots at the closest soldier. Each shot slammed into the soldier's body armour. Kane cursed under his breath when he quickly noticed he did little to no damage to the soldier besides pushing him back and forcing him to go into cover. As another hail of bullets ran across the hall Kane was a split second too late as a bullet grazed Kane's arm. Causing light bleeding, Kane sucked in a breath of air trying to ignore the burning pain. There was a faint

"Move up!" heard within several gunshots. Panic soon began to return through Kane when he brought out his hand with the pistol and started firing blindly. His finger and hand getting sore at the heavy recoil from each shot. Throughout his blind execution, Kane actually managed to hit one of the oncoming soldiers when he heard a scream. Possibly just injuring them. However, none of that soon mattered when his weapon was no longer firing. Pulling his hand back Kane saw the ammo counter was now red with a zero shown. He scrambled to get on his feet, another bolt was fired from Helix before they backed into the suite. The firing soon stopped and was replaced with a heavy series of footsteps sprinting to their location. Kane moved to dash behind the couch. It didn't even take a few seconds before the room began to light up. Bullets being fired in random areas of a living room and kitchen. While in his cover, Kane ejected the empty mag from this pistol. Just letting it fall to the floor when he searched his pants desperately for a fresh one to reload. Helix floated up to fire another bolt, however before he could release the shot the soldiers didn't hesitate this time as they shot him up. Some of the bullets deflected off Helix's shell but one managed to pierce his screen.

"N-NO! Helix!" Kane shouted. Watching his little buddy sputter in the air before falling to the ground. As much as Kane wanted to go to him in an attempt to both comfort and repair him. The gunfire behind him reminded him of the current danger he was in. After a struggle, he finally reloaded the pistol. Seeing the shadows of the soldiers closing in. He moved back and quickly pulled up the pistol to fire a shot at the closest soldier's face. One of the others shouted

"NOOO!" Before suddenly running in. Kane couldn't even react before feeling the soldiers boot smash into the side of his face. His vision blurred immensely. Kane laid there as he then saw a hand come in to rip the pistol out of his hand. After a painful blink, he saw the barrel of a rifle right in front of him. Kane's eyes widened. His breathing quickened as he tried to brace himself for death. Only to hear a muffled.

"Stop! We're taking them alive! Cuff him," The other ordered. There was a moment of silence, the soldier who aimed at Kane looked at him before she replied with a low,

Austin Patten

"Yes, sir." She placed her rifle on her back and brought out a pair of cuffs. Quickly cuffing his hands together. When the others left, Kane couldn't even get a word out before she kicked him in the stomach. A very faint wheeze was heard before her fist met his face.

Then it was all black...

CHAPTER FOUR

"Alan, you must stay still!"

Though only minutes had passed by, it felt like hours. The pain had surged dramatically the moment the doctor got to work. With a panel opened along his mechanical wrist. Doc wasted no time getting to work. Using a handful of tools that Alan nor Hans knew much about. Though the poking mixed with the electrical pain was horrible, Alan had been able to keep himself still. Even though this has not been his first time on this table Alan wished he would be used to this by now.

"A-Ack! H-how bad is it doc?" Alan asked, his voice a sharp whisper in pain. The doctor though decided to stay quiet. Concentrating on his work.

"I think you're doing fine sir." Hans tried to chip in, hoping to calm his master down. Though in all honesty, if Alan was afraid, he did an excellent job hiding it. His face stayed serious besides having to wince every now and then from a sudden shot of pain.

"Thanks Hans." Alan said, trying to make a smile for him, but it didn't last.

Austin Patten

It was after a few more painful minutes before the doc closed and sealed the hidden panel on Alan's wrist.

"There, I apologize for being silent with you, Alan. But I needed to be fully concentrated. This is still relatively new technology to us..." He said with a slight bow, getting his tools back to his case. Alan sat up, flexing his mechanical fingers. Being more than relieved that the pain was gone. Though he couldn't seem to help but give a sigh,

"Well, technically you're wrong, doc," he corrected. Watching the doctor paused for a moment, who rubbed his temple lightly before clearing his throat and continuing to gather his tools.

"Your arm and other robotic components should be good Alan." The doctor added abruptly. No longer facing Alan, he gave a light nod before leaving. At first, Alan was tempted to force the doctor to face him but chose not to. In the end, the doctor had done his job. So without another word from either the doctor left.

Hans didn't wait any longer before making his way to his master. Bringing out a hand for assistance. There was a light chuckle from Alan as he extended an arm of his own to accept the help.

"Thank you, Hans. Don't know what'll do without you." He said. Stretching out his arms once he was back on his feet. Feeling more than relieved now.

Ignition: Unknown Criminal

"You think these...problems will be over soon sir?" Hans asked, hated seeing him in this immense level of pain so often. His hands were together now, back straightened as he was ready to work as soon as Alan needed him. Though the only thing Alan could really offer as a response was a shrug.

"I honestly don't know..." he replied quieter than he meant too. It wasn't exactly a whisper, though silent enough that the old man needed to put a hand to his ear.

Before either could continue, a sudden beep in Alan's office soon made Alan jolt.

"Oh no..." Alan dashed into his office, seeing the noise coming from one of his various consoles on his desk. The repeating loop of electronic beeping was emitting from one of the communication terminals. Alan knew he didn't even need to check who was calling. Pace now quickening, Alan yanked a coat from his closet. Zipping it up while walking to the door. Hans seemed to have been done already, wearing an all-black coat of his own. The moment his eye spotted Alan he had opened the door and closed it behind them as they left the large living quarters. Security guards were stationed on each side of the door, both giving a nod to Alan.

"Sir," they both said in sync. Alan gave a hasty nod of his own as he made his way to the garage.

"I Informed a team to escort us to the embassy," Hans reported, checking his holo watch. The yellow light soon turned green with a *Ding*. Hans then placed his arm down and turned back to his master.

"They're ready sir." Though Alan had acknowledged the information. He just kept on walking, if anything his speed only increased. There were a few more minutes of silence until Alan finally decided to reply, "Thank you, though it'll take more than a squad of union soldiers to protect me from this incoming nightmare."

Governor Oni stared silently at the holo table with the rest of the appointed government officials. Through the silence of the group, the repeating sound of beeping echoed in the room. Everyone watched the flashing red light that was accompanying the beeping. Waiting for their galactic leader to answer. A minute or so would pass… then the beeping would end.

"That's the second time he failed to answer..." Oni muttered sourly. Closing his eyes, Oni pinched the bridge of his nose. Ears turned back mumbling a curse in his main

language. Everyone else only heard a handful of meows
followed by some hisses.

"Curssssssing our galactic leader will do usss no
good." Governor Shek warned. Giving a hiss of her own.
Standing from her seat, as if daring the lykoi to keep going.
This took a few of the other members off guard since
gwarians were usually quite passive. Watching Oni intently
when his eyes opened. Bringing his attention back to her he
rose a paw.

"Fair enough governor, my apologies." he said.
Which seemed to be good enough for her. The gwarian
soon sat herself down. Though she seemed to have calmed
down. Shek couldn't resist giving a glare at Oni, who chose
to simply ignore her. His whisker giving a twitch from the
annoyance of her stare.

Before the possibility of this escalating farther, a
muffled commotion was heard outside of the door.
Everyone turned to the door. Trying to listen in to what was
going on. There were hushed apologies followed by a
rather sudden,

"They're waiting for you sir." The voice came from
Hans. Nearly everyone was able to recognize him as a
handful of sighs filled the room.

"About time," Oni huffed, crossing his arms.

48

The door then opened.

Backs were straightened at the sight of Alan. A few throats were cleared while some watched intently. Closing the door behind himself, Alan made his way to the end of the table.

"You're late."

The words echoed throughout the room. Some eyes were widened from the harsh tone that came from Oni. Alan seemed unfazed, keeping a neutral face as he gathered his thoughts for today's meeting.

"I apologize..." He started, taking a seat. Facing everyone as his hands rested on the table.

"There was another issue with my..." Alan stopped to lift his robotic hand, flexing his fingers. A few began to murmur among each other. Most just nodded in response.

"We understand Galactic Leader." Governor Jun spoke up, bowing slightly in his seat. His own robotics shifting, creating a light hum as he moved. Alan smiled at the anvol's kind words. He appreciated that at least someone was actually able to understand. Since anvol's were entirely mechanized beings. Alan could only guess how horrible a glitch on the entire body must be like. Part of him shivered at the thought.

Governor Shek then cleared her throat loudly too soon to gather everyone's attention.

Ignition: Unknown Criminal

"Well, now that everyone'sssss here. Shall we prosssseed?" She hissed kindly, facing Alan with the others. Alan took in a breath, already quite aware of what this meeting is about.

It's solving that's going to be the issue. After a few seconds of silence, Alan stood up. Pressing a button under his side of the table to activate a holographic keyboard. The screen appeared right after. Using a hand to swipe it forward. The screen then was placed in the center of the table, expanding in size. Everyone gazed at the blank screen, hearing the faint beeps from the typing.

A video played on the screen.

The official's expressions stiffened. Screams of agony and a ripple of gunshots filled the room. The sight of countless bodies falling to the ground, to then see Union marines and specter's move in. Many voices shouted orders while others attempted to flee the massacre.

Then the video stopped.

Oni was the first to break the silence afterward.

"As we all know, our intelligence had assumed there have been rebels housed in Gwars for..." He sighed, glaring at governor Shek. "...some time. Thanks to the additional information I had received from the Union station posted on Gwars." He reported confidently. Eyes were now on

Shek, since her homeworld was her responsibility. There were gonna be plenty of questions coming her way. Though hidden under the table, her purple hands were clenched tightly. A low growl could be heard.

"Ssssssending troops on my planet wasn't necessssssary!" She bursted out, her hands slamming on the desk. Startling her assistant sitting beside her. He whimpered softly as he looked up Shek standing up. A sharp finger then pointed directly at Oni.

"An attack this big sssssshould've been discussed before pointing weaponsss at my people!" The gwarian Governor was breathing heavily after her little rant. Everyone, especially Oni could tell she'd wanted to continue. But she forced herself to stop, though she kept on standing. Alan then rose a hand, bringing everyone's attention to him.

"I agree with governor Shek. This was more than unfair to you and your people. Regardless of the information Oni had." His eyes narrowed at the now slightly wounded lykoi. Earning a smirk from Shek as she crossed her arms.

"But Galactic Leader I only-" He then was cut off by Alan.

"However, as unjust as this was to the gwarians. It seems you've dealt a powerful blow to the rebels. That is something that has pleased me." It was now Oni's turn for a smirk. As the gwarian couldn't help from her eye twitching.

"T-this is absssurd!" She hissed! Though Shek soon turned down the hostility. Taking a seat and bowing her head.

"My...my apologisessss Galactic Leader." Alan was resting on his hands as he listened. "Itssss...the reports of what happened to the city of Teros was devastating to ussss all. I'd hope there would've been lessss casualtiessss."

As Alan took a moment to process everything that had happened, Oni's ears dropped slightly. Admittedly, he was so proud of his achievement of conquering such a large rebel cell. He never really noticed the possibility of civilian loss at the time.

"My deepest apology Governor Shek." He said mournfully. The gwarian governor peeked her head up. The sad expression still on her face.

"An apology won't bring my people back," she shot back coldly. Oni seemed struck by the reply. Alan rose a brow, his eyes trained on the guards. In case anything were to happen.

"But..." Shek continued.

"I appreciate it..." she finished. Handing a small smile back at Oni. Who nodded, visibly showing his relief.

"Now." Alan abruptly started. "We need a plan of action from here on out. Starting with Gwars." He turned back to Shek. She gulped lightly.

"What would the galactic leader like?" She asked with a hint of nervousness had slipped in her voice. Typing on the keyboard, he removed the video file and brought in a text document. Titled: *Bill 217*.

Both governor Shek and her assistant's eyes widened at the new document.

"Bill 217?!" She blurted out. Honestly terrified seeing that in front of her… again. Alan nodded silently. Opening the contents of the document. Now everyone could read it. Though everyone had only kept their attention on the core specifics of what the bill would do:

Bill 217:

Bill 217 will enable the enactment of an updated set of mandatory laws and regulations for the citizens living on worlds under the bill.

These laws include but are not limited to:

-Increased security both planetside and orbital.

-Enforced Curfew, effective for all citizens

Ignition: Unknown Criminal

-Increased number and intensity of Identification checking within the planet under bill 217

The list of restrictions, rules, regulations and the fact the U.G.G would be able to pump more troops into Gwars devastated the governor.

"When I first proposed bill 217 to your homeworld governor Shek, it was meant to only be temporary. A sweep of the planet from the intel we had prior." He began, keeping his eyes locked onto her. He paused, seeing everyone's faces at the corners of his eyes. No one dared interrupted. Since they knew exactly how this was going to turn out.

"However...after recent events. I think we can all agree that bill 217 must be enacted on Gwars." He said coldly. "I am sorry Governor Shek, but after finding a rebel force as large as this. I can't believe that this is the only one hidden on your planet."

When Alan had finished, the silence that followed after was deafening. No one spoke a word. A few gulps were heard, one was from Shek's assistant. Who had been just as if not more nervous about this. It was Governor Genx who broke the silence. His large self sitting up. The hellion had a somber look on his face, the scar alongside his cheek only made it more saddening.

"I understand your concerns, Shek." Though he tried to keep his voice at a normal volume, there was still quite a boom coming from him as he spoke.

"When 217 was pushed onto Kell. The struggle for my people was terrible." His facial expression began to fight with his emotions. Trying to find the words to show that he knew the pain, but also wanted to show a sign of hope.

"Your people, however, like any powerful race, like us, will adapt. Learn how to survive in these new conditions. And with time. 217 could not only make your citizens but YOU stronger." Genx had intentionally raised his voice as he pointed at her.

The Hellion took everyone off guard with that. The large blue creature soon took a seat after. Alan and his fellow human associates couldn't help but cringe slightly at Genx. His demon-like appearance, even down to his short wings brought a trickle of fear down his spine. Shek, however, was less than intimidated by him at this moment.

"Thank you governor Genx."

"Well, It'll still be down to a vote." Alan added. Turning his head around the whole table in case anyone wished to add anything else. Though the quiet stares answered that.

"Alright, all in favour of bill 217 being in effect on the planet Gwars raise your hand." It was simple, though most found it a little too simple galactic leader Alan wanted laws and rules to be decided as quickly as possible. Not wanting to wait for weeks or even months for an answer. Nearly everyone in the room, Alan included, raised their hand. In fact, the only officials who didn't raise their hands were Shek and Genx. Even with Genx's kind words. Shek still couldn't help but feel...guilty. Her head drooping.

"Then it is decided." She said quietly.

After that, most of the officials began to leave, formally saying goodbye to each other before exchanging a handshake. Governor Oni finished shaking Alan's hand.

"I'll make sure to spare some troops once the bill's have been officially announced," he offered, which made Alan smile.

"I'd appreciate that. Thank you Oni, take care." He thanked. The Lykoi nodded before heading out himself. Alan then turned. Seeing only Shek and her assistant left.

"So, I-I guesssse we have to...um...let our people know, yessss?" he said nervously. Unsure of her mood at the moment. He was about to place a hand on her lap to try to comfort her. Then suddenly Shek wrapped her arms around him. Hugging him tightly, though she was pretty quiet. Alan could hear the faint weeping from the governor as he began to leave. Closing the door behind him....

———

"Thank you Zensssss." Shek thanked. Sitting beside her assistant as they took the transport back to gwars. She rested her head on his yellow shoulder. Zens smiled softly. Keeping a hand on hers.

"Your mosssst welcome governor Shek," he replied. Looking ahead, he could see the other gwarian guards with them. There were a few talking amongst each other. Just small talk. Most were excited to head back home. Even with the bill being enabled.

There was a muffled *Whump* followed by being tugged back. The jump to Gwars had finished. Both Shek and Zens looked out the window. The orange and pink planet grew larger and larger as they flew closer. Shek sighed as she stayed rested by Zens. At that moment she felt safe...calm. Even relaxed. Her eyes fighting to stay awake. Zens messaged her hand gently.

"Maybe you sssssshould rest? You sssseem exhausted." He commented. Noticing the light-coloured bags under her eyes. They didn't seem too noticeable but she must have been tired. And he knew it may only get worse from now on. She nodded, allowing her eyes to be shut.

"Mmm...Wake me once we land," she ordered gently. Resting on his shoulder as she began to enjoy her nap. There was a light snore as she slept. Zens couldn't help but find it a little cute. Though he forced himself to keep the situation serious. Trying to remove the blush that was forming on his cheeks. Besides he knew his chances with her would be slim to none. The various colours from the planet began to shine through the window. A vibration was soon felt as they flew through the planet's atmosphere. Zens decided to simply enjoy the quiet time he had with her. Knowing, sadly, it wasn't going to last.

CHAPTER FIVE

Kane was barely able to get another cough out before another fist plowed into the side of his face! Making the already existing bruise worse while shooting blood across the wall. Kane felt his vision blur. His face ached followed by blood dripping down his nose. Kane then blinked out of his thoughts, noticing after the third punch the soldier had stopped. As he painfully brought his eyes up he saw a hand placed on the attacker's shoulder. He soon found his head to be very heavy and soon found it slumping back down.

"That's enough corporal. You got your three hits in. Now let the prisoner be." The other voice ordered. Hearing two sets of footsteps walk away from Kane, he felt his tired eyes close…

"We should kill him now." A voice growled. It was faint, but Kane was able to hear it. Even on the other side of the transports thick doors. His head was spinning, aching. From both the physical pain and the fact he was suddenly a wanted criminal. His emotional distress has hardly calmed since he was ambushed by those soldiers. And after surviving two firefights, the last thing Kane wanted to do was stay awake. Let alone think. However, he forced his head up anyway.

The first thing he noticed was how tight the space was. It was as if he invited four armed guards to his bedroom. Two of the guards were stationed on each side of Kane. The other two sat across from him. Not a word was said; there was just silence and the light rumble of the road.

The argument behind doors continued. It was quieter this time. Kane noticed he was unable to listen this time as it was far too muffled for him to understand. Not that it mattered, he could guess it was probably about him. The door then suddenly opened, making Kane jump a little in his seat.

A lykoi stepped out. Her helmet in her hand as she stomped towards Kane. Without any indication of a warning, she swooped her hand in to clutch his face. Forcing it to face the door.

"This criminal must be dealt with now!" She snarled, her grip tightening. Kane groaned in pain. Even with gloves on, Kane could feel the rather sharp pain of her claws on her grip.

Coming out of the door was an anvol. The screen of his rectangular face projecting a grim expression.

"I understand your pain corporal but we have strict orders to bring him in alive if possible. Thanks to you, we were able to do just that." He said. Walking up to her to remove her hand off Kane's face.

"Now take a seat, we should be back to the nearest union facility soon." He said walking back to the front of the transport, closing the door behind him.

She mumbled something that Kane couldn't exactly catch before slumping down across from him. Her arms crossed with her eyes narrowing down at Kane. Which made him straighten his back. Was it because he was frightened of her? Most likely, but it felt like an instinct to do so. She huffed at the sight of him, the human criminal has been nothing but a clear danger to both the squad and her. To think that someone that was able to assist that rebel trash was able to live in such a loyal world to the U.G.G practically disgusted the lykoi soldier.

"W-where's Helix?" He whimpered softly.

Kane's eyes showed nothing but pain and exhaustion. The lykoi's ears only flicked lightly at the sound of his voice.

"You mean that anvol cybel?" She asked with a sneer, "Why? Do you miss your pile of trash?" She spat. Enjoying the glare she received. A grin soon widened on her face. "Oh, we have him. I'm sure he'll make a wonderful set of trays once we are done here." She continued.

"Don't you lay a finger on Helix!!!" He suddenly boomed. Attempting to stand up, making the lykoi flinch. The guards on each side took hold of Kane's arms, keeping their weapons close.

"Remain in your seat prisoner." One of the guards started. "This is your only warning." Kane could tell he was dead serious and didn't want to take his chances. So, he did as he was told and took his seat. The lykoi pinned her ears back. Keeping her eyes off of Kane as she scoffed. Hating that she actually was intimated by the prisoner.

Kane was able to easily sense this and chuckled under his breath,

"Sorry about that ma'am, didn't mean to scare you that bad." No one laughed, other than himself. But it seemed to be enough to trigger something in her as she attempted to lunge at him.

"Why you son of a-" A hand then abruptly took hold of her, yanking her back from Kane.

"Enough of this!" The voice boomed, coming from the anvol. His screen showed an angered expression glowing red. The lykoi's heart sank at being barked at. The screen soon began to back to a black background as the blue text like face on the screen went back to a neutral look.

"Besides, we have arrived. This may continue during interrogation." He said plainly. Which made Kane gulp.

The transport soon came to a stop. The door opened, the evening sun shining into the interior of the vehicle forcing Kane to squint his eyes. He then felt the soldiers get him up and escort him off the transport. With the anvol still aboard, once Kane had exited the large vehicle drove off. Eyes forward, Kane looked up at the U.G.G base. Along the walls were several guards patrolling. A few mechs were patrolling the outside of the wall as well. Kane had noticed they mainly consisted of *Sentry* mechs. Which made sense for a rather small base. They were medium-sized mechs outfitted with a heavy chain gun, excellent at handling infantry, though it also was able to swap its ammunition to be more effective against light vehicles and mechs. Other more powerful variations may have lasers and even rail guns instead of ballistics. Some also included a missile rack for an extra punch. Though unlike most mechs it had no arms, the sentry made up for its speed regardless of being larger than light mechs. Thanks to its improved leg design alongside a set of boosters on each leg.

Ignition: Unknown Criminal

As the guards escorted their prisoner closing to the entrance, they could feel the vibrations along the ground as the sentries stomped past them. Knowing that either of those mechanical terrors could obliterate Kane within a second horrified him. He kept his head down and kept walking towards the base. It wasn't long before the giant, heavy doors opened revealing more union troops within.

Once inside, Kane saw soldiers at work. He noticed a few platoons doing push-ups. A crew had been repairing a pretty beat up looking *Sentry*. Kane had wondered if that was thanks to the ship that had saved him. To which he still had no idea who that was. At first, he had hoped it was Gwen. Though Kane quickly realized that would've been impossible since the ship was far too large to fit in the city. Followed by the fact he definitely didn't have that kind of firepower on his ship. Plus he never got any word from Gwen since they landed. Kane soon noticed some of the soldiers staring as they were eating at the outside tables. The rest seemed to be busy with patrolling or moving to different sections of the base. It felt like no one was out of place here, except for Kane.

Both Kane and the guards were stopped as an officer soon moved towards them. The lykoi seemed to have gotten a little annoyed by the sight of him, though forced herself to keep her feelings invisible. As the officer approached closer, the squad came to a halt and saluted the officer who after giving a salute of his own, nodded.

"At ease." Tilting his to the side, he rose a brow at the sight of Kane.

"So this is him? For someone who was able to take down a spec ops team I had expected...more." The officer commented, seeming disappointed. The lykoi simply ignored the comment and cleared her throat,

"Where would you like me to place the prisoner sir? And if you don't mind me asking..." She brought her attention to the tired and beaten prisoner. His head stayed down as he didn't dare to speak.

"When would I be able to assist with the interrogation?" She asked plainly. The officer raised a brow at the question.

"We typically don't have soldiers assisting with interrogation," he stated, sounding a little annoyed. As if that was more than obvious. The lykoi took a breath.

"I understand that sir… but this is… personal." Kane became quite confused about what she meant by that. The officer, however, didn't show any change in his demeanour. Shaking his head, he signaled his soldiers to move in to apprehend the prisoner. The officer only glared at the lykoi, knowing full well he didn't have to reply to the statement. A hand then came onto the lykoi's shoulder, turning her head back, she saw that it was one of her squad-mates.

"Let's go Fay. This...this is over." Fay's ears drooped slightly in defeat. Watching the new set of guards escort Kane to the base.

"Yeah..." Was all that came out from her. It was faint, but others had heard. He squeezed her shoulder softly. A light tug was added. Fay got the hint and began to leave with the rest of her squad. A feeling of guilt washing over her.

A few painful hours had passed.

Kane was staring at the desk in front of him. The cool metal seat sent a chill down Kane's spine as he was forced to wait. The barely lit room was dead silent, every corner cramped around Kane. Blood dripped down his face while his chest ached creating a slight abnormality to his breathing. Sitting alone, with Kane nothing but his thoughts to keep him company. The many worries inside began to flood in. However, before he could find himself dwelling for too long the door then swung open.

Austin Patten

"Back to get the same answer again?" Kane croaked, yet managed to let a chuckle escape despite all that has happened. The one who had entered, an anvol, seemed less than impressed. His screen showed a rather neutral expression.

"Your resilience and attempts of sarcasm won't keep the information you have on the rebels Mr. Lons. " He stated confidently. Taking a seat in front of Kane. The low hum emitting from his body was faintly heard. Placing a case by his seat, he sorted the handful of papers in his hands, taking a moment to organize himself before bringing his digital eyes to Kane.

"Although, I believe such...barbaric methods may not be required." Wiping the blood off his face Kane took in a breath.

"Is that so? I don't know what else I can tell you." He sighed with a hint of frustration. "I know you already read the reports of what I've said to the others. Yet, here you are." He waved his hand to the anvol, who nodded, placing hands together on the desk.

"Yes, this is all true. Though unlike the others. I think there is the possibility of you being innocent."

Now that got Kane's full attention. For a second, a smile actually appeared on his face. Although it didn't last long, skepticism kicked in soon after. The anvol seemed to be more than prepared for it. Watching Kane intently as his face shifted, observing the internal battle to trust the anvol or not. Then he finally asked,

"W...why would you help me?" Kane asked rather fearfully, his eyes now locked onto the anvol.

"To put it simply Mr. Lons, after looking into nearly all that the U.G.G has on you. It seems you have had a few violent encounters." He started, raising a brow on his screen. Kane nervously twiddled his thumbs.

"However, there had never actually been any U.G.G forces actually harmed by your encounters. That is...until now." The anovl didn't bother to check on Kane this time as he continued. Who only became more and more worried. Listening to the report of what has happened today. From the delivery gwars to him defending himself from the union soldiers.

"I must admit, Mr. Lons, assuming this is accurate you managed to hold your own pretty well. Even the cybel assisting you was impressive." He added, bending to the side a little to grab his case. Gently placing it on the table and opening it. Inside, Kane's eyes widened. It was Helix. Though it seemed like he was cleaned up. The damage, the hole that pierced his screen became very visual to Kane. He forced himself to not change his expression at the sight.

The anvol then ejected helix's memory chip, revealing that it was still intact.

"I must say, you are a man of luck Mr. Lons. The chances of this surviving after taking a shot like that..." He paused, looking at Kane sternly to emphasize his point. Putting the chip down by the case. Kane's eyes followed for every moment of the process. Wanting to do nothing but snatch it right then and there. But with his current situation, it would be pointless.

"I can tell you care greatly for the survival of your cybel. Which as an anvol myself, I can greatly respect." He stated, Letting his face loosen a little. Kane nodded,

"Yeah?...So what happens next then?" He asked plainly. Still not knowing where this was going.

Without warning the anvol's right arm shifted to the side, pointing at the camera recording at the two. Firing a pair of electronic darts at the lens. Kane barely caught it before hearing a light spark.

"W-what the hell?! What did-" The anvol suddenly leaned over and cupped his hand over Kane's mouth. Shushing him instantly. Once Kane got the hint the anvol removed his hand, standing up he walked behind Kane and removed his binds. Staying quiet, Kane turned up to the anovl with a mix of confusion and worry. After the quick *snap,* Kane was free. The anovl then walked to the table, taking both the chip and Kane's left hand. Placing the chip in his hand and closing it. Looking down at Kane, the light of his screen illuminating Kane's face. "Your welcome. Now get up." Getting to his feet, Kane watched the anvol stick his head out of the door for a few seconds.

"It seems clear for now." Though before he could continue Kane had placed a hand on the anvol's shoulder.

"Wait, who are you?" The anvol turned his head back to Kane closing the door.

"Oh yes. I guess this must be quite confusing for you. I'm Dusk." The anvol replied simply. Kane opened his mouth, getting ready to fire another set of questions before a sudden explosion rocked the entire room! Kane had slipped from the violent shaking to then feel a cool mechanical hand take hold of his arm.

"That's the signal." Dusk said, bursting the door open as he grabbed a pair of *Lance* plasma pistols from his suit. Getting his balance back, Kane looked back at Dusk.

"Signal for what?" Offering a *Lance* to Kane, a smirk was then displayed on dusk's face.

"Escape."

Austin Patten

———

Fay alongside her squad was sent flying across the courtyard. Her back smashed into another soldier as they collided into the floor. Attempting to clear her blurry vision from the hard landing, muffled orders and screams filled her ears. Soon followed by a flurry of gunfire. One of her squadmates soon caught up to her.

"Corporal Fay! Are you alright?" He asked professionally yet showed his genuine worry for her as he offered a hand down for her.

"I'm good." She replied sternly. Taking his offer as he helped her to her feet.

"Thanks." Taking her union assault rifle. The other only nodded before carefully grabbing the unconscious soldier that softened Fay's landing and pulling him over his back.

"Let's get out of here!" He yelled, sprinting to the nearest vehicle for cover. Fay wasn't far behind as she began to observe the scene. Platoons of soldiers began to pour out of several buildings. Most armed with the standard-issue union rifles similar to hers. All firing at the attacker while attempting to take cover themselves. A large mix of non-combat personnel was in a panic. Jumping over for cover and following the soldiers that led them to safer

71

Ignition: Unknown Criminal

locations and away from the fighting. An unknown ship suddenly flew into Fay's view, its weapons quickly charging up before unleashing a wave of energy projectiles! Soldiers scattered as far as they could before being mowed down by the firepower. Fay watched in horror as more troops were helplessly being blown to pieces. A handful of squads prepared themselves to fire back. Fay pointed at the nearest building for her squadmate.

"Get him to cover!" She shouted, flicking the safety off her rifle.

"What about you?" He asked while running.

"I'm taking this bastard down." She huffed, equipping her union rifle before catching up with one of the squads just in time. Hearing the squad leader ordered,

"OPEN FIRE!" Everyone then got out of cover and shot at the ship. Fay soon squeezed the trigger and felt the kick of her rifle as the automatic weapon got to work. Soldiers behind her also added to the shooting. However, hearing the click of her magazine being depleted, she tried to reload but another burst of projectiles sent a squad beside her flying! Fay quickly ducked down for cover. The other soldiers soon realized how pointless it was as the shields of the ship easily absorbed the ballistics.

Austin Patten

"Everyone get down! Mech support is inbound!" A voice boomed out of one of the *sentry's* external speakers.

That was until the *sentry's* arrived. Six of the massive machines stomped over, firing their chain guns at the aircraft from different sides. Two of them walked right past Fay with a THUD! One of their giant feet stomped right beside her! Shaking the ground with each heavy step as they made their way closer to the enemy. Another pair used their boosters to jump behind the spacecraft to engage its engines.

Fay got herself to hide by the base's walls with her squadmate. Peering her head over to watch the mechs do their work. A platoon soon caught up to Fay, using the wall for cover as well as more soldiers hid. As the *sentry's* kept on firing, Fay could hear some of the mechs swap to the heavier ammunition. The chain gun had a slower rate of fire with a lot more punch with each shot. The ship then zoomed across the base. Trying to avoid the oncoming fire from the mix of mechs and infantry as heavier weapons were soon being deployed.

"Who the hell is that? Are they insane??" The soldier that had stuck with Fay asked, softly placing the wounded soldier on the ground as one of the platoon's medics rushed over to check on him.

Ignition: Unknown Criminal

"I have no clue...but I have a pretty good idea of what they are after." The platoon's gunnery sergeant soon heard that. Walking up to her, a fellow lykoi at that.

"And what might that be corporal?" She sighed, hoping that she was wrong. Though after hearing recent reports of a ship taking out the squad that was sent to capture Kane...she knew that after escorting that criminal here that it was too easy to guess. After shoving a fresh magazine in her union rifle her attention returned to the sergeant. Her eyes became cold.

"Kane..."

CHAPTER SIX

It was distorted, but Alan saw it.

An explosion.

Then another.

His eyes widened as he stared at his holo-watch. Seeing the live feed play on the news. A fighter craft had been attacking a U.G.G base on Para V. Union forces stationed have been deployed and have been scattered trying to take down the one ship. One of the first things Alan noticed as he watched was how fast and nimble that ship was. Zipping past several buildings to avoid oncoming fire. In fact, it looked like that ship hadn't even taken a scratch. A few mechs soon came into view of the feed.

Sentry's

They wouldn't stand a chance...

"Is everything alright sir?" Hans asked. Stepping beside him to see the holo-feed playing from Alan's watch. The walk home was peaceful at first. It had begun to rain in the enormous city. A crackle of thunder was heard in the distance. Hans held an umbrella over the two. A series of taps crashing on the umbrella as the two watched. After a few more minutes of silence between the two, Alan cut off the feed. Closing his eyes as a sigh came out of him. Hans stared at his master intently.

"Sir?"

"...That ship...It's for Kane Lons… Isn't it?"

"...I...I would believe so sir."

Alan's eyes eventually opened, turning to Hans. Hans froze as their eyes locked. A gulp was made as his peripherals noticed Alan's mechanical arm. Its fingers wiggled before gripping into a fist. Alan's attention then turned to the ships flying above them, past the umbrella. Through the thick, grey clouds a mix of civilian and military craft flew above the vast city. Adding small specks of light in the dark sky. Hans soon joined him.

"What are you planning to do sir?"

"I think it's time I meet Kane in person," Alan answered plainly, continuing to stare up at the seemingly endless number of ships. Watching as both lanes of ships either entered or exited the atmosphere of the planet. While others were flying around the city.

"Then perhaps we should head back a little sooner." Hans offered, using his holo-watch to call in a ride. Alan kept quiet, bringing his head down to view the many people that were walking along the streets as well. A few would have recognized him. Usually getting excited to actually meet the galactic leader in person. Though Alan kept it casual by offering a smile, easy small talk and then ending it with either a handshake or even a hug. When he'd watch the person he interacted with would leave, he couldn't help but feel his smile become more...genuine.

Within twenty minutes a black Hover-Limousine stopped by Alan's home. Stepping out, Alan began to walk inside, Hans was close behind. The same pair of guards as before gave Alan a swift salute. Alan then stopped in front of the two before shaking one with a strong and confident handshake.

"Take the rest of the night off you two. You've done well today." He said the two took a second to look at each other. A smile shown on their faces, the one who was shaking Alan's hand nodded his head.

"Thank you, sir, we'll see you in the morning." He replied with a gruff voice. His hand departing from the handshake.

"That you will, take care, Jacob." With that, Alan began to enter further in his home while the guards began to leave.

At his office, Alan had prepared his communication terminal to speak with General Corgan, a rather impressive hellion. Alan sat back as he waited for the transmission to be answered. Corgan was one of the first non-human generals to oversee such an important world under the U.G.G. Especially after his bold tactics against the Bruticus Syndicate. A growing band of hellions and humans banding together to create the "2nd Wave." Alan could almost feel the headache returning as he recalled the event. The 2nd Wave was an event that was believed by the Bruticus Syndicate. The 2nd Wave would essentially wipe out all intelligent life within the galaxy. When it came to how and when the answer became very vague and inconsistent. Though, that didn't change the surprisingly strong faith they had for the 2nd Wave. In fact, due to the size of the U.G.G the leaders of the Bruticus Syndicate, the Chosen Hands had targeted Harmony as the cause of the 2nd Wave. At first, the U.G.G hardly saw the religious faction as a threat. However, as their numbers grew, the religion strengthened and with a sizable number of planets under their banner. People began to notice the Bruticus Syndicate as something more than a few crazy fanatics. Especially when they became the 6th largest faction. Just under the Forged Union.

Then there was the attack on Paris Prime. One of the farthest worlds of the U.G.G, a large mining world that was discovered in between the borders of the U.G.G and the Bruticus Syndicate. It held minerals and ores used for an impressive amount of vehicles and ships. Tension grew as the U.G.G practically rushed in a colony ship to claim the planet. At first, when the order was given by the G.L of the time, Ben Geo. He had hoped to make it a smooth transition, have the colony ship place the U.G.G banner to claim the world before the Bruticus Syndicate would have any idea the planet even existed. Unfortunately, when reports came in that the Bruticus Syndicate already had a ship in descent when the colony ship jumped into the system. Ben gave the order to discreetly take the ship out. Hoping to make it seem like the ship was destroyed by an accident. Since no matter how advanced your ships were, the risks of space were always there. Though the operation was a success, the colony ships weapons were able to take down the Bruticus colony ship. It turned out one of the Hand's sons was part of the crew. He was enraged, followed many of the people in the Bruticus Syndicate. Saying both on the planet and in the media that the U.G.G were bloody murderers, who were willing to take down innocent and holy lives for their own greed. Although part of that was true, the U.G.G had done an excellent job hiding the truth of the event to not just it's people but their allies as well.

Within the span of a few days after the U.G.G officially claimed Paris Prime and began mining

Ignition: Unknown Criminal

operations. Bruticus Syndicate ships had jumped into the system. A huge fleet, consisting of mainly *Carriers* was sent to destroy the very operations and make an example of the people working on them. At the time, all there was to defend the world was a handful of corvettes and destroyers alongside the union station. Though Admiral Janne fought to the best of her abilities, giving the warning to General Corgan and his troops for the incoming invasion. Her ships were only able to stop so many of the hundreds of dropships and *Carriers* flying towards the planet. Corgan's situation was just as poor as the admirals, if not worse. Under his command, he had a fair amount of infantry consisting of roughly two battalions to defend the colony and the main factory. Though, in terms of mechs and vehicles, it was next to nothing. There were a handful of *Dune* APC's which were armed with a few light machine guns and an anti-missile battery but wouldn't help much with an entire invasion force. Other than that he had the colonies automated turrets to assist with taking down incoming dropships. Before the union station was destroyed, Admiral Janne was able to send out an S.O.S to the U.G.G. Giving hope to the forces below as the battle soon got to the ground. General Corgan barely got an hour to assemble his troops before the ships were spotted! From there, a constant battle for the survival of the colony had begun...

The reports of the battle on the ground were quite vague. However, all that mattered was that General Corgan managed to keep the enemy at bay till U.G.G reinforcements came. Within a day or so, the battle was won. The Bruticus Syndicate had sustained heavy losses at the end. While Corgan on the other hand... had managed to hardly use anyone. In fact, the reports claimed that he kept his losses under forty percent!

Corgan soon answered the call after a few more minutes of waiting. The tall dark blue hellion stood at attention, nearly instantly saluting at the sight of Alan!

"Good evening sir! How may I assist you?" He asked with his deep and gruff voice. Alan sat back in his chair.

"At ease, general. I called to ask about the situation with Kane." Putting his arm down, the hellion cleared his throat.

"I assume you've seen the news, sir?" He questioned, managing to keep any hint of fear unnoticeable. Alan only stared before replying quickly,

"Indeed I have, It's not every day I hear a prisoner managed to cause so much damage...even with help." He said sternly, getting right to the point.

Ignition: Unknown Criminal

A few pictures of the situation soon appeared beside Corgan, high-res 3d holo images that Alan used his fingers to get better angles of each one. All of which showed different shots of the base. A few even showing the ship that is attacking it. It was a *Kret,* a Lykoi hybrid of a fighter craft and a dropship. *Kret's* were fast, durable ships mainly used to drop shock troopers or special forces.

"This ship seems to have been pirated, we have yet to discover which band of pirates this has attacked us." Alan tapped his fingers along his desk. Continuing to swipe a finger along with an image of the battle. Plenty of fallen soldiers laid along with the compound. A few *sentries* were scattered within the exterior of the base. A mix of the mechs was still standing, regardless of the damage, they sustained they kept on fighting the craft while a few had been littered on the surface, destroyed.

"Are we certain these aren't rebels?" He asked. His eyes locked on Corgan's.

"There's a possibility sir. Though, I trust Admiral Scone from allowing rebels to pass the blockade. Especially in a world like Para-"

"He didn't stop Kane…" Alan retorted. "People can change sides in this conflict quite easily it seems." Alan got to his feet. "I want him taken alive, Corgan. If the reports

I've been receiving are correct. Kane had assisted in supplying the operations held on Gwars." The hellion quickly brought up newly completed reports from the integration, projecting them to Alan's screen.

"From the time in interrogation he's been through. We managed to get practically nothing out of him. Claiming that he was innocent and had no idea about the rebel for-"

"I'm already aware of this Corgan." Alan interrupted again. Since the same reports have already been sent to him by those performing the interrogation. His hands became fists as he became further irritated. Before sitting back down with a heavy sigh. Lifting his eyes back to the general.

"Destroy the ship, take Kane alive. I'll be at Para V within twelve hours." General Corgan managed to give Alan another salute before Alan ended the transmission. The black screen reflected Alan's half mechanical face. Getting back to his feet, he walked out of his office.

Hans was standing at the deck, looking down at the thousands of people within the city. The sun shined brightly in the sky, a couple of reptile-like birds soared high above the house. Hover-cars flying throughout the roads, while groups of people of every race walked along the pathways. A soft breeze soon came on the deck, hitting the older man's face gently. A smile beamed off his face as he breathed in the fresh air.

"Beautiful isn't it?" Han's turned, to see Alan walk beside him. Placing his hands on the railing he took in a deep breath.

"Ahhh... Harmony is truly one of a kind isn't she?" He asked again, feeling the cool air brush against his face. Hans kept the smile on his face as he nodded,

"Indeed sir, Harmony was quite the lucky find." His face then softened.

"I wish you were able to see it more often." He sighed dolefully. Alan's smile also began to disappear from the comment.

"You heard that?" Hans kept his attention at the city.

"Didn't have too…" Alan brought his head to face the city as well.

"You think this conflict will be over soon? So we can actually enjoy some peace and quiet? At least...for a while." Hans asked. Spotting a group of kids. His smile returned as he watched them play at a park. A game of tag. A game that is so simple and yet so enjoyable. Especially to the young mind. Like many people, Hans missed being able to have that simple mindset. Of just having fun. Enjoying the day till the sun came down.

"Yeah, I do," Alan replied, staring up at the clear blue sky. Seeing a large Union *Titan* soar through the sky. The gigantic U.G.G Battleship nearly made the whole city black as it flew past during its patrol. Hans, however, kept on watching the children. Noticing the gwarian child stopping to look up at the massive ship in awe. Reading the "WOW!" from his lips. Pointing up at it and turning to grab her friends. Who all stopped in their tracks to join in to stand and watch the *Titan* flyby. A few waved up at the huge ship, others only stared in utter awe. Probably imagining themselves piloting such a ship.

"Please, sir. Just win this war. For them." Hans pleaded softly. There was even a croak in his voice. Alan looked at Hans, an expression filled with a mix of confusion and concern on his face. When he realized Hans wasn't looking back, Alan looked down, trying to find what he was talking about.

It was their smiles that grabbed him. Seeing the kids play together again once the *Titan* was out of sight. Alan swore he could hear the laughter from up there. The joy from that small group alone was inspiring to the cyborg. Reminding him of much simpler times.

"I promise Hans," He placed a hand on Hans's shoulder. Looking at him sternly.

Ignition: Unknown Criminal

"For the good of the U.G.G, its children especially, I will win this conflict." Hans then finally turned to Alan, his smile back on his face.

"Thank you, sir."

CHAPTER SEVEN

A duo of Union soldiers barely got a few seconds to react as a sudden door burst open before Dusk quickly opened fire on the pair. Two green bolts slammed into the soldier's faceplates. Dusk waited for the bodies to fall before pushing up. Kane was close behind, *Lance* in both hands as he checked their rear.

"All clear on my end," Kane said, which only made Dusk chuckle.

"It's only clear on *your* end thanks to me. Have you even fired your lance yet?" The anvol asked with a chuckle.

"I-I'm working on it!" Kane quipped back. "I just-" Dusk then placed a finger on Kane's face.

"Ah ah. I believe it when I see it, Mr. Lons." Kane scrunched his face as Dusk removed his finger, who pushed up right after. As much as Kane wanted to say a comeback of sorts, he kept quiet, only sighing with a chuckle before catching up.

When Dusk detected Kane jogging up behind him he checked the map he had downloaded of the base.

"We shouldn't be too far from the nearest exit." He started, seeing additional enemies on his HUD. "Though

Ignition: Unknown Criminal

I'd recommend we hurry." Dusk then turned back with a smirk plastered on his screen. "Unless you want to be interrogated by a less friendly and handsome anvol." He teased. Kane only shook his head as he caught up.

"Heh, well, you managed to get half of that information correct." Kane shot back with a grin. Dusk's face swapped to a more shocked expression as Kane came right beside him.

"Ha! Not bad Mr. Lons." He smirked digitally. However, both of these expressions became serious once they stopped at the next door. With their backs at the wall, Dusk wasted no time as he typed in the keycode he had. After a beep, the door unlocked.

"OPEN FIRE!!!"

A squad of union soldiers immediately fired their rifles at the opening door. Forcing Dusk and Kane to stay hidden behind the sides of the door.

"Get back Mr. Lons!" Dusk barked, but Kane hardly had time to react as the soldiers pushed through the door! The first two instantly brought their attention to each side, one facing Kane, the other at Dusk. Kane didn't think twice before lunging himself at the soldier in front of him. His *Lance* slipped out of his fingers as he took hold of the soldier's rifle with both hands. Forcing the weapon upwards when the soldier tried to fire, spraying the roof with bullets. Meanwhile Dusk backhanded his soldier's face, shattering the protective glass on the faceplate of his helmet. Knocking him back, Dusk swiftly brought his *Lance* and fired twice at the soldier's chest. Kane continued to struggle to keep the soldier from shooting him. Twisting the rifle left and right as the weapon kept on firing. Dusk attempted to aim his *Lance* at the soldier's back, however, the other two soldiers from the squad quickly rushed in. Taking his attention away. Before the first could bring his weapon up, Dusk blasted his face with a green bolt, his body slamming into the wall. The other soldier fired quickly, managing to shoot the *Lance* out of Dusk's hand as he opened fire on the now defenceless anvol. Hearing the click from the soldier's rifle. Kane, with all of his strength, pushed the soldier into a wall. Using the few seconds he had, hurriedly Kane scooped up the fallen *Lance* and with both hands having a tight grip he quickly fired three times into the soldier. Dropping him before he had a chance to reload. He then turned to Dusk, who was using his arms to protect his lightly armoured head as he was pinned at the wall. The soldiers fired shot after shot into him while stepping closer. Kane aimed his *Lance* at the soldiers before rapidly pulling the trigger. Using every shot in his magazine to take them down. With dark burns scorched onto their backs, they smashed into the floor. Without even waiting for more soldiers to enter, Kane dashed to check on Dusk. Who was still sitting at the corner of the wall, his face peeking from his arms.

"Dusk! Holy shit, are you alright?" Kane asked worriedly, checking him over. Dusk then stood up almost instantly, making Kane jump a little.

"Of course! Good work Mr. Lons! I guess I owe you one." He chuckled fist-bumping Kane's shoulder. Dusk didn't bother to check on the smouldering remains of his *Lance* and just picked up one of the union rifles laying on the floor. A smirk came across Kane as he checked the door.

"I gotta admit, you're in a pretty good mood for nearly being killed." Dusk reloaded his rifle and snagged a few extra mags before walking out the door.

"I knew you had me covered."

Outside of the base, Fay had been ordered to stay with the wounded. There were many due to the several airstrikes from the enemy craft. Fay's ear twitched at the high pitch screams and howls of agony from the wounded.

Looking back at a squad of crippled soldiers resting along with the debris of the base. Knowing there were more than enough soldiers watching the main entrance. Fay kneeled down by the squad. They all turned to face her, all with a similar look of fear and anguish. Fay began to open her mouth, wanting to say something, anything that could bring these people some comfort. But nothing came out. Instead, Fay kept her mouth shut and began to inspect the soldier's wounds. Most of them were burns, some of them were extensive, covering large portions of their bodies. Specialized gel from the field medics has been added to help with the pain. Though she could tell from there faces that it was still more than noticeable. Each and every mark on these men enraged her. Fay's breathing became heavy as she held up one of the soldier's arms. His hand was no more, nothing but a black stump remained. Looking at the man who the arm belonged to, only angered her further. The pale young man looked right back at her. Human. He couldn't have been older than twenty.

"W-well get him right?" The soldier rasped slowly. Fay grabbed her canteen and brought it up to his mouth.

"Drink." She ordered softly. The soldier stared at the canteen intently before opening his mouth. Fay then gently poured the cool water until he closed his mouth. Pulling it away, she then replied to his question,

"Yes, either here right now. Or if that bastard does manage to slip between our fingers…." Her grip tightened on the canteen as he looked right into the soldier's eyes.

"May I have a drink as well?...Please?" The soldier beside him asked weakly. Another human. He reached out his hand. Fay gently placed her canteen in his hand. Watching him take a drink before sharing it around his fellow squadmates. As they drank the water, Fay then noticed the empty canteens laying beside them.

"Corporal Inne?" A voice called out behind her. She turned back to the same soldier that had been with her before the attack began.

"You don't have to call me by rank Axel." Fay replied sternly, yet casually. Getting back to her feet she followed him.

"We got some new orders. The sergeant just filled me in. What's left of our squad is being ordered to assist the 214th platoon at guarding one of the emergency exits." Axel reported, speeding up when he noticed Fay increasing her speed to a jog.

"Then we better get moving...Private Vission." She added, with a smirk of her own. Even though Axel kept his helmet on, she could bet there was a grin hiding under it.

"Dusk!? Dusk! What's going on down there?! U.G.G reinforcements have landed! And *A.A Sentry's* are being deployed!" There was an explosion heard as the pilot continued to yell at Dusk. Kane was able to faintly hear it as they ran through another hall.

"Understood, I'll have Mr. Lons at this exit." Dusk informed the pilot. Kane heard Dusk's internal fans get a little louder before he said back to the pilot. "Meet you soon." Dusk then turned to Kane once the transmission ended.

"Our transportation should be ready at the next exit. Though with union forces having us surrounded it's gonna be hot. I recommend you stay behind me, Mr. Lons." Dusk advised. Kane nodded while sprinting beside the anvol.

"Good to hear...sounds like our ride is going through hell though," Kane added. Dusk tilted his head as he thought.

"That's one way to put it," Dusk said as he brought a finger to his screen.

Dusk soon broke his train of thought once they got to yet another door.

"This will lead us to one of the staff rooms and then an emergency exit. If my radar is being accurate, union troops are only being deployed in this area. So they'll be the least prepared here." Dusk said, taking out the union rifle he had holstered. Kane did the same with his lance. With that, after a quick type of his code the door unlocked.

The room was only lit from the outside due to the windows shining brightly inside. Papers were littered along the floor, with tables and chairs flipped over throughout the room.

"Stay low Mr. Lons, union soldiers may be able to spot us. We should make this quick." Dusk warned, going to a crouch before moving in. As Kane stepped in, the faint smell of coffee hit him. To his right, he noticed a few mugs, still full of hot coffee.

"Wow...these people really did leave in a hurry," he mumbled under his breath. Dusk, still in front peeked up slowly to check the window.

He was correct.

His digital eyes moved left to right as he scanned the area. A few platoons of infantry, APC's and *Sentries* were waiting outside. Though Dusk had expected this. However, there were faint orders being barked outside. Turning his head to where the orders came from he noticed a few squads of soldiers pushing forward with *C.D.B's* in front. His orange eyes widened at the sight, his head turning so quick it spooked Kane.

"Mr. Lons, we need to leave. Now." Kane was a bit surprised by the sudden urgency. Though, he got a pretty good idea that if Dusk was starting to worry it was for good reason. So with no arguments, he nodded. "I'm right behind you." He whispered back. Dusk tightened his grip on the union rifle, staying crouched he moved closer to the exit.

"You're going to hear a certain...noise." Dusk started, looking up at the window during moments of this talking. "When you do you must brace yourself Mr.lons," Dusk warned further. His fans got a little louder as they moved closer. Kane felt his chest becoming tense from the wait. His heartbeat thumping hard while sweat formed on his hands, coating his *Lance's* grip.

Then it happened. A sudden electronic wave boomed through the room! Before Kane could try to shout to Dusk, there were more electronic waves sent into the room! Suddenly while Kane's ears were still ringing, trying to recover the glass above them began to shatter from incoming gunfire! Dusk started to pick up the pace, he turned to Kane to shout something. Something he didn't catch before Dusk lifted the union rifle over his head to fire blindly out the window. As the ringing began to slightly fade, Kane heard nothing but gunfire ripping into the walls around them. There was a muffled hum heard from behind the gunfire.

"D-Dusk! What is that?!" Kane panicked. Without any warning, Dusk took hold of Kane's arms. Yanking him into his chest just before an explosion erupted through the wall Kane was hiding behind. Kane looked back at it for a second as his face paled, but before he could look for long Dusk grabbed his face and brought it to his screen.

"You need to keep moving Mr. Lons. They are tracking our movements, plus," Dusk paused, pulling Kane behind him when he noticed a squad of soldiers sprint into the freshly destroyed wall.

"Anvol!" One of the soldiers yelled. "Get-" He was abruptly cut off when Dusk fired his union rifle. The one who shouted was rippled with bullets as he crashed into a table. Before the others could react Dusk gunned them down since they had no cover. The rest collapsed on the ground. After a quick reload and chucking the empty magazine on one of the bodies, Dusk yanked Kane by the collar of his shirt. The hail of bullets only continued to fire through the windows. While practically dragging Kane along the floor, Dusk used his union rifle to force at least some of the soldiers into cover, hitting a few in the process. Though with the *Cover Detection Bots* shields deployed, they started walking closer. Kane, on the other hand, spotted another squad entering the room. With a slight struggle from the shaking from being dragged across the floor, he lifted his *Lance* and fired at the soldiers. Four green bolts flew through the air. One slammed into a soldier's chest while another was a headshot. However, the other shots only smashed into the wall behind them.

"Man down!" Was shouted by one of the two survivors. Before Kane could continue to fire, Dusk got to the end of the room and placed Kane behind one of the metal tables while taking cover as well.

"How's that ship coming along?" Kane shouted, reloading his *Lance*. Dusk was still keeping his attention to the soldiers as he switched the rifle to burst fire.

"Shouldn't be much longer Mr. Lons." He replied, waiting for an opening to return fire. Which he soon did as the shooting began to die down. Dusk brought his rifle up, seeing another head peek the anvol nearly instantly pulled the trigger to fire a spray of bullets into her head. The last one of that squad then brought up her rifle and began to spray blindly at the pair, forcing Dusk to fall into cover again.

Austin Patten

"Dusk? Dusk?" I'm about to land the Jade! Are you ready for thisssss?" The Pilot screamed through his internal communicator. To which he then swiftly replied,

"Yes, Mr. Lons and I are at the door as we speak." Dusk then stood up, firing rapidly to keep the soldier pinned, returning a light smirk to Kane.

"Told you." Then his digital face became serious once he kicked the back door open.

"Now stay extremely close Mr. Lons." Kane didn't hesitate, within a few seconds of getting back to his feet he was practically hugging Dusk. "I'm ready, let's get out of here." The *Kret* then suddenly landed, its main guns opening fire to cover the two. The door on the side opened, revealing a gwarian with a *Rift Carbine* in her hands. The dark yellow gwarian waved her hand over impatiently as she made a hiss like whine,

"Come on!" She then quickly brought her attention to platoons firing at the ship. Lifting her *Rift* she began to shoot at the incoming soldiers. Dusk didn't need to be told twice. With Kane right beside him, they sprinted towards the *Kret*. Dusk's heavily armoured body did an excellent job providing protection for Kane as they moved through the open field. Dusk fired his union rifle at the crowd of soldiers as Kane did his best to stay close. They were nearly at the ship when Kane spotted one of the *Sentry's* charging up one of their weapons. "Dusk! We need t-" There was no time for warning. The heavy round came crashing right in front of Dusk, sending the two flying into the ground.

Ignition: Unknown Criminal

Kane tried to desperately get back up, blinking his eyes to clear the blurry vision from the hard landing. Turning to his right he saw Dusk, who was motionless on the ground.

"Dusk!?? Hey! Dusk!" He screamed, seeing the screen was blank. Kane soon noticed one of his arms was blown off from the explosion, though the rest seemed intact. Looking back at the Kret, he saw a hellion and lykoi appear. The lykoi held an *S7-SMG,* spraying the area with bullets while the large red hellion dashed towards Kane. A gantlet on his wrist deployed an energy shield, protecting him from the incoming fire. Thankfully they weren't too far from the ship, so the hellion caught up to them quickly. Without as much as an introduction, he lifted Dusk over his back and barely made eye contact with Kane before bellowing,

"RUN!" To which Kane instantly followed beside the hulking alien. One of the Kret's weapons fired a smoke grenade, hiding the ship from further attacks. It was only seconds from there that they got to the ship. The lykoi had already headed back inside while the gwarian gave a hand to help pull Kane inside. Closing the doors right behind him.

"Hurry!" She hissed, though her tone was more worried than aggressive. Taking Kane's hand she brought them to one of the chairs in the Kret. She sat Kane down before strapping on all four of the seat belts, tightly. She then sat beside Kane, doing the same for herself. The ship already in the air by now, muffled explosions were both heard and felt as the pilot continued to maneuver the ship off the planet. Red lights were flashing while the ship continued to fly.

"I hope everyone is sssecure back there! We are leaving this place NOW!!" Another gwarian barked from the cockpit. Kane felt the ship rock and shake. The g force slamming into this chest like a rock as the ship increased its speed.

"Whoa, there's a lot of *U4'sss* here!" The pilot shouted.

Kane felt the entire ship shake abruptly in response.

U4's Kane thought, those were the standard fighters used by the U.G.G. Small, triangle shaped ships used to primarily swarm their targets.

"Hold on, Kale! Bring that human in the cockpit!" The other gwarian shouted!

"You got it Fesh!" Kale replied, jumping out of her seat once she was unbuckled. Kane already finished unbuckling himself as Kale then grabbed his hand, suddenly forcing him onto his feet as they ran to the cockpit.

"Here he is!" She said. The second gwarian, also dark yellow, spotted Kane as she stood from the pilot seat. "You're supposed to be some kick ass pilot right?" Fesh asked, pointing at the seat. "Then get us the hell out of here." Kane didn't dare to argue with the pirate, he felt her place a headset on him before allowing him to take a seat. Once seated he was quick to figure out the controls to the ship. Fesh then pointed at Kale.

Ignition: Unknown Criminal

"Kale, you and I are taking the rear missile launcher, Ryko, may you mann the A.A gun?" She asked. Ryko nodded, "Sure can." As the three sprinted to their stations, Kane already began to veer towards the rear of a handful of *U-4's*. Knowing he'd have no choice but to take them down. With a heavy sigh, he pushed down on the triggers to fire the *Kret's* main weapons, two heavy laser cannons. Watching the red bolts soar towards the fighters before completely decimating them.

"Wow, good shot." Ryko said through the headset.

"Thanks." Kane said back, hearing the muffled sounds of the A.A gun opening fire behind him. Kale and Fesh were just as quick to fire the missiles as well. Kane just needed to get them out of here.

"Ryko! We need some help with the rear! We're getting swarmed with fighters!" Fesh shouted, Kane just barely heard the volley of missiles being launched.

"On it." he said. Kane only kept the *Kret* moving higher and higher. Hoping to outrun the fighters. Only to then spot a squadron of *U4's* fly towards him, most likely exiting from the orbiting stations above the planet. With lasers suddenly shooting down towards the *Kret*, Kane swung the controls to the side, attempting to avoid as many oncoming lasers as he could before firing the *Kret's* lasers towards the *U4's*. This forced the squadron to scatter as nearly all of them were destroyed by the barrage. Though, the situation only became more desperate as the several Union stations came into view. With a jerk on the controls to the left, Kane evaded oncoming laser fire from the stations. Having only a few scratch the outside of the ship. However, he wanted to keep close to the stations as they were essentially his only source of cover from other fighters at the moment. To avoid the firepower on the stations, Kane moved the ship under them. More fighters were being deployed from the stations as the *Kret* flew closer, including the station Kane was flying towards. Making a sudden maneuver up, Kane opened fire on the *U4's* gunning from the front. Watching the series of heavy red lasers effortlessly smash through the rows of fighters. Kane swiftly avoided the debris left from the remains of the fighters, moving the ship under the station. It didn't take long for *Corvettes* and *Destroyers* to arrive. However, they didn't seem to try to fire while the *Kret* was so close to an ally station, which worked perfectly in Kane's favor. As strong as the *Kret* was, it wouldn't stand a chance against ships as large as those.

"Any idea where I'm taking us exactly?" Kane asked, keeping the ship near the station as the others fired at the seemingly endless amounts of *U4's* coming from behind.

"There should be coordinates already in the nav computer! Just get us away from this station quickly and hit the jump drive!" Fesh yelled. Kane didn't hesitate from there, after briefly looking for an opening, he slammed on the acceleration to fly the *Kret* away from the station. It was only a matter of seconds before the *Corvettes* and *Destroyers* noticed and began to fire. Unleashing a hail of lasers and ballistics in Kane's direction! Quickly forcing the ship to dash from side to side, Kane narrowly missed the incoming fire as he flew towards the closest *Corvette*, using it as a wall from the other large ships. Flying near the *Corvettes* gun batteries, Kane fired the *Kret's* lasers to damage the weapons from being used before flying past them.

"Okay, we are nearly ther-" Kane was then cut off as he felt the Kret suddenly slow down.

'The station has us in their restraint beam!" Ryko shouted! "Anything you two can do on your end?" Kane yelled, giving the Kret everything he can. Though slowly but surely the ship continued to go backwards. In a matter of seconds the *U4's* caught up to them as laser fire passed the cockpit. Ryko's breathing started to quicken, Kane could only imagine how fighters were trying to take down.

"Get ready to punch it!" Fesh shouted. Kane braced himself in his seat, more than ready to jump out of the system the moment he can. A sudden nearby explosion shook the entire ship. Kane grunted as he tightened his grip on the controls.

"Whatever your planning, better hurry it up Fesh!" Ryko yelled. Then, all of a sudden Kane felt the restraint beam getting weaker.

"We fired everything! That station won't be disabled for long!" Fesh warned, and Kane wasted no time preparing the jump drive. Moving the Kret at full speed, he aimed the ship towards the location already in the nav computer. After a few more agonizing seconds the jump drive was ready. Without a word he pulled the lever to jump.

After a moment of silence, other than the hum of the engine at work, Kane heard Kale whoop.

"Wow! I didn't expect a rescue mission to be so much fun!" Kane couldn't help but cough softly before chuckling,

"I'm glad at least some of us enjoyed ourselves." Getting to his feet, he placed the ship on auto pilot for the jump before exiting the cockpit. Ryko was the first as he jumped down from the A.A gun with a sigh of relief.

"That was impressive flying for a cargo pilot." Though, at this point, after finally realizing he was safe, Kane noticed how tired he truly was. The lykoi tilted his head a little.

"...You alright?"

"Yeah, mostly, just tired." Ryko then helped Kane to one of the chairs, buckling him up once he was seated. Then almost instantly Ryko watched as the human crashed.

"Well, enjoy the nap then." He said, hearing Fesh and Kale climb down the ladder.

"That was awes-" Ryko nearly sprinted up to Kale to cover her mouth.

"Hmmf?" Kale asked in a muffled voice. Ryko then pointed to the sleeping human. Fesh rose a brow while Kale made a muffled,

"Ohhhhh…" Ryko then removed his hand.

"Alright, good work you two. I'm very pleased we're able to still be standing. Now, Kale, since you've already met, stay with the human. Ryko and I will go check on how Jok is doing with Dusk." Kale nodded, which was enough for Fesh, who then waved Ryko to follow.

Kale walked to Kane, tilting her head as she was now able to actually observe the human.

"Wow, what a messy thing you are." She commented. Though she felt a little bad.

"Sorry, I didn't mean that in a bad way. I guess you been through a lot huh?" She then asked, though only got slight snoring as a response.

"Oh! Your welcome for saving you by the way." She said, taking a seat by Kane. Her hands on her lap as she bounced gently in her seat, enjoying their "conversation."

"You know, I guess you and Dusk would have been dead by now." She said.

"But you're not! Meep!" She then slammed her hands on her mouth. Silencing herself, she brought her head down to check on the human. Who was still sleeping. She sighed as she brought her hands back down.

"Sorry about that, I can get a little excited you know?" A smile was brought back on her face as Kane shifted lightly in his sleep.

"Yeah, you get it." Kale then looked around the empty area. Nothing but a few beeps filled the silence between them as Kale looked at the human.

"Well, you can sleep now. But I am here if you need it." She said softly. Sitting back in her seat, guarding the human as ordered.

Austin Patten

"Oh, and welcome to the Jade. Home of NightWave…"

CHAPTER EIGHT

"All I need to know, Jok, is if Dusk survived or not."

"He just took nearly a direct from an *Ark Sentry.*" Fesh stated. The hellion merely nodded as he worked on repairing Dusk. The Anvol's chest plate was removed as the large hellion carefully examined the components inside.

"I noticed Fesh, I was there when he was laying on the ground." Jok shot back coolly. Which made Fesh twitch her ear as she glared at the working hellion.

"Excuse me?" Jok then sighed, quickly realizing his mistake.

"My apologies, It's been a while since I've needed to repair Dusk, I enjoyed the break." He said, which earned a chuckle from Ryko.

"Well, the man has a point." Fesh brushed off the remark, leaning beside Jok,

"He's going to make it though, right?" She asked again. Her tone was more gentle than before, sounding disturbed this time. This was her secret weapon against Jok. Showing her emotions over her command. In fact, the large, red hellion was already softening.

"Yeah, Dusk will survive. I promise." He said, turning a soft smile. But quickly brought his attention back to Dusk,

"But I need to concentrate. You should go check on our friend. Or make sure Kale hasn't disrupted anything yet." Jok suggested. Fesh quickly got the hint and nodded.

"Fine, don't take too long." She ordered, sternly but there was a hint in her voice that made hellion laugh.

Ryko was first to leave with Fesh right behind him. Walking past Kale, she was humming a gentle tune as Kane was still asleep. It wasn't long before she spotted the pair.

"Oh! Hey guys!" She shouted in a whisper. Waving to them happily. Fesh then gently nudged Ryko towards Kale,

"Keep her company. I'll keep an eye on the flight." Fesh ordered her tone cooling.

"Wait, now?" Ryko tried to ask but was quickly cut off.

"You heard me, plus you owe you her from last time." Fesh reminded Ryko. Who placed his hand on his chest.

"Hey, I did it to protect your sister." Ryko said back, trying to defend himself, but Fesh wasn't having any of it as her reply was her closing the door on him. With a sigh, Ryko then walked up to Kale.

"Hiya Ryko!" Kale whispered, patting on the seat beside her. Though hesitant at first, Ryko did take a seat beside Kale.

"Hey Kale, how are ya?" He asked calmly.

"Me? I'm great!" She answered gleefully, shifting her position to rest her head on Ryko's lap. Placing her feet on Kane's lap as she got comfortable. Ryko raised a finger before pointing it at Kane's lap.

"Is that necessary?" He asked, seeing her two toes wiggle as Kale rested.

"What? I don't think he minds. Right, Kane?" She asked the sleeping human, who didn't reply. Though Kale gently shook him with a foot to make it seem like he was giving a nod.

"See? No problems here." She stated, looking up at Ryko with a smile. Which admittedly, Ryko found pretty cute.

"Alright alright, you win." He said, booping her snoot gently. Earning a giggle in response. Kale then nuzzled his lap softly as Ryko then leaned back into the chair. There was a light hum in the room as the Jade continued the jump.

Ryko then nervously rubbed the back of his head,

"Hey, I know we're technically still on a mission...though I wanted to apologize for what happened in Gio." He said gently, looking down at her. Kale looked up at Ryko, her smiling fading.

"Hey, it's okie Ryko. I was only a bit scared." She reassured. Though it didn't seem to mean much as Ryko soon wrapped his arms around her.

"You say that, yet you were in tears. While I was...gone." He croaked, feeling tears well up in his eyes.

"Aww hey, that's not fair. I know why we had to split up... We all do." She said softly, hugging him back. Ryko squeezed her gently as he forced the tears back.

—

Ryko and Kale remembered the event so vividly...

The dark streets being only lit from the neon signs on from the several shops littered in the cities of Gio. Though Kale was an adult woman, she was quite frightened to be alone in such an unknown place to her. Fesh had gone to speak with the dealer for the current mission, Dusk was with her while Jok was stationed to protect the Jade. Then there was Ryko, who said he needed to blow off some steam. Kale then asked to come along, wanting to help him in such a dark time. Kale hardly saw Ryko sad, maybe disappointed or stressed. Though at this moment, Kale worried that he was becoming nothing but depressed.

"Hey, Ryko?" Kale hissed shyly, stepping towards him nervously. Her hands were fidgeting together gently. She looked up at the lykoi, her eyes almost glowing from the several colours in the area. Ryko found a small smile form on his face.

"Of course Kale." He said, already answering her question, waving her over. Her face almost glowed from the response as she power-walked towards him.

"So, where are we going?" She asked, taking Ryko's hand as she leaned closer to him.

Ignition: Unknown Criminal

"Well, how about we get something to eat." He said, moving closer to another set of shops. Kale nodded softly,

"Ooo I'd love that!" She replied gleefully. Ryko only laughed softly,

"Of course you do, if there's food nothing's stopping you." This only made Kale giggle,

"Yep!"

They walked to a noodle shop in one of the many shopping districts. People of all races walked along the busy malls. More neon was resting on the buildings and the sides of posts, trying to shout different advertisements to all of the potential customers below. The hot noodle bowls tasted surprisingly fresh, especially with how far they were from the core worlds. Yet, none of them wanted to ask. At least Ryko didn't when he turned to Kale she didn't even seem to notice as she simply ate. Happy to be with him instead of alone.

"Mmmm, wow! Good find Ryko!" She beamed, enjoying another slurp of her noodles. "I wasn't expecting this to be so good! I do always seem to think that human food is weird...till you try it!" This only made Ryko happier, even calm. Seeing Kale being so joyful herself. Even if it wasn't that rare of a sight.

"Heh, yeah. They're definitely better cooks than lykoi." Ryko chuckled. The two allowed themselves some silence to enjoy the food. These ramen noodles weren't always the most filling meal, though the price usually made them worth it. Plus, Ryko knew they would need to head back to the Jade soon. Placing the empty bowl on the table, Ryko soon gave a sigh,

"Alright Kale, time to go." He said, seeing her tipping the bowl in her mouth to finish the broth. With a sigh of relief, she placed the bowl down once she was done drinking.

"Alrighty! Let's go!" She practically yelled, jumping up from her seat. Ryko placed a finger on his lips as he stood up.

"Shhhh, not so loud! We are still here on a mission. We can't risk being spotted out here." He said sharply. Walking up to Kale, seeing her mood going down, her face drooping down.

"Right, sssssorry." She hissed softly.

"Hey," Ryko said, using a hand to bring her chin up. Her face at eye level with him.

"You're fine, Let's just head back, ok?" He asked gently. To which Kale nodded, suppressing the tears back.

"Oh come on, I know you're stronger than that. I wasn't even mad." He said, lightly scratching the bottom of her chin. Making Kale smile in return.

"Yeah yeah, your right." She said while enjoying the soft scratches.

From that point on they were ready to leave. That was until someone had stepped out of their seat, placing his drink on the table. As Ryko started to step out of the eating area outside, a hand suddenly took a grip of his arm. Before Ryko could have time to react, the man's fist came flying and smashed into his face! From the quick motion, Kale turned around to see Ryko already preparing a fist of his own. Clenching it hard before lurching his body forwards punching the stranger under the rib. Who collapsed to the ground immediately after, his arms wrapped around his chest as he gasped for air. With the quick help from Kale, Ryko got back up.

"We need to get out of here, It's an am-" A blue laser suddenly fired across the pair and slammed in the wall behind them. People suddenly rushed out of their seats. Screams filling up the shops as more lasers and bullets were soon being fired! Pulling out an *S7-SMG* from her handbag, Kale carefully fired at the direction the bolt came from. Trying to avoid the fleeing people desperately trying to get away from the firefight. Though the initial panic only made it harder for Kale to continue firing as more innocent people filled her view. While their attackers had no issues firing blindly into the crowd. Kale watched in horror as bodies began to fall on the cold concrete.

"O-oh my gwars…" She muttered.

Ryko then grabbed Kale, snatching her weapon and stuffing it back in her handbag. Ignoring her confused reaction as he tugged her towards him as he hastily moved towards an alleyway.

"Are you crazy!? You can't be firing blindly in public!" He hissed, his tight grip moving them along.

"I-it wasn't blind!" Kale said back, wanting to defend herself. "I was trying to force them to hide." She continued much quieter now. To which after a moment of silence between them, Ryko nodded,

"O-ok that's fair. And…" He hid them by the wall at the end of the alleyway. Peeking over he was ready to run if they came sprinting down, but it never happened. He sighed heavily as he loosened his grip on Kale's hand before letting go.

"And, your plan worked." He admitted, turning back to her, with a slight grin. "There always seems to be at least one way you manage to impress me." He added. Kale only smirked before fear slowly kicked in,

"You think those were Dafek's Pirates?" Kale asked, looking up at Ryko.

"I'd bet on it." He answered quietly. "Come on, Fesh is probably worried sick by now…Especially if these guys are onto us out here." Ryko kept a hand on his holster as he turned around, trying to hastily come up with a route.

"Yeah follow me." He said, leading them through a set of sidewalks. Keeping their heads low, they pushed through the crowds of people, lightly so they didn't draw any attention to themselves. Which was the opposite of the pirates chasing them. Looking back every so often, Ryko would spot them getting closer.

"Kale?"

"…I see them too."

"Kale?" Ryko asked again, much more rigid. Making her turn her head slightly in his direction.

"Kale, keep moving to the Jade, Let Fesh know that Dafek has found us."

"What about you?...Ryko?"

Ryko however, didn't reply. In fact, When Kale brought her face to where he was walking, he was gone. A shiver soon went up her spine, the realization of being alone always strikes her hard. With a deep breath and looking back down, taking one step at a time she kept on moving. For added protection, she placed a hand on her *S7* so she can be prepared for anything.

The sound of gunfire soon filled the street! Kale forced herself not to look back. The fear she kept locked in her gut was thrashing inside. Wanting to make her panic, though Kale managed to just keep on walking. She did quicken her pace but avoided running like the other people once the shooting started. It was proven to be quite difficult as people would shove past her. A female hellion even pushed her hard into a wall of a coffee shop. Nothing broke but Kale felt the air from her lungs being forced from her from the harsh impact.

"O-ow." Kale soon fell to her knees. Within a few seconds catch a breath, she got back up.

"You better come back alive Ryko…" She muttered to herself as she continued to push through the crowd.

Originally, Kale was going to wait until she was further away from the fighting before contacting the Jade. Though it seemed Fesh was already becoming impatient, hearing her communicator going off Kale answered as quickly as her shaky hands will allow her. A 3D-Holo Projection of Fesh's face was shown on the little device.

"Kale! Where are you?! Dafek's pirates are scouring your location an-are you, are you crying?" Fesh asked, bringing her voice down. Oddly enough, Kale didn't even notice until Fesh mentioned it. The cool streams of tears flowing down her face. Though she simply nodded,

"Yeah, I'm on my way...I-it's Ryko...H-he's holding them off for me. I'm...a-alone." She whimpered quietly. Fesh mumbled a Gwarian curse before replying,

"Alright, Kale, we are on our way, Just stay safe alright?" Kale held back another set of tears before saying back,

"O-okie...L-love you Fesh." Then real softly Fesh then said,

"Love you too." Then the call disconnected.
The fighting was only getting closer, no doubt Ryko was merely trying to buy them time. Time Kale needed to keep moving. With her *S7* still in her hand, she began to pick up her pace to a jog, still attempting to blend in with the chaos within the crowd. Kale had been able to handle the near-constant shoving from the people. Being almost knocked out by that hellion definitely gave her the heads up she needed. Kale knew not to underestimate the civilians, especially when in a state of fear-induced panic. When Kale felt she was making some good distance from the gunfire behind her, that soon meant little to her when she heard more shooting but this time in front of her. Swiftly pulling out her *S7-SMG* she lightly brought her finger on the trigger, bracing herself for the pirates knowing that she would have to get past them. It wasn't long before the first one came to her sights, a female lykoi. Her orange and white clothing gave her away. Before the pirate could raise her *Rift-Carbine* Kale already had her sights on the pirate. Quickly tapping the trigger to fire a controlled burst into

her upper body. She was flung backwards from the burst fire and slammed onto the concrete. Other pirates soon screamed at each other from the crowd. Soon enough, another pirate came into view, firing a basic pistol. Though Kale briskly ducked, avoiding the shot as the bullets hit a human straight in the chest behind her. Kale then tapped the trigger of her SMG again, the series of bullets blowing through the pirate's leg. Who wailed in pain as he dropped to the ground. However, the wounded pirate wasn't able to scream for long as the crowd ran towards him!

"W-wai-!" He was quickly cut off as the crowd of all races trampled him! His body being mangled and flattened in the ground. Kale felt nothing for him as his screams eventually stopped. Knowing that he was more than willing to gun these people down to kill her.

Another pirate appeared to attack, though this time from Kale's left! She almost didn't notice him as he lunged towards her! With a modified, electric knife in his hand, he swung aggressively towards her! Due to his speed in the ambush, Kale was half a second too late to dodge the attack as the blade sliced her left shoulder! She hissed in pain as the cut itself wasn't deep, the shock made her arm go numb and limp. The *S7* soon dropped from her hand. The pirate chuckled at seeing his enemy now defenceless.

"Heh, too easy little snake! Now come over her-!!" The pirate was suddenly silent as a green laser bolt slammed onto his face! Sending his body to crash into a fleeing gwarian! Looking where the shot came from she spotted Dusk! Couching at an opened side door of the Jade. With a *Dravis Sniper Rifle* in hand, Dusk aimed the long silver weapon before charging it up to fire another bolt at a fourth pirate ready to ambush Kale. Right after the pirate collapsed to the floor, Kale's communicator soon went off again. With a quick answer Kale already began to speak,

"Thanks Dusk! Where's Ryko!?" She then asked. Looking back at the crowd, hearing the gunfire only continue.

"I can't seem to spot him, though If I know Ryko he's most likely already spotted the Jade. We are going to land by the coffee shop, Luvers Of Caffeine. I'd make haste Kale." Dusk advised, ending the call. Watching the Jade move, Kale attempted to sprint towards it. This time she had to push others out of her way. Usually, she would be the first to help, but she knew well enough in this situation that would be impossible. If anything, the longer she stayed the more they were in danger.

With a sharp turn around a corner, Kale spotted Luvers Of Caffeine. On the roof, the Jade was hovering, both Dusk and Jok suppressing more incoming pirates on the streets. As fewer people were on the streets, Kale's cover was only being diminished. Kale rushed towards an abandoned hover car. She took in a breath of air. Wanting a few seconds to breathe, Her right hand clenched on the burning wound on her limp shoulder, the numb effect was wearing off. Without a weapon, Kale knew her only chance was to make a run for it...and hope Dusk and Jok had her back. Then after wiping the remaining tears from her face, she braced herself and stood. The first half a dozen of pirates didn't even notice her. They were hiding behind other hover vehicles dispersed along the street. Using the element of surprise to her advantage, Kale dashed towards the closest pair, hiding behind a hover car right in front of hers. Since they were both crouching, Kale swung her leg to the side at the first one, her boot smashing into the back of her head! The pirate's head hurled at the door, knocking her out instantly. The second brought his head up only to meet the bottom of Kale's boot as it swiftly collided with his face, pulverizing his nose and jaw as he crumpled on the ground.

"One of them is here!" One of the pirates across the street shouted. The other few that were taking cover soon brought their attention to her. While staying hidden from Dusk and Jok, they began to fire their weapons at Kale! She yelped as she was forced to crawl to another side of the hovercar. However, that soon also became a bad option as more pirates began to close in on her.

"O-oh no…" she squeaked to herself. Seeing pirates moved closer to her cover, hearing a spray of gunfire to keep the Jade distracted. Turning to her right, she saw the first pirate make a move! With a baton in his hand, he darted for an attack. Mustering the energy she had, Kale flung herself to the side. Hearing the metal weapon smash into the hovercar from the brutal swing. While on the ground, Kale kicked her foot at the lykoi's knee, breaking it as it bent backwards. He screamed in agony, dropping his weapon and falling to the ground. As the others soon rushed in, Kale felt a hand grip on her left shoulder. Kale hissed in pain as the pirate's hand forced her to her feet. She attempted to use her good arm to swing an elbow to the attacker's face. Which smacked right into his nose, but his grip was still tight. If not stronger now. Making her cry out more, Kale barely had time to notice the approaching fist crashing into her chest. Winding her as she coughed the little air left in her lungs. Surrounded and pinned, Kale was finding the fear clawing further within her as she flailed perilously from the several hands holding her on the hovercar.

Then with a sudden boom of a *Hize Hand cannon,* the grip on her shoulder was loosened. A loud ringing filled Kale's ears from the shot. Soon after, all of the hands on Kale were gone as she fell to her hands and knees. From both the wounds and exhaustion Kale found herself unable to look up. She heard muffled shouting followed by several gunshots above her. Including that heavy *Hize,* which gave her much needed hope. That hope only accelerated when she felt a soft hand take hold of her, now facing Ryko.

"Hey, Kale, I'm so sorry." He said through tears. Though Kale only smiled,

"You survived…" She said meekly. Ryko nodded, wrapping a hand over her with his *Hize* in his other hand. The large black pistol glowed yellow around the sides.

"Alright, we should be clear to move. You ready?" He asked hoarsely, feeling tired himself. Kale sighed, forcing her head up,

"Yeah." She said weakly, though determined.

Ignition: Unknown Criminal

From the hovercar, the two moved along the street. Ryko soon realized he had to do most of the work as Kale was pretty much leaning on him. Though he didn't mind as she clearly struggled through some combat before he got to her.

"Just stay awake, Kale, Please..." He asked softly, Pushing closer to the coffee shop, he heard Dusk and Jok firing down at the pirate's behind them. Keeping them pinned so he can keep them moving. Although Ryko needed to quickly raise his *Hize* when he saw a pirate sprint through an alleyway! With the pull of the trigger, a round, yellow laser disintegrated the pirate's chest! After taking him down, Ryko burst into the coffee shop. Becoming extremely grateful that it was empty as he was now having to carry to the passed out gwarian. With the *Hize* in his holster, he used both hands to bring Kale up the stairs. As Jok was reloading his *Rift* he saw Ryko kick the door to the roof open. Going in a full sprint towards them!

"Dusk! Move, Ryko is here!" Dusk moved his orange eyes before displaying a smile,

"Ah! You're correct!" He said before stepping aside for the lykoi carrying Kale.

"Fesh, we got them! Go!" Jok boomed. Fesh didn't even reply before closing the door, taking the Jade off-world at full speed.

"Besides, we kicked butt AND completed our mission!" Kale chimed in, nuzzling softly. Which helped quite a bit as Ryko sniffled. "Now stop crying, you never cry Ryko." Kale practically ordered, crossing her arms. That got a smile out of him.

"Yeah...Yeah, your right. Though we can't all be as stone-cold as Jok." He said.

"I heard that!" The hellion boomed from his workspace, which made the pair chuckle. After a minute or so, the chuckling died down as Kale was very pleased to see a smile on Ryko's face.

"There you go." She teased. "Now, stop blaming yourself, the past is the past." To which Ryko tilted his head,

"It was a few days ag-" But Kale pressed a finger on his lips.

"Shhhhh. Shush you, past is the past." She stated again, Grinning playfully. Ryko brought his head up, rolling his eyes halfway.

"Ok, you win. Past is the past." He repeated.

Fesh opened the door to meet the two. Though before she started speaking, she paused at seeing Kale resting on his lap while her feet were kicked up on Kane's lap. A finger was raised as her eyes went to Ryko, who only mouthed,

"Don't ask." With a slow nod, she decided to go with it.

"Right, well you two should get cleaned up and ready to go. We have just jumped in the Raxin Prime

System. We should be landing on Jez within a few hours."
Fesh ordered. As Kale then stood up, Ryko then replied,

"Well hold on, you two get ready together first, I'll
wake up the human." Kale then added,

"His name is Kane." Ryko then corrected himself,

"I'll wake up Kane." Which made Kale smile in
response. As the two were starting to leave, Ryko then
added in half shout,

"And please try to take under an hour this time."

The pair then said in union,

"Yes, dad."

CHAPTER NINE

"I apologize to wake you sir, but you may want to see this."

The voice came from the ship's speakers from Captain Vail. Alan's eyes opened right after. Laying in his bunk, the bottom of the top was the first thing his eyes caught on. With a sigh, he sat up. Rubbing his organic eye before standing on the cool metal floor. Alan knew by the tone of the captain's voice, Alan wasn't going to be pleased when he got to the bridge. So, as he got changed into a fresh set of clothes he mentally braced himself for what he was gonna find out.

Stepping out of the bunks, Alan moved briskly towards the bridge. As he moved through the various halls of the Hollan, A U.G.G Y-Class Capital ship, Alan would nod and even salute back the many soldiers and workers onboard the enormous vessel. Alan understood he needed to respect the environment here, even if it's a ship. People sometimes treat ships like this their home, since they have the right to raise and be with their families on them. Most living quarters that house families are within the thickest areas of the ship. Alongside being the closest to the escape pods. This allowed morale for the many soldiers aboard to be increased dramatically, as they no longer needed to have a long-distance relationship with their loved ones for months or even years. An added bonus for the Union as the children will not only get their standardized education on the ships but will also have the opportunities once to train as crew or soldiers if they choose too. Having work upon their graduation.

There had been many arguments on the ethicality of having children on military ships, especially when sent to combat. Though to many members of the U.G.G, including Alan, this is seen as necessary as it would only show the future of the U.G.G the importance of the strong will, courage and sacrifice it takes to be a part of the U.G.G, regardless of your profession. It was harsh to a lot of citizens since the chance of any of these ships being destroyed in battle is a real possibility. Though Alan passed the law to be mandatory for naval personnel to have their families live within their vessel for a minimum of twenty years. When it's passed, whoever became the next elected G.L would not be able to immediately remove it. As time passed, Alan soon noticed stability on many of the core and colony worlds improved as the next generation was much more prepared with the new life on the Capital ships. Alongside the numbers of the U.G.G's fleets and armies rising.

The moment Alan stepped in the bridge, all of the crew stood in attention at the sight of him.

"G.L on deck!" The captain barked, his hand swiftly moving to form a salute. A human, Captain Vail had a long-form. Standing over Alan by a foot. His hand only inches away from his round spectacles as the salute stayed. Alan quickly replied,

"At ease everyone." Once the words came out of his mouth, everyone got back to work. Alan walked up to Vail, who held a grim expression on his face.

"Sir, Corgan had contacted the bridge while you were resting. Kane Lons had escaped Para V." He said with his hands behind his back. Vail watched as Alan walked past him to observe the planet before them. The first thing Alan spotted was the series of fires burning through one of the defence stations.

To think that rebel was such a deadly pilot.

He noted to not underestimate him. Looking around the rest of the defences, Alan spotted several destroyed fighters along with the damaged stations. Blown to either small debris or large chunks still in flames. Many good people died today, Alan soon realized. Letting out a breath of air. Unaware of his hands clenching on the railing in front of the window. His cybernetic hand started to crush the metal.

"Shall I get Corgan for you, sir?" Captain Vail asked, clearing his throat as some of the crew watched their G.L nervously. The captain stood his ground, prepared to give the order but Alan shook his head,

"That won't be necessary captain, I'd rather not hear excuses for his failure at this time." The captain was surprised by the answer, though nodded his head waving everyone to get back to work.

"Understood sir. The fleet is at standby for your orders." He said, Watching the view from his position. With a few minutes of thinking, Alan began to give orders to the captain,

"Contact the admirals of each station, get as much information about the crew Kane was with and where they jumped. Then contact the base Kane escaped from, send me the troops that dealt with him personally." The captain was swift,

"Yes sir!" Was the immediate response before giving orders to the crew. Alan turned to see everyone on the bridge hard at work. Vail did good work keeping his people in line. Something Alan was impressed to see as he began to exit the bridge,

"Send the troops to my quarters, you have an hour captain." With that, Alan left.

———

Fay rested by the leg of an *Ark Sentry*. Feeling rather pissed that Kane got past her squad and the rest of the platoon she was with. A lykoi curse escaped her lips as she leaned on the massive mechanical leg. Axel was standing beside her, his rifle still in hand.

Austin Patten

"Those damn *Krets*, never knew how strong those ships are." He commented, thinking out loud.

"They are used by Special Forces for a reason." She said back, "I'm just surprised that the bastard managed to get a crew with one." Axel took off his helmet, revealing his dark bald head.

"Yeah, I just wonder how command plans on catching him now." That only made Fay scoff.

"Hey," Axel started, getting Fay to look at him this time. "I'm sorry about Glin. He was a good man, and a great soldier." He said gently. Seeing the pain in Fay's eyes.

"Would've been a great father too…" She added cooly. Her hands became fists. "That is...before that rebel took him away from me." Her breathing was getting heavier as the memory replied in her mind. Kane, on the ground, firing straight in her husband's face.

"Damn him. Damn him!" She screamed before suddenly turning around and punching the *Sentry's* leg. Uncaring of the pain shooting throughout her hand. She panted, both Axel and the soldiers were taken quite off guard by the sudden attack.

"He...he will pay. One way or another." She mumbled as tears rolled down her face. Pulling her hand away, she sighed seeing it wasn't broken. Turning herself to rest her back on the *Sentry's* leg. Using an arm to wipe the tears away. Slumping down, she allowed herself to sigh. As everyone began to divert their attention back to their duties and each other. Leaving the lykoi to her own accord. All except for Axel, who took a seat by her. When Fay looked in his direction, she noticed he stayed silent. Which she

127

didn't blame him for. Besides, though she kept quiet herself, she did appreciate the company.

However, the sight of their squad leader caught both their attention. Both of them scrambled to their feet before saluting. Fay nearly tripped from the speed of getting up, thankfully Axel quickly brought a hand to catch Fay. His hand taking hold of her arm. To which Fay used to swiftly balance herself out, soon joining Axel with the salute.

"At ease." He said calmly, ignoring how sloppy Fay's recovery was. Looking down at his military-grade holo-watch, he waved at them to follow.

"Our unit is leaving, let's move." He ordered, removing his face from the holo-watch to leave the area. Fay tilted her head at the order, holstering her rifle behind her as she walked beside their Sargent.

"Sir?" Fay tried to ask, however, the sergeant only raised a finger, silencing her.

"Not now, Corporal Innes, these orders are coming from someone far higher than myself." He stated, leading them to a transport ship. As they moved briskly along the remains of the battlefield, Fay noticed platoons already receiving orders of their own. Some were staying put, while others were sending troops into the base. Repair and Medical crews soon came onto the scene, rushing in aid the wounded of the living and machine. As the three moved through the crowds of soldiers, the sergeant soon spotted their ride, where the rest of their squad waited.

"There they are, Let's pick the pace." He ordered, picking up his pace to a jog. Fay and Axel soon joined him. As they stepped inside in silence, the doors closed behind them. Fay soon brought her head down, wanting nothing but to avoid eye contact with the rest of the squad. Seeing almost all eyes on her. Since they all knew Fay hadn't been able to properly mourn. The sergeant wasn't blind to this either, turning around to see her strap in.

"You can request temporary leave if you need Innes." The sergeant said softly, seeming to sound concerned. However, Fay only straightened her back before looking back at her superior.

"Unless that becomes an order, I'm staying sir." She replied sternly. To which the sergeant only nodded, taking a seat of his own.

"Very well. In that case, listen up everyone." He said, removing his helmet, revealing his human face. Revealing a dark-skinned, well-shaven human. Snapping his fingers, he made sure all eyes were on him.

"We are being posted on the Hollan." He started, placing his helmet on his lap. Seeing the change of everyone's faces.

First, it was a shock...or more like a surprise. Everyone looked at each with the same stunned faces. Being positioned on a Capital ship usually required skills that stood from the crowd. Whether it was specialized training in combat or engineering. You needed something more than the core training of your profession to be even considered. Yet, they just heard the news that they were being positioned on one. Normally excitement would be second, though the sergeant rose a hand to grab everyone's attention again. As the initial mummering began to die down, the sergeant sighed, seeming unsure how this next part was going to go with the squad.

"We are going to speak with the Galactic Leader, Mr. Dokes." The sergeant eventually said, after a long pause. It was as if the air changed in the ship once he finished. Not a word was spoken after, just silence and expressions that showed awe...and fear.

It was quiet for the rest of the ride. The mood only darkened when the transport flew past the Union stations. Fires and large cracks covered a few of them. Fay even noticed the crew rushing inside and out trying to get repairs underway. A few ships from undamaged stations were flying towards their injured brethren. Deploying additional repair crews to assist with the repairs. The square vessels hovering close to the damaged areas of the stations as various tools and crew members were being utilized to help. Although, the environment suddenly became quite horrifying as remains of U-4 fighters laid scattered along the outskirts of the stations. Large chunks were ripped out throughout each craft. Some were even just small pieces of metal floating in space. While others were much more intact. However, their cockpits were destroyed, sending the pilot out in the cold vacuum of space to suffocate and eventually die. In fact, a few of their bodies could be seen alongside their destroyed ships. As if they died together.

Austin Patten

Spotting the Hollan, the enormous capital ship hovering away from the Union stations. No doubt the crew aboard could see the end of the battle to capture Kane. Or at least the remains of it. The ship was a massive, long, smooth rectangle of metal and firepower. As the transport flew along the side of the Hollan, everyone would see the wall of turrets and weapons sticking along the heavy armour the capital ship had. It seemed nearly impossible to not be in awe at the sight. The Y-class was the largest of capital ships the U.G.G had. Used only for large scale invasions and space combat. While also being home to the thousand who operate the enormous vessel. With the many defences laid on the ship were also plenty of windows peering over the thick wall of the ship. Fay wondered how many people had their eyes trained on them. She guessed at least hundreds. Though none of that mattered once the pilot grabbed everyone's attention.

"Keep advised, we are landing in the Hollan within five minutes." He stated. Turning back, Fay noticed the hanger becoming closer as the transport moved in.

The transport soon entered the hanger of the Hollan, landing softly.

"On your feet everyone. The G.L had waited long enough for us!" The sergeant barked. Putting his helmet back on. Everyone did the same, feeling the smooth fabric slide along their faces. The dark green HUD's loading back up. A squad member, Private Eran pressed the button to open the side doors. Leading the soldiers out, the sergeant gave no warning before jogging out of the craft. In two rows, 2 in each row, Fay with the other soldiers kept a steady pace behind the sergeant. People in the hangers turned from either their conversations or work to see who was exiting the ship. Fay caught a handful of crew members repairing a *U-4* fighter stopping to watch the squad exit the hanger. Moving past the other crew and soldiers aboard the Hollan. On the sergeant's HUD, a green line was creating the path to the G.L's office, which was surprisingly closer than he expected. Though he knew no one was gonna be complaining. After arriving right after being in combat for hours, everyone needed rest. However, this needed to be done, especially if Mr. Dokes wanted to actually speak with him and his squad in person. A trickle of sweat was felt down his forehead as he took another turn in the series of hallways. He never really gave much thought of why the G.L wanted to see them personally. He could only assume it had to do with Kane escaping. It was his team that had secured him in his apartment complex. What he didn't know was if it was if this was his squad being punished for Kane's escape or not.

Keep it together damn it.

It was only one more turn before the sergeant began to slow down. Spotting an elevator. Two U.S.T's, Union Shock Troopers stood at each side of the elevator. One of them tightened their grip on their union rifle. Which only made the Sergeant's barrier weak further. Though he pushed forwards, walking briskly before them. A salute offered, his squad behind him quickly saluting themselves.

"At ease." The commanding shock trooper said, already aware of their reasons for arriving. Without further word, he unlocked the doors to the elevator and brought a hand to gesture them to enter. Other then a nod, the Sargeant kept quiet as he and his squad entered the elevator. Everyone brewed in silence for the ride up.

Then the elevator stopped, the doors opened. The whole squad froze in their spot. There he was, Alan Dokes. The U.G.G Galactic Leader standing in the room before them. His back was facing them as he looked out the office observation window.

"Take a seat everyone." The cyborg listened, shifting lightly in his position as the soldiers moved into a seat. Fay realized there were only three chairs available. Allowing the others to take a seat, in silent agreement Fay and the sergeant decided to keep standing. Alan then turned his head back, his body following with a datapad in his hands.

"Number 2465, Your Squad's ID." Alan started, using his thumb to scroll down. "Part of the 17th Defense garrison of Para V, your squad was more well known as Kilo. Hmmm, a common human military name for a unit." Alan stated, sounding rather fascinated by the fact. When he lifted his head from the datapad, he could see how uncomfortable everyone was. Which was understandable given the circumstances. Fay uneasily removed her helmet as she listened.

"Kilo and Echo squads were sent in to extract Kane Lons from his apartment after he eliminated a squad sent to capture him silently. It was soon discovered that he had

Ignition: Unknown Criminal

additional assistance with an unknown team aboard a *Kret*."
Alan sighed, bringing down the datapad. Which still
showed the digitally printed report.

"Though all of you were aware of this...well most of
this. That and you managed to apprehend him. With the
loss of an ally." Alan mentioned, pausing after the last bit.
Bringing his head to face Fay,

"I'm so sorry for the loss of your husband Fay
Innes." Alan then said. Fay found herself straightening her
back. Though her ears drooped from how genuine the
Galactic leader sounded. To actually mourn the death of a
fallen soldier. One that meant the world to her. In an
overwhelming moment of memories of Glin. His handsome
face, his uplifting attitude and his laugh.

God...if I could hear his laugh again....

It wasn't until she felt the sergeant's hand rest on her
shoulder did Fay notice the tears rolling down her face.
Alan, at the other end of his desk, waited patiently for her
to wipe her tears.

"So, I'll get one thing out of the way, none of you
are being punished for Mr. Lons escape. There had been far
too many unknowns to accuse anyone of that." Alan
watched, even felt the tension fall from the squad in front
of him. Most of them sighed in relief as if they had been
ordered to hold their breath until the hidden question had
been answered.

"I'm glad to have calmed everyone down." He said,
offering a smile of his own, though imperfect thanks to his

half mechanical face. "Although, it's time to discuss why you're all have been asked to join the Hollan. As you all are probably aware. It's not every day a squad from a defence garrison is taken to join soldiers aboard a capital ship. Let alone a Y-Class. Let alone *my* Y-Class…" Alan said.

"Though, I've made an exception this time. Sergeant," Alan began, bringing up his head to face the large, bulky soldier. "Your squad will be assisting a task force I've assembled along the Hollan to hunt down Mr. Lons." Alan then pressed a button under his desk to make a holographic keyboard and monitor appear. The sergeant only offered a silent salute to respond to the information provided by Alan. With rapid speed, the cyborg G.L typed along with the keyboard, hitting the enter key with an electronic click.

"I've sent you the location of your team's bunks. This is where your private quarters are. Welcome to the Hollan. You'll be given crew member access. So you can go to all the common and public areas. I doubt I need to tell you to not go into areas that are restricted…right?" Everyone shook their head, giving a nearly united,

"No, sir." Alan nodded,

"Excellent. In that case, you're all free to go. Thank you for your time, I'm excited to work with you all." Everyone was surprised at the casual attitude, though no one complained. Those that were sitting got back to their to join Fay and the Sergeant in one last salute. The G.L merely continued to work, from the reversed end of the screen. It seemed that the G.L had plenty of work to continue. Without another word, the sergeant led everyone to the elevator.

Once the elevator stopped at the bottom, No one within the squad nor the guards spoke a word to each other. When they got out of hearing distance of the guards, it was Axel that broke the silence.

"Well then, that went way better than I thought it would." Others nodded in agreement.

"Alan has always had a way with people, it's one of the many reasons the man became the G.L." Private Eran added. "I mean, he even knew about Glin. I've never heard of someone with that level of power care about the loss of a soldier. And never the G.L." With that said it was Fay's turn to talk.

"Yeah, I don't think his death could've been more respected. He didn't get the death he deserved, but at least he's sacrifice has meant more than just to us...So it's going to count for something, right?" No one had an answer for her. Only silence. Till the sergeant chipped in.

"Yes, Glin won't be forgotten, Fay. None of the soldiers that died on Para V today. They all fought to the death to take that criminal down. This time, as the G.L mentioned, we will be prepared for him and his allies." He said gruffly.

As the squad continued to walk through the large halls of the Hollan, many crew members began to look at the soldiers with less suspicion now that the G.L has given them actual status aboard the ship, even if it technically wasn't the status of the soldier. Fay, alongside the rest of her squad, at least felt to be more welcomed to the ship. That feeling only increased when a lykoi cleaner was spotted with her child. Both of them were cleaning the walls of the hallway. The small girl smiled brightly at the soldiers, regardless of how filthy and battered they looked.

"Whoa! Look, mommy! The soldiers that are helping us!" She beamed. Waving with her free hand with a scrubber in the other. The woman looked back as well, seeming quite happy seeing such a bright smile on her child's face. Fay, being the only one with her helmet removed smiled back. Waving her free hand as well. Though, she honestly had no idea what to say back. However, that didn't seem to change much from the child as she only giggled. Though the mother soon got back to cleaning.

"Yes Vear, now come on. Let them be, they clearly need some rest after the day they had." She said.

"Okie mommy." The child replied, soon turning around to continue scrubbing alongside her mother. Though, when she looked to the left, seeing the soldiers turn she quickly shouted one final,

"Thank you for stopping the bad guys!!!"

Axel smiled softly as they were at the door to their bunks.

"Cute kid, I nearly forgot entire families were living on these ships." He said, waiting for the sergeant to unlock the door. The red screen on the door soon flashed green, unlocking the door and opening it for the squad to enter. There was a large room that they walked into. To the left was a closet to store their weapons and gear. Which they all did, double-checking the rifles were on safety before storing them. Further in the room was a couch and holo TV, a small kitchen with the essentials. Even a dining table was provided. At the end of the room were 5 doors.

"Those are bedrooms right?" Private Erans asked, to which the sergeant nodded.

"Good, I'm crashing then." He said before taking his boots off to claim the first bedroom. Though she waited till she was inside, closing the doors behind her, Fay replied to Axel's comments regardless of it being a bit late,

"One of the many perks of working on such a massive ship. You'll be away from your homeworld for years mostly. No one ever wants to be away from their kids as they grow up in the background." Axel nodded, as everyone else began to head to their personal rooms. Fay walked towards hers, though stopped halfway to look back at Axel.

"Hey, thanks. For helping me....with everything today." Axel only nodded before softly slapping her shoulder.

"Anytime Fay, We'll get through this. For him and the rest of the squad." Though his face soon shifted to become more serious.

"Just, stay strong alright? Do whatever you need to do, but don't fall apart on us." Fay nodded, a hand on the door handle to her room.

"Thanks, I will." She said before heading in and closing the door behind her. The moment the feeling of privacy hit her, she walked to the bathroom. Flicking the lights on. Whipping open the shower curtain, she turned the faucet to get a hot shower started. Taking her uniform off as fast as she could, she tried not to practically rip the thing off. She just dropped it all on the floor before stepping in. Sighing at the hot water raining down on her body. With another sigh, the feeling of loneliness hit hard...and with it came the third set of tears.

CHAPTER TEN

"Hey, you're awake."

Ryko simply stated, seeing the human's eyes open slowly before trying to close again.

"Hey now," Ryko said, lightly slapping Kane on the cheek. Or at least it felt soft by his standards. Ryko noticed a red mark along Kane's face as he jolted up.

"Whoa! I'm up I'm up!" Kane yelled. His head darting side to side. Seeing nothing but Ryko and the interior of the ship he escaped in.

"Oh," Kane said, seeming embarrassed by the noise he made. Ryko chuckled,

"You're fine, sorry for the rude awakening. We should be arriving soon." Ryko explained, getting to his feet to stretch. As Kane continued to wake up, he watched the Lykoi stretch what seemed to be nearly every muscle on his body. After a few extra minutes Kane soon joined him, almost immediately yawning the moment his feet touched the ground. Stretching his arms up and high. Moaning lightly while doing so.

"So, I never exactly got your name," Kane mentioned, trying to break the silence. The silence Ryko was actually enjoying as he stretched. Though he knew how much most humans enjoyed conversations. So he decided to not be rude any further and answered,

"Ryko." He said, stretching his back on all fours. Getting back on two feet. "You're Kane right?" Kane smiled as he also stretched his back, staying on two feet as he bent it back.

"You got it."

A few more minutes of silence followed as Kane didn't exactly know what else to bring up. They both just continued their stretches. However, it wasn't too long before they finished. Ryko picked up the same awkwardness Kane felt as they stood by the chairs, only hearing the light hum of the Jade in jump speed. Turning back to Kane he attempted starting a new topic,

"So, guess I should thank you for getting us out of Para V, that flying was pretty incredible, you've impressed me so far." Not only did Kane's smile return, it was tad larger than before from the compliment.

"Now that's surprising, someone impressing dad that quickly?" Fesh said with sarcasm. Walking from the cockpit. While Ryko rolled his eyes from the comment. Kane was soon baffled by the name,

"Dad?" He asked looking back and forth at the two. "Am I missing something or-" Fesh was quick to snap at Kane,

"Not biological, you idiot!" Suddenly stepping closer to jab a finger at his chest. Her face squinting with annoyance from the question she interrupted. Kane brought his hands up in defense, stepping back to only fall back in his seat. Looking up at the rather pissed off looking gwarian above him.

"Fesh, be easy on the human." Ryko said, crossing his arms. To which her expression changed rather quickly when she turned back to Kane. A grin was slapped on her face as she offered a hand.

"Alright, guess we need him alive anyway." She said.

"Lucky me." Kane said back, accepting her help. When she got him back to his feet, Fesh gave him some space as she rested her back along a wall across from him,

"Sorry about that. It's just that isn't the first time I've heard the question...or someone being an ass because of it." She scoffed. Ryko then said,

"I think what she's saying is that we are a family, just in another sense. We met when-" Ryko was gonna start, when he noticed Fesh pointing at her wrist. Knowing full what that meant, he continued,

"Well, long story short, I found Fesh and Kale as children. No parents to be found as they were alone on one of the nastiest colony worlds." Ryko sighed. Kane tilted his head,

"Which one? ...If you don't mind me asking." He asked carefully, looking at Fesh for almost permission to know. To which she nodded with a shrug, knowing full well Ryko was gonna answer either way.

"Fold." Ryko replied. Kane's eyes widened at the answer. Fold was a dangerous world, known for having one of the most deadly environments in U.G.G space. From brutal lightning storms and Planet-Quakes. Fold was plentiful in reasons why someone wouldn't wish to live there, let alone raise a family. The only reason the U.G.G even bothered to colonize the planet was because it had enormous pockets of minerals and ores.

"I was a miner on Fold for a few years, jobs were high paying and...I had a few debts to pay off. Unfortunately, with time and space the loans won't find an end to find you. So, after surviving on that horrid planet long enough to pay off the loans I was ready to finally leave. When I got to the spaceport, I noticed both of them digging through a trash can. No one did a thing, just kept on walking as if that was a normal sight. When I soon learned their situation I offered them to come along with me. And well...here we are." He said, expanding his arms out to show what the event led to.

"And you did wonderful dad!" Kale added gleefully! Rushing out of the cockpit to hug the lykoi. Ryko smiled brightly at this, hugging Kale back.

"Thank you Kale." He croaked, managing to not shed tears. Kane at the very least smiled at the sight.

"You know, for hardly knowing me for a day you've been quite socal." Kane commented.

"OH! That's dad for ya! He is a huge socal butterfly when he can get the chance!" Kale replied, soon giggling after, "I bet Fesh already told him to keep this story brief right?" This made Ryko blush in silence as Kane chuckled.

"Yeah, I'm sure she did." Fesh then stood back up, soon actually realizing Kale was here.

Ignition: Unknown Criminal

"Wait, Kale, you were supposed to be monitoring for when we entered Jev." She said, already walking back into the cockpit.

"Oh yeah! I already got the clearance from Draz! Auto-pilot is taking us to the spaceport!" Kale replied. Though Fesh still went inside anyway. Just to be safe.

Though she came out seeming good,

"Good job Kale, we should be on the ground in ten minutes." She informed, heading back to the cockpit. Kale stuck out her tongue playfully.

"Told you!" Ryko then loosened his grip on Kale, looking back at Kane,

"So what's your story Kane?" He asked, actually taking a minute to look at the human. Who seemed to be quite harmless looking. Most people would agree humans were the weakest of the five known species. Although many knew to never underestimate them. When Ryko eventually decided to become a smuggler, his opinion of a human's ability had changed dramatically. When strength wasn't an option they were usually quick to either flee or find another way to take their opponent down.

"I mean, you don't seem to look like the rebel type." Ryko added. Kane was quick to change moods from the question,

"That's because I'm not. Someone is telling lies about me." He replied with frustration stuck in his voice. Both Kale and Ryko became puzzled at the reply.

"Wait, what are you saying?" Kale asked.

Austin Patten

"I'M SAYING I'M NO REBEL! I DON'T KNOW WHY BUT THE WHOLE U.G.G THINKS I'M SOMEONE TRYING TO HELP THOSE BASTARDS BUT I'M NOT!!!" Kane suddenly exploded.

"I'M-I'm...I'm...just me." He tried to continue, feeling lightheaded as he fell back to his seat.

Kale tightened her grip around Ryko while he instinctively had his hand pressed against his *Hize*. Kane just laid back, in all honesty he was still exhausted. The few hours of rest he managed to get only did so much on him. Especially after nearly the whole day was just fighting, torture...followed by more fighting.

"I'm...sorry." Kane croaked, his throat aching from screaming at the top of his lungs. Ryko nodded,

"Hey, it's alright. We had no idea. We believe you." He assured. Kale also gave her head a nod letting go of Ryko. Moving to sit beside Kane. Kale knew if the human did try anything she'd be more than prepared to deal with him. Though Kane sounded...genuine. Something she doesn't hear often from people other than her family.

"Yeah, you're a good guy Kane." She said softly. Kane sighed, his eyes starting to close.

"Hey, no no no." Kale said, getting up to slap him awake. Feeling the sudden slap woke him back up.

"H-hey. I'm up." He yawned. Though Kale's face told him she wasn't convinced.

Ryko then moved towards the tiny kitchen,

"Do you drink coffee?" He asked, getting the coffee machine started. That seemed to have gotten the human. He practically jumped onto his feet at hearing the word

145

"coffee". It even startled Kale enough for her to step back, for a moment at least. Though she too jumped in response. Hugging the human.

"I think that's a yessss!" She hissed cheerfully! Kane stayed silent but nodded a smile. Which was enough of an answer for Ryko. It was only a minute or so of a wait before he came back with a hot cup of the black goodness for Kane.

"Here you are. I'm sorry that you have to drink it black. Don't exactly have room for cream." Though Kane didn't seem to care as he took the cup, taking a fast but small sip.

"Mmm...Thank you Ryko. You're a saviour." Kane said with a chuckle. Feeling more awake from the small amount of coffee entering his system, the regret of exploding at the people who saved him began to sink in.

"And...I really am sorry for just...taking all of that out on you two. That wasn't fair." Ryko waved it off,

"Kane, don't worry about it. For someone who clearly doesn't go head first into combat often. I can imagine this taking a toll on you." Kale was about to chime in, but then Fesh appeared.

"So that explains the horrifying screeching in my ship." Fesh interrupted. Her arms crossed as she entered the room again. Kane blushed slightly from embarrassment.

"Y-yeah…"

There was a low hum from the ship before everyone felt a light bump under them.

"That, and we are now on Jev. Finish your caffeine and then meet me outside the ship." She ordered sharply, exiting the ship from the side door. Kale followed her out. As both Ryko and Kane were trying to drink their coffee as fast as they could, trying to not burn their tongues in the process Kane suddenly remembered something!

"Wait! What about Dusk? I haven't seen him since that hellion took him." Ryko took a moment to pause drinking.

"That hellion is Jok. He's a good man, rather intelligent for his kind. He's our doctor." Kane laughed a little at that, feeling relief.

"For both organics AND machines?" He asked. Ryko smirked with a shrug,

"Putting it simply, yes. We are very lucky to have him though. I'm sure I've lost count on how many times he saved our lives."

"Now this is true." The almost booming voice said from his office. Walking out Kane saw that tall, bulky red hellion enter. The lab coat must have been specifically tailored for him to fit such a large being.

"It's good to actually meet you Kane. Sorry that our first time was soo...intense." Kane took another gulp of his cooling coffee.

"It's no problem. If anything, I think you saved both of us there. Thank you for that." Jok only laughed,

"As you heard before I seem to have quite a skill for that." Jok looked out the door to see Kale trying to buy the two some time from Fesh,

Ignition: Unknown Criminal

"Although I'd hurry up. That mechanic can only hold Fesh for so long." Kane then did one final drink before rushing over to the kitchen with Ryko to place the cup in the tiny sink.

"Thanks for the heads up Jok, We'll see you soon." Ryko said before the two exited the ship.

I'm aware it's bad!" Fesh shouted at the human mechanic as others were moving past him with tools to begin work. "I'll pay the fee the moment I get paid, you don't believe me? Ask Draz." She spat in irritation, seeing the others catch up.

"Alright let's go, Drazz is waiting for us. I'd rather not make her wait any longer." She said as they walked into the city. One of the first things Kane noticed were no guards at the ports. No one checking the people as they either entered or left the port.

"Is this lack of security normal on Jez?" Kane questioned, watching everyone walk in freely. Kane was used to flying for many U.G.G worlds, both core and colony. Each time he went through several security checks, questions and scans before being able to actually enter the planet. Yet here they were, On a U.G.G colony world and there was nothing.

"Well, even though Jev is officially a U.G.G world. It's more technically a neutral world." Ryko answered, "It's like a Hub for smugglers, pirates, mercenaries or people who just want to escape life under a government." Kane was surprised about the answer. He always assumed life in the neutral worlds would be dangerous, which he still believed, though at the moment he couldn't seem to help but find some attraction to the world. Especially now.

"You don't think the U.G.G would check the neutral world's first?" Kane asked worriedly. Fesh was next to chip in,

"Of course, but Jez is well protected. If the U.G.G were to send in troops on the planet, they would have to push through hundreds of thousands of trained professionals. Plus a lot of them hold grudges…" Kane nodded, seeing a few of these "professionals" shove past him.

"It's a harsh life on Jev, but you do your job and it pays well. Draz can be a tough person to work for. But if you manage to please her you'll definitely be rewarded for it." Kane then began to wonder,

"So wait...why are you bringing me here?" Ryko then moved behind Kane. The three of them formed somewhat of a circle around Kane. Kane quickly noticed the change of mood, almost a warning if he tried anything.

"W-whoa hey now guys. You have me." He assured, raising his hands beside him.

"I don't know, but she paid well enough that we didn't ask questions." Fesh answered. Kale then began to ask,

"Is there any chance you know Draz?" Kane shook his head quickly at that. At most he's had offers to help, even join from messengers. Though he never got to meet her in person,

"No no! I don't deal with smugglers...well...often..." Ryko smirked at that,

"That's a story you're telling when we meet again." Kane's heart almost stopped,

"W-what do you mean?" Fesh glared at Ryko for saying that, soon sighing before facing Kane again,

"This is temporary Kane, no offense but you are cargo to us." She stated plainly. Knowing there is no other way to put it then bluntly. Kale felt guilt rushing through her whole body as she saw how Kane saddened a little from that,

"Right." Kane said.

"W-well we-" Kale tried to say, only for Fesh to shush her.

"No more talking. We deliver Kane to Draz and get our next assignment." Fesh said coldly, watching her sister intently. Who soon nodded, keeping her head down once Fesh removed her hand from Kale's mouth.

The walk along the city felt long and awkward. As what Fesh ordered, no one spoke a word after her talking to Kale. Other than the boost of energy from the caffeine, Kane still felt tired. And horrible, knowing he was a tool for someone he didn't even know. With that first feeling soon came fear.

Do they think he was with the rebels? What if they were going to recruit him? Or kill him? He had no idea who the rebels enemies were and he doubted it was only the U.G.G. If they were based on a world like Jev who knows what kind of people may be trying to put a knife in their back. As this fear crept further and further within him, the idea of escaping became far more alluring to him. With his head down he tried to spot the weapons everyone had around him. For the most part they were all handheld. Even the massive *Hize* that Ryko had holstered. Although Kane had enough common sense to realize how the odds were with taking them. Huffing softly, he brought his eyes back to the ground. Watching his feet take step by step along the pavement. The dirty, cracked sidewalks led them closer and closer to Draz. Kane could only assume that she either worked for the rebel's...or possibly not. If that was the case that's mean so would his "escort". None of them mentioned being in alliance with them. Only that they worked for Draz.

Once they got close to Draz's location, Kane looked up to see an enormous club.

"Draz is in there!" Kane exclaimed. Breaking the long silence. Though Fesh was annoyed from Kane talking, she couldn't exactly blame him. Draz's club was the largest in Jev. Many are always surprised by the sight! Some would call it the "The Partying City" for both its popularity and size. The doors were standing a massive twenty five feet! Kane forced himself to stay quiet after the sudden outburst. Yet his face showed the continuous shock and awe he had. Which seemed to have lifted the spirits of everyone. Even Fesh cracked a smile from the reaction. There were four bouncers at the door. Two gwarian, one human and one hellion. When the four spotted Ryko and the sisters, no words needed to be exchanged as they silently allowed them to pass.

Inside, the club managed to seem even bigger. The whole place was littered with people, booming synthwave and strobe lights. Though one thing that Kane noticed as they moved into the club was that most if not all of the people at the club were near the walls. This included the DJ and the bar. Tables were spread out but stayed within the fenced restrictions. There was a fifteen feet wide area completely open from the entrance to all areas of the club. All with the gigantic doors. Though everyone seemed to find it normal. Even with so much space exposed. Kane would see the odd person sprint along the open areas to reach another. What was the rush?

Fesh led the group to a table at the bar.

"Drazz is busy with another client, got the message when we landed. So, we wait." She stated simply. Taking a seat beside Kane. Who made sure to not seem intimidated by her presence being so close. Though he did gulp when a new question was formed in his mind.

"Do you think she got me to, well, kill me?" Fesh quickly shook her head,

"No, Draz has a handful of enemies, but she rarely bothers to send people to hunt them down for her to kill." Kane looked down at his hands.

"Oh. I see." Ryko found himself wanting to help ease the mood.

"Look, sorry if it seems harsh. That this may seem to be like another job to us. Jok thought the same thing when we were assigned to bring him in. Draz, she looks for people to assist her. Not make more enemies. Or to just *crush* people without reason." He said rather softly.

"So don't seem so damn frightened. You're gonna be fine. Worst case scenario is that she lets you go. The only way your gonna wound up dead here is if you did something stupid. Really stupid. But even then…" He added with a shrug.

A smile was starting to peer along the edges of Kane's face.

"Thanks, Ryko, you have no idea how much I needed that." He said with that smile stuck to his face. Ryko laughed lightly,

"Oh I'm sure we could all tell. Never seen someone shaking in their boots like that." Kane was half a second from defending himself before Ryko cut in,

"But! I can't blame you, this," he said, his arms showing the whole club, "is all new to you. I'm sure Draz will cut you some slack."

Another ten minutes had passed, Ryko offered to get a few drinks for everyone since they were already at the bar. While Fesh was willing to accept some alcohol, both Kane and Kale asked for some non-alcoholic beverages. The people were surprisingly fast at Draz's club. They hardly had to wait five minutes before the drinks arrived. Kane enjoyed it simple, just a glass of milk for him. Bourbon for Ryko, Gin for Fesh and some kind of gwarian juice for Kale. When Kane took the bottle from Kale, he

153

couldn't begin to try to pronounce the drink. He just sighed before handing it back to her. Earning a giggle from Kale as he happily enjoyed a sip. The music was becoming far more catchy and the three noticed Kane was enjoying it. His feet were tapping to the beat, while his head bopped with the beat.

"You dance?" Kale asked, her head trying to follow Kane's lead. Kane chuckled at the question,

"Oh nah, not really. I just know when I hear a good song. Music like this can help make any day better." Kale seemed a little confused by the statement but still enjoyed the swaying to the beat. So she simply continued, trying to keep with the beat.

Ryko smiled at seeing the two happy. Even if it was short-lived. It was only a few more minutes later before the large doors at the end of the club opened. One of Draz's advisors soon activated his holo-watch to signal Fesh. Who stood the second she read the signal,

"It's time." Kane, followed by the rest got up to head to the large doors. Just like at the city, Ryko, Kale and Fesh formed a circle around Kane. Fesh at the front and Ryko and Kale on the sides.

With a push of a button, the advisor opened the door. When opened the sight that Kane saw next almost made him drop his jaw. Though that stopped halfway when Fesh slapped his shoulder hard. Shutting up any comment he was gonna have. Draz was sitting before them. Sitting in what seemed like a normal chair you'd find at the dinner table. She wore jeans with a T-shirt that had gwarian words written along with it. To most, she seemed just like another normal gwarian. The only problem was her size! Draz was sitting high above them at twenty feet!

Well, that explains A LOT about this place....

Kane thought to himself, swallowing down hard at who he was looking at. A Gwarian Giantess. A rare breed of gwarians. Most assumed they were either extinct or practically trapped on Gwars due to their size. Yet Kane was facing one right now. In fact, she called for him. Not only was her size something to behold, but she was also an even more rare morph! Drazz was grey with white dots speckled along her whole body!

"It'sssss good to finally meet you Kane." Drazz started, relaxing into her enormous chair. Her back was straight with her feet planted firmly on the floor. It would have only taken a few more steps before her shadow would be able to swallow them all. Kane nervously replied to the towering gwarian,

"It is?" Draz nodded,

"Of course it isssss!" She then brought her attention to Ryko and the others.

"Wonderful work NightWave! Your paymentsssss will be sssssent you soon." She said rather cheerfully, before suddenly pointing to the door. "Now leave. I need to speak with Kane in private. Your next assignment will be given to you ssshortly." The three then turned around and left.

The moment the door was closed behind them, Draz looked down at Kane.

Ignition: Unknown Criminal

"Alright, time for me to be sssstraight with you." Draz began, crossing her arms. "For ssstartersss I know you're no rebel." She said, finishing with a half chuckle. "I mean look at you. After reading your profile I was amazed that anyone in the U.G.G believed that you were with them. You're harmlesss!" She laughed. Her booming laughter sent vibrations through the floor as Kane just had to stand there awkwardly as he was being practically insulted. "And they claimed you were able to fend off squadssss of union forcesss! Ha! How does their newsss come up with that crap?" She asked, though never expected an answer.

As the laughter began to die down from her, Kane lifted up a finger asking,

"So, If I'm so harmless and useless....why am I here?" That was when the laughter stopped completely. With near-instant speed, she looked back down at Kane.

"I never said you were uselessss." She hissed. "Harmlesss, yes. But I don't need only people who can fight for me, Kane. You do have a ssskill I need." She said, sounding far more genuine this time. Kane was skeptical but questioned anyway,

"Like what?" Draz rolled her eyes at that,

"Don't be sssstupid Kane, we both know your one hell of a pilot. You may have not killed any union forcesss but you've done a good job escaping piratesss, smugglersss and raidersss just as, if not more, competent than them." She shot back.

"I even remember a member of the Dead Nebula sounding pretty pissed that a cargo pilot managed to slip past him." She added with a smirk. Kane chuckled nervously as he rubbed the back of his head.

"Fair point. Granted, he was pretty sloppy himself." That got another chuckle out of Draz,

"Ohhh better hope he doesn't hear that or he'd tear you to pieces. Those hellions are well known for that." She warned in her chuckling. Kane gulped, starting to shake. It was quite obvious for Draz to notice.

"But! That won't happen, when you join me I'll send anyone to kill him if he tries. Or I'll *crush* him myself depending on my mood." Kane's eyes widened, now seeing why Ryko used that word earlier.

"When I join you?" He dared to ask. Draz's smirk soon slumped down to something far more serious after hearing that.

"Yesss, that or you will probably die. Either by the lovely occupants on Jez or the Union trying to hunt you down." Kane was quick to try and defend himself,

"But you're the reason they are hunting me!" Draz was just quick to snap, suddenly standing over Kane! Stomping right beside the human! Her foot created a massive shake in the room!

"I'm the reason you aren't rotting in a cell to only get tortured to death!!!" Falling to his back, Kane shakily rose his hands over him.

"O-Ok! You have a very very good point." Sitting back down, Draz sighed,

Ignition: Unknown Criminal

"Look, regardlessss of what you say. You owe me. Work for me Kane, I pay well and you will be doing good work." She said, waiting patiently for Kane to get back up.

"So...I'm becoming a smuggler as well then?" He asked. Draz merely shrugged,

"Essentially, yes."

"Oh."

That was all Kane could muster in response. He was still so exhausted, it didn't take long for the coffee to wear off. Draz also saw this, the little purple bags under his eyes followed by the sloppy movement.

"I don't expect you to like or trust me yet, Kane. But I want to help you, even if it'sss because I need your skills. It'sss common sssense, a win-win." She said, trying to use human terms to help her. Though, Kane still didn't seem that convinced.

"Well, I also know you have a chip for an anvol cybel."

Draz added.

"What if I was willing to give you a new chassis for him in exchange for your first assignment tomorrow? From the looksss of you, you need the sleep." Kane chuckled weakly at that, as sleep sounded amazing. However, it wasn't nearly as amazing as the idea of bringing Helix back. With a wobbly nod, Kane accepted Draz's offer.

"A-alright. You win." He said. A smile was then planted on Draz's face,

"Good choice, Greg, if may, can you get Kane a new chasis for his cybel?" She asked one of the human servants. Greg nodded,

"Of course Ms. Draz." He replied obediently, leaving the room.

Within a few minutes, Greg returned. He briskly walked up to Kane before offering the new chassis to Kane. It looked almost identical to Helix's.

"Thank you," Kane said politely, pulling out the chip that contained Helix's memories and personality. Kane inserted it in the slot before turning the cybel on.

Kane waited patiently as the boot up started. Helix's face was showing a circle loading screen that was animated to continue a loop. Kane just watched intently as Helix was starting up. Soon, the cybel began to float from Kane's hand. The loading circle disappeared and was replaced with the default smiley face. For a moment Kane's heart sank, seeing the default face just blankly staring at him. Did something happen to the chip? Or was Dusk lying? However, before more of those questions could flood his mind. The smiley face was suddenly changed into a "?". Then quick it began to type,

"Kane? :O". Kane's face changed from anguish to shock and awe within a fraction of a second. A tear or two even rolled down his face.

"Oh my god! H-Helix? Is that really you?" He asked. Seeming to be in disbelief of what he was seeing. However, he was soon given a quick response with Helix flying up to his cheek to nuzzle him. Kane brought both of his arms up to hug the little robot.

Ignition: Unknown Criminal

"Oh, I've missed you too, buddy."

Draz found it surprisingly difficult to not find the moment adorable. Especially at her size. She never expected Kane to be so emotionally attached to his cybel. Then again, in every report that cybel was always with him. If she had to guess, Helix was most likely his only friend for a long time.

"W-whoa. Hold on?" Kane then asked. Pulling Helix back suddenly, Helix's screen then typed out,

"What?". Kane tilted his head,

"Since when could you talk? Or type?" Before Helix could try to reply, Draz quickly answered,

"The chassis is a new model then what he was originally in. The older modelsss were limited to text like emojisss, I'm sssurprised you were using ssssuch an old model for ssso long." Kane shrugged at that, never seeing the point in upgrading his chassis. Helix always seemed perfect to him.

"It's nice to have an improved way to speak with you. :)" Helix typed, the letters animating to the side so it could fit the whole sentence on that small screen.

"Ssso, now that you have been able to see your friend again, I expect you to hold your end of the deal?" She asked, raising a brow. Kane was quick to nod. Though Helix typed,

"Deal?" Kane smirked,

"I'll explain soon, bud." Although one problem suddenly struck his mind.

"Wait, we have an issue," Kane said, looking up at Draz. With her arms crossing again she asked,

"What?" Kane was nervous to admit the problem but he knew it had to be addressed.

"My ship, I don't exactly have it." Draz sighed in relief that it was it.

"Oh, heh, don't worry Kane, I got you out. Of course, your ship isn't with you." She chuckled.

"Right." He said back, a little embarrassed.

"You'll be with NightWave again to get your ship back, on the sssame day I need you to get my cargo the U.G.G will be escorting your ship off of Para V to scrap it. With the Jade and alongside a team of pirates, you'll stop that from happening." Draz said, answering the next question Kane was ready to ask.

"Alright...just one more question, then we are gone for the night," Kane said. Draz sighed, nodding her head for him to ask.

"What about the possibility of the U.G.G sending a fleet here? I mean….I asked Fesh about this. She claimed it would have been crazy for them to try but…" He ended with a nervous shrug.

Draz was silent for a few seconds before bursting out laughing,

"Jez is MY world! If Alan dares to send troops here…" She didn't even bother to finish the threat, sounding dead serious in the end.

"Now, you and Helix get moving. Get some rest. Enjoy the day off….but then you get your ssship and my cargo. Understood?" Kane nodded,

Ignition: Unknown Criminal

"Yes yes, you got it. Right Helix?" Kane asked, turning to the cybel resting on his shoulder. Even though Helix was still very confused on what is going on, he trusted Kane time and time again. That habit had no chance of changing now. Helix typed,

"Yep! ^w^". A smile was then on Kane's face after seeing that. That seemed to be enough for Draz,

"Alright, now leave. Meet with NightWave, you'll stay at their home tonight."

"Sounds great." He said as he walked out.

"Hmph." Draz huffed, finding pride in how easy it was to get Kane on her side. Standing on her feet, she enjoyed stretching out as she was sitting all day having to coordinate for her plans. Draz was about to get ready for some shut-eye herself. That was before she was interrupted by one of her advisors.

"Ms. Draz you have an incoming transmission for you." Draz rose a brow, not expecting any calls at this time.

"From who?" She hissed. The advisor rubbed his neck nervously,

"Um...Unknown."

——

"Oh! You can sleep with me tonight! Since Fesh stopped doing that since we were kids!"

Kale cheerfully offered. While Fesh scoffed and rolled her eyes, Helix suddenly bursted in front of her! Typing an angry,

"He's with me! >:(" His chassis covering Kane's face. Kale jumped a little from the abrupt appearance of the cybel!

"EEP!" Kane then gently took hold of Helix,

"Whoa, hey now bud. They're fine." He assured. Although Helix wasn't so easily convinced, turning around to face his human. Typing,

"Are you sure about that?" Kane nodded,

"Yes, I'm sure, they are the reason I'm standing here tonight." Helix had his screen blank for several minutes. Kane felt a sense of worry as the wait for a reply became longer. Though Kane then read Helix's reply as he typed,

"Fine, but we should head to their home alone, we need to talk...in private." Kane just wanted some sleep, he knew he was at the point where even if he did have the energy to split off from the others, he would hardly be able to get any of the information Helix would try to give. So, Kane shook his head,

"No. We can talk in the morning. Please." It wasn't hard for Helix to recognize how tired Kane was, it must have been far more difficult to escape then he assumed. Feeling rather bad, he floated down to his shoulder.

"Alright, tomorrow we can." He typed,.

The crew of Nightwave hardly heard anything Kane was saying to his cybel friend. Watching the pair come back. Fesh, very slightly leaned closer to Ryko,

Ignition: Unknown Criminal

"Is this going to be a problem?" Ryko only looked at her for a second before Kane began to speak,

"Sorry about that! Helix is not used to me hanging with others often." He said with a chuckle, hoping to bring down any possible tension. Unlike the other two, Kale didn't feel any of that tension, she was just happy to see Kane happy again.

"Awesome!" She cheered, walking beside Kane as Fesh and Ryko kept quiet to lead the way.

"Soooooo…."Kale began to start, "My offer still stands." She said, watching Kane look at his Cybel, who presented a thumbs up on his screen.

"Sounds good to us!" Kane replied. Which made Kale leap happily before wrapping her arms around him, "Yay!"

The group was moving through a rather crowded sidewalk as they moved deeper into the neon-filled city of Heav. Kane widened his eyes at the sight of the large city. Walking past several buildings glowing throughout the city.

"Wow, this place is gorgeous, never seen such a colour city before." Ryko shook his head at the statement, though with a chuckle,

"Doesn't surprise me at all, Most places in the U.G.G are pretty dull. Just concrete and metal…" This was quite accurate unless it was for grabbing the attention of a customer almost everything on U.G.G worlds had a similar design for their cities. In that it was similar to the designs of the 2010s, only with modern materials. Which was decided by Galactic Leader Franklin. He found certain designs being nothing but a problem based on different species. Whether it would be too small for hellion to fit or not enough sunlight for a gwarian to bask. So, to help remedy the problem, the G.L brought in many architects of every race together to design homes, commercial buildings and other essential places for cities within U.G.G territory. It took months of constant back and forth, redesigns and even flaws after the designs were accepted before everything was perfected. Though, when brought to the present, everything works for everyone in a practical sense, it heavily affects the look and feel in the cities as everywhere nearly feels the same.

"Yeah! Ryko is right! Most of those worlds feel so boring; that's why we live here! Always something new!" Kale happily added, clapping her hands together. Kane was still in awe from a park they walked past, his head following it as they moved forward. It was a small park planted beside a condo. A hover-playground was assembled consisting of a slide, a few sets of monkey-bars, an anti-grav trampoline and a set of swings. A smile was soon sent onto the group's face as everyone watched a couple of kids enjoying themselves in the park.

"For a neutral world, it's definitely quite peaceful." Kane noticed, seeing the people go about their evening.

"We try, life on neutrals can be hard, very for most. But we try to show the galaxy we aren't just here to hide criminals and pirates." Ryko explained. After not saying a word for the whole walk, Fesh finally decided to chip in,

Ignition: Unknown Criminal

"Mhm, everyone here are people just like those in the U.G.G worlds. We just didn't want to live under a G.L." She sighed, crossing arms.

It wasn't long before they reached the home of NightWave, It was a rather small house sat in the middle of others. Though they were quite similar in size, shape, colour and even overall design was a different story. The home of Nightwave was two halves of a cylindrical house. The top half was floating a meter or two above the bottom, thanks to the use of grav-lifts on each support beam on the lower half. The colours were a mix of mustard yellow and light red. Which was quite an interesting combination to colours to Kane based on his expression,

"This is… new." Kane said carefully, wanting to use his words correctly.

"We enjoy the newfound freedom of designing our homes." Fesh said, answering Kane's next question. Who was stopped halfway raising a finger.

"I see." Kane replied. "Now I'm just as interested to see the inside." Kale then jumped, literally.

"OH! Then you'll definitely love my room then! It's wayyyy more interesting than the others! Especially Dad's!" She exclaimed, sticking her tongue out playfully when Ryko shouted,

"Hey! I like to keep it...you know, practical." Ryko attempted to defend himself.

"Ha, you mean boring." Fesh chuckled, which made Kale giggle. Kane offered a smile and a shrug to Ryko.

When Ryko unlocked the door to the house, the first thing Kane noticed how clean the living room was. A couch, a few coffee tables followed by a holo-tv mounted on the wall rested neatly. A bookshelf sat beside the holo-tv, though there were mostly holographic pictures along the shelves, Kane noticed a few actual books were on the top shelf. A handful of pictures hung along the walls, most were pictures of Kale and Fesh as children, though one picture that stood out was a triangle one. It stood on the coffee table right beside the couch. In the middle of the photo was Ryko, with both Kale and Fesh in his arms. Kale was hugging his chest while Fesh held a smirk with her arms crossed.

"The girls rooms are upstairs, not gonna lie, you look pretty terrible, you should get some rest." Ryko said, watching Kane shakily remove his shoes. Fesh agreed, catching Kane from nearly tripping on the floor.

"Yeah, we can give you a proper tour in the morning." With Kane's arm wrapped around her, Fesh turned to Kale,

"Can you get your bed ready?" Kale smiled immediately and began to rush to her room!

"You got it sis!" Kale then jumped on the grav-lift and was shot up the upper level. If he wasn't so tired, Kane would have been quite surprised by what he saw. Though, he was at the point where walking was becoming more than a chore for his tired body.

"Stay with me Kane, cause There's no way I'm carrying you." Fesh hissed, feeling him slow down. Using another bit of energy he had left, Kane forced his legs to take another step, then another. Till they soon got the grav-lift themselves. Kane felt the sudden rush within and outside of himself as the grav-lift shot them up. Before slowing down to lightly shoot them out into the hall on the second floor. From there Fesh led Kane to Kale's room. Whose door was open for the two to enter. With his head drooping down, Kane didn't get a good look at her room before they gently placed him on the bed.

"Think you can handle him from here?" Fesh asked, to which Kale nodded with a smile on her face.

"Oh of course! You and dad relax, I'll be down soon!" Kale answered confidently. Which was enough for Fesh as she left without a word. Kane closed his eyes the moment he realized he was in bed. He heard a window opening, a cool soft breeze then entered the room. He sighed in relief, enjoying the coolness of temperature as the house did feel rather warm. A hand then patted his forehead gently,

"There you go, Sleep well Kane. I'll be back soon, need to be with Fesh and Dad first." She said softly before leaving. Though Kane had no idea what she meant by that, his tired brain didn't allow him to think about it much before he drifted off to a long-awaited rest.

CHAPTER
ELEVEN

The seemingly endless sea of space always fascinated Alan. With every trip, every look in the telescope and even just on his homeworld, the unknown beauty of space was something special to him. Sitting at one of the observation decks, Alan enjoyed a drink while sitting on a leather couch facing a large window facing the void of space. A soft tune of chill electronic music played in the background. Taking a sip of his drink, Alan sighed as he rested back on the couch. Watching every star and planet glide along the window as the capital ship sailed forward.

Though when he heard the door open behind him, that was certainly unexpected.

"Mr. Dokes?" The voice asked, seeming a bit...shy. Odd, though Alan nodded before replying,

"Of course, please come in." The person then entered, closing the door behind him. He heard footsteps getting closer before looking to his right.

"I'm sorry if this is a bad time, I tried to see you in your office but the guards told me you were out and-" Alan chuckled to cut her off,

"Hey, it's more than alright." He assured, soon seeing I was one of the soldiers from the defense garrison. The one who was in tears at his office, Fay Innes.

Ignition: Unknown Criminal

"Ah, Ms. Innes, this was an unexpected visit." He said, quickly noticing her uncomfortable posture, "Well take a seat, don't seem so nervous." The soldier seemed surprised by how casual he was acting. Which happens more often than not. Taking a seat on the couch, Fay couldn't help but smile lightly,

"You usually like this...you know. Not professional often?" She then asked, which made the G.L chuckle.

"Yes, I know it may not look as good for someone of my authority, but I can't stand having to be that serious all the time. Trust me, it gets old real quick." Alan laughed. Though as the laughing died down, he turned back to Fay,

"Though, I doubt that was merely the only reason you came here. Unless you wanted to enjoy the view as well?" Fay's smile soon slowly went down,

"Not...Not quite." She said, scratching her neck nervously.

"Alright, well your gonna have to tell me eventually." He said, taking another sip. She nodded from that,

"Yes, yes of course. I just... for starters I wanted to thank you for mentioning the loss of my fiance" She said, swallowing down hard. Feeling a lump in her throat as she forced herself to shed no tears. Alan placed his drink on the table before placing his hands on his lap.

"You're most welcome, Fay, though I never met the man in person. I'm more than sure he was a great man. I'm just ashamed he had to go in such a fashion." Alan then paused before continuing, "The sergeant did inform you of being able to go on leave, correct?" Fay nodded slowly.

"Yes. I just...want to finish this one last mission. It's the least I can do for him..." Alan paused to think as both of them looked out the window. Then, getting up, he moved to the counter to pour himself another drink,

"Do you want anything?" He asked, placing the bottle of his choice down. Fay did think about it for a good few seconds before declining,

"No thanks, I'm fine." Alan then placed the bottle away before sitting back down. When taking another sip, he noticed Fay staring into the window.

"It's easy isn't it? Just to watch and wonder."

"Yeah, a simple reminder of our place in the universe I guess..."

"Oh? What do you think that is?" Alan asked, seeming interested by the statement. Fay shrugged as she sunk back into the couch.

"Does it not...I don't know, make you feel so tiny?" She tried to ask back. Alan only shook his head,

"No, not at all actually." Alan answered. "I know where I am and where I'm needed, that's more than enough to allow me to feel as big or small as I need to be." He continued.

"Well, I mean, you are the Galactic Leader after all." Fay shot back. Alan however pointed a finger at himself,

"True, though I started exactly where you are. A soldier fighting for the people and the Galactic Leader before me. Hence the prosthetics." Alan said, showing his mechanical arm to Fay. Stretch then clenching his fingers into a fist. The sleek silver metal that was his arm moved very robotically yet was rather impressively smooth with each movement.

"You know, I'm surprised you were able to afford such improvements on a soldier's salary." Fay said. Looking at the entire mechanical half of Alan. Since she remembered the few reports she's read about him, it was a *sonic* grenade that blew him in half.

Alan then looked down, seeming defeated.

"I didn't, I couldn't remember how they had kept me alive during the operation. But when I woke and soon realized what had happened. I knew I would have been in a life debt for that. But then my father came in. Paid the whole debt off right there, if I resigned my position." Fay was shocked,

"Wait, you mean the head of Dokes Industries??" Alan nodded, "Remember when the company had to lay off during the so-called crash in the 2090's? Well, the only reason Dokes Industries was even affected was because of me..." Alan sighed.

Fay was silent for a second after that, thinking about how the G.L before he survived his career in the Union military.

"Damn, that's harsh. Did your father give you hell for that?" Alan nodded,

"Ohh yeah, though he clearly cared about his son more than the profit margins." He said, feeling a tear roll down his face.

"I'm surprised you're willing to be so open with me. I mean...you hardly even know me and yet you talk to me as if I was your best friend." Fay pointed out. Alan smiled, not even bothering to wipe his face.

"It's easier than you think, to open up to a stranger. But then again, why should I see you as a stranger? We are both here for the same reason. To catch the same criminal that has done you, myself and many others in the U.G.G wrong." Alan had made a good point. Fay agreed that they both had similar goals in mind, it was just the fact that they had such different roles and levels of power that made her surprised.

"Thank you sir. I hope we continue to elect people like you in the future. It seems to be more than rare these days." She explained.

As the conversations began to cease. The two just enjoyed the view as they passed another set of stars in the darkness of space. The relaxing music continued to fill the room. However, Alan was soon interrupted when his holo-watch received a message. After reading the message that was sent to him, he sighed.

"Well, I'm sorry that it was short. But I am requested at the bridge." He said, getting up. Fay smiled,

"Have fun sir." Alan chuckled before walking out the door,

"Stay safe Ms. Innes."

CHAPTER TWELVE

The morning suns of Jev rose in the sky. Shining brightly in Kale's room, even with the curtains down. Kane groaned as the bright light landed along his face. Kale was sleeping on the floor beside him. A few blankets were placed down to make the ground a bit more comfortable to sleep on. Turning to his side, Kane tried to avoid the incoming sunlight gunning towards the rest of the room. However, that soon did very little for him when it was Helix that floated down to lightly push his face. Beeping softly before displaying,

"Wake up." on his screen.

"Mmmm...Five..more minutes." Kane groaned in his sleep. Though they both knew Helix wasn't the type to wait. So he would bop him again....and again. Until eventually Kane would at least open his eyes.

"Alright, I'm up." Kane sighed, using an arm to help him up. Helix beeped happily! Even twirling in the air displaying,

"YAY!" beforing flying up to nuzzle Kane.

"H-hey now. Don't be so dramatic, I was only sleeping." Kane said, though he couldn't help but smile as he rubbed the cybel on the side of his "face".

"He's quite the loyal little guy isn't he?" Ryko asked from the end of the door. Both Kane and Helix seem to have turned to face the lykoi at the same time.

"He wouldn't leave your side all night. That and he wouldn't let anyone near you. Just look at Kale." He said, gesturing Kale that was laying on the ground. Kane nervously laughed at the sight,

"Sorry about that, again, we don't normally stay with people for long. So this will take some getting used to. For all of us." With how genuine Kane sounded, Ryko nodded before waving him to follow.

"Come on, let her sleep. The girls hardly get enough of it anyway." Kane stood up awkwardly raising a foot over and around Kale. Trying not to fall or step on her. In fact, if Helix didn't spot him nearly slipping over her tail and zoomed down to catch him before falling. Then it would've been game over. Though thanks to Helix's save, Kane sighed in relief.

"Thanks buddy." Kane whispered with a thumbs up.

Heading down the hallway. Kane remembered how they were supposed to go down. Through the other grav-lift. Kane looked at it nervously before Helix pushed a little. Kane reacted and moved back.
"H-hey!" He shouted in a whisper! The cybel then floated up, displaying a " -_- ". Kane blushed from his fear and looked back at the grav-lift.

Ignition: Unknown Criminal

"I-I'm going! Just...hold on." With a few sarcastic beeps, Helix floated down. With a sigh, Kane stepped down, feeling the grav-lift gently pulling him down, soon pushing him out and on the first floor. It felt so odd for him, but he was grateful to be ok. Kane and Helix then heard sizzling. Followed by a rather delicious smell.

"Take a seat!" Ryko shouted from the kitchen, "Breakfast will be ready soon!" That worked for Kane, who then sat on the couch with Helix landing on his lap. As the two waited, Kane looked around the living again, actually feeling awake now he properly examined everything. Looking at the picture of Ryko and the girls beside the couch, he carefully picked up the picture. Hearing the cooking continue in the background. Kane just looked at the picture, seeing how happy the three seemed. It's hard to believe that this was the life they had to live now. Then again, they still seemed rather happy.

When Ryko entered the living room with two plates in his hands. He noticed Kane with the picture in his hands,

"Careful there, you have my favorite one with the girls and I." Ryko warned. Kane smiled at that,

"I can tell. It's a gorgeous photo. I'm happy you were to get a physical copy." Ryko then returned the smile, placing Kane's plate down.

"Yeah, no kidding. You can imagine how rare this is to do in parts like Jev." Putting the picture back down, Kane took his plate and began to eat his breakfast.

"Oh yeah, It's expensive enough within the U.G.G."
Ryko nodded as he also started to eat. Kane then noticed
something when he looked around in the house.

"Wait, where's Jok and Dusk?" Kane asked. Ryko
allowed himself to swallow before answering,

"Jok prefers to...well live on the ship. Guess he
enjoys the silence. He's working on the repairs on Dusk."
He said with a shrug. Kane nodded,

"Honestly I can relate a little...Not that I mind living
here. You guys are great! I'm just more used to that kind of
lifestyle…"

As the two ate, it wasn't long before Kale
practically jumped down the grav-lift!

"Ohhhhh breakfast smells amazing dad!" Kale said
gleefully. Covering his mouth that was full of food, Ryko
replied before Kale could walk in the kitchen,

"Your food is on the counter! Please leave Fesh's
plate alone." Kale walked in the kitchen before whining,

"Aww but Fesh hardly finishes her breakfast
anyway." Ryko looked at the kitchen entrance, shooting a
look Kale already knew was there.

"Kale." He said sternly.

"I know dad…." She shot back with a giggle,
coming back into the living room. With a plateful of food.
Taking a seat beside Ryko, she was quick to start enjoying
her meal. Eating much faster than the men.

"Mmm! This is delicious dad!" She said with a
mouthful of scrambled eggs. Kane brought a hand to cover
his eyes from the view. While Ryko shot her another look.
Kale only blushed before swallowing.

"Sss-sorry." She hissed, embarrassed.

"It's alright, just a little unused to that." Kane replied, "Not like I see Helix eating." Helix looked up at Kane before displaying a pair of rolling eyes at him with a smirk. Which got a laugh out of the three.

Soon after, Fesh was awake as everyone heard the *whoosh* of the grav-lift drop her down.

"Morning everyone." She said with a yawn. In union, all three said a good morning to her.

"Ryko, is there coffee?" Ryko nodded with a smile, "It should be done by now." Ryko then turned to Kane, who seemed quite interested at hearing those words.

"Can I guess you'd like some as well?" Kane nodded,

"Yes please." A smile came on Ryko's face.

"Good, I'll be right back." With that, Ryko was on his feet and walked into the kitchen. As he prepared coffee and Fesh grabbing her breakfast, Kane turned to Kale.

"Its really is a nice set up you three have here. I'll admit, I'm impressed." Kale smiled sweetly and bounced in her seat.

"Really? I'm so happy to hear! Most people think the house is...either well ugly or "illogical."." She mocked at the end, sticking her tongue out. Kane smiles back, enjoying the positivity around him. It was a rather nice distraction from thinking about the work ahead.

After a few minutes, Ryko and Fesh came into the living room. Fesh held her plate of breakfast in one hand with her hot cup of coffee in the other. Ryko on the other hand held two cups of coffee. Kane soon stood up and offered his seat on the couch for Fesh,

"It's yours." He offered. Fesh seemed surprised by the gesture while Ryko claimed his seat.

"You sure?" Fesh asked, tilting her head. Kane just nodded.

"Yeah, I can stretch my legs anyway." A smile managed to peer on Fesh's face.

"Thanksss." She then sat down, taking a sip of her coffee once the plate was on the table. Ryko then lifted a cup of coffee for Kane,

"Why here you go Mr, Gentlemen." Though it was clearly sarcasm, Kane ignored it as he happily took the cup before enjoying the first sip.

"Oh yeah...thank you Ryko." Kane said with a sigh. Enjoying just the scent of the wonderful beverage. Ryko chuckled before enjoying a sip of coffee himself. Meanwhile Kale just rolled her eyes,

"Dirty bean water drinkersss. Dad, is there juice in the fridge?" She asked, feeling thirsty herself. While still enjoying his sip, Ryko nodded. Kale dashed out of her seat with her empty plate. Placing it in the sink once she entered the kitchen and poured herself a glass of Druffle juice. Soon returning to the living room. Kane rose a brow at the sight of the dark blue drink in Kale's glass.

"What kind of juice are you drinking?" He asked. Kale only giggled,

"Druffle juice silly!" She replied, as if it was an obvious answer. Which to a gwarian it was.

"Druffle? I take it that it's not human." Kane replied oddly. Which only made Kale and Fesh chuckle,

"I mean, you can try it. But you may need your stomach pumped afterwards." Fesh said back.

As breakfast was coming to an end, everyone that still had plates brought them to the sink. Fesh, Ryko and Kane gulped the rest of their coffee and added the mugs to the dishes as well.

"Alright, I can get the dishes done quickly, girls, you get ready." He then turned to Kane and smirked,

"And get him a fresh pair of clothes while you're at it." Kane then looked at him with a confused look.

"What do you me-" Kale then suddenly wrapped her arms around him! Lifting him up like he was nothing!

"Oh! Great idea dad! His clothesss are filthy!" Kane gasped at how sudden this was, while also being carried to the grav-lift. Helix beeped as he watched his human being carried away, flying after Kale. Fesh, sighed with a smile stuck on her face.

"I'll make sure she doesn't go overboard with him." Ryko chuckled while cleaning the dishes,

"Oh I know you will." Fesh then turned to head to the grav-lift to head to Kale's bedroom.

The girls usually took a while but not this long. Ryko looked at his holo-watch, it showed that twenty minutes had gone by.

"Girls! Come on." He insisted...again. Crossing his arms as he waited for their arrival. A shook his head, knowing this shouldn't be taking this long. However, before he was tempted to march up there, he heard the *whoosh* of them coming down. First was Fesh, then Kale. Both of them wore rather casual looking clothing. They both had jeans followed by T-shirts, although they had dramatically different designs. While Fesh wore a rather simple grey shirt, with a logo "**FGBG**" imprint on her chest. Kale's shirt was a more colorful mix of orange and white. Both shirts seemed to fit their dark yellow selves. However, under each of their shirts was an advanced set of bullet proof vests. To most, the vest would be nearly impossible to notice thanks to how slim they were. Though Ryko had seen more then enough individuals with the light armor to easily spot the slight bumps it showed.

Last was Kane, who dropped down behind the two with Helix planted on his shoulder. Ryko immediately noticed he was wearing Fesh's clothing. Since Kale's taste was definitely more suited for her. Kane wore a pair of jeans as well, though he had a black T-shirt with the same "**FGBG**" logo printed on his chest.

"I assume the FGBG doesn't stand for anything?" Kane asked. Fesh just shrugged,

"For Gwarians By Gwarians," She replied simply, "The first brand by only gwarians. I see it as just another shirt though."

"Alright, enough chit chat about clothing ladies, we are already cutting close as it is." Fesh and Kane soon caught up to Ryko, shoving their shoes on before following him and Kale out the door. Fesh was quick to start asking questions as she stepped up beside Ryko,

Ignition: Unknown Criminal

"So, you got the details of the mission?" Ryko had been preparing himself for this, though sighed anyways.

"Yes but no." With a brow raised Fesh faced Ryko,

"What's that supposed to mean?" Kane and Kale were just as confused by the answer as they listened from behind. Ryko scratched his arm as the older sister simply crossed her arms.

"Well, I did get the original mission, but it changed."

"Changed how exactly?" That question came from Kane. Since he was the first to be informed of the mission before them. Hearing it suddenly change grabbed his attention in more ways than one.

"The objective is still the same, it's just not for Draz specifically anymore. She made a deal." Ryko explained.

"A deal?" Fesh spat, sounding irritated by that. "Last time she made a deal and had us handle it we nearly got shot in the back!" Fesh hissed! Though Ryko was calm.

"Yes, I'm aware of that Fesh. And I'm sure Draz is as well." Fesh kicked a rock that was on the sidewalk in frustration. Keeping herself quite. Kane then came beside Ryko while Kale moved beside her sister. Soon enough she managed to get a conversation started to keep her mind occupied. Kane on the other hand still wanted to pry a little further.

"So, who did she make a deal with?" Ryko looked down, keeping his voice down as they moved through the now bustling city.

"You ever heard of the Xhell Corporation?" Kane shook his head.

"Never heard of them. Are they a branch with the U.G.G?" A brief chuckle escaped Ryko from that.

"Wow, they really do hide a lot from you people don't they?" Kane just shrugged at that.

"I mean, you're a cargo pilot. How have you not encountered them before?" Ryko asked. However Kane could only find himself shrugging again,

"Maybe they aren't as far spread out in the galaxy to find them in the routes?" Ryko nodded a little at that,

"Fair, however for a Corporation alone the amount of worlds under them is rather disturbing. Alongside their growing power in the galaxy." Kane became curious as he leaned in more, just enough to hear better while not being too obvious,

"How much "Growing power" are we talking about?"

Ryko, looked around with just his eyes, not moving his head an inch before replying,

"Not entirely sure, but from rumors and friends I've been told they passed the Kolan Empire, in fact I've been told Xhell Corp quite literally bought out many of their worlds after losing a major war against the United Minds and the U.G.G." Kane's eyes widened the information. He never knew much about the war against the Kolan Empire. On the news or the Holo-Stations he would hear the media say how much of the growing threat they were becoming. That the Kolan Empire forced many planets under them. Using the extra population to simply grow their armies. So

Ignition: Unknown Criminal

Galactic Leader Alan made the call to go to war when the United Minds requested assistance.

"With each world under their control, they gain more people to place under their workforce. In turn, more profit. Then the cycle continues. The work is usually brutal, more often than not people would work themselves to death for them."

"So, I take it, that's who Draz made the deal with then? I'm surprised she would trust people like that." Kane thought out loud. Ryko kept his head down,

"It's a shame, a lot of people under the Xhell Corporation are good people. Just working for the wrong bosses." He said sorrowfully.

"You seem like you would know some of these people personally." Kane said, Ryko then brought his eyes to face Kane. The pain in those eyes visible for Kane to notice.

"That's because I did. It didn't last long but I did offer to work for the Xhell Corperation's Mining District on Fold for a while before eventually leaving. Unfortunately most of the people I worked with were still saving up for a ride and had to stay."

After that, Fesh was soon calm. Able to control her anger by the fact she is helping the Xhell Corporation and stay focused.

"Back to Para V huh? At least we'll actually get some back up thissss time." She said as the group continued to walk through the city to spot the spaceport the

Austin Patten

Jade landed in. When they got to the entrance of the port. A small group of pirates moved in. The one in front, a lykoi smirked as he looked at Ryko.

"I see you've got yourself another person to join your little crew Ryko." He quipped. Before Ryko could even bother to reply, Fesh stepped in, shoving the lykoi.

"Out of the way Fluke. Or does he need to whoop your ass again?" Fesh hissed. Fluke on the other hand only kept that smirk slapped on his face.

"Back off Fesh, if I wanted to speak a little girl I would have looked at you." Fesh's eye twitched a little. Hissing again as she walked up to Fluke with a clenched fist.

"Why you son of a-"

All of a sudden Kane's fist came flying into Fluk's face. Directly on his nose. The lykoi never saw it coming as his head flung back. His hands were quick to cover the broken nose before crashing on his back! He screamed and cursed in pain. The two others behind him growled at Kane.

"This little crew saved my life you trash can!" He shouted. While Ryko and the other two seemed stunned by the act. Helix flew beside him. Displaying,

"Get back you animals!" followed by many angry loud beeps. Helix then revealed several new weapons Kane wasn't expecting. Including a plasma gun, stun gun and an emp launcher. One of Fluke's men raised his hands up slowly.

"W-whoa..hey. We don't want any trouble. A-any of that kind of trouble anyway." He shakily said. The other man helped Fluke to his feet. Who still held his broken nose with a hand before glaring at Kane.

"This isn't over human." He growled. Kane ignored him, turning back to the others while they left.

"Seems over to me." He said under his breath. Fesh then walked up to Kane. Smacking him at the side of the head.

"Ow! H-hey!" Fesh then crossed her arms.

"That was risky and iditoitc of you." She said, though sighed before smiling slightly,

"Though...I don't mind seeing Fluke being punched in the face. So thanks." Kane then smiled as they followed Ryko, who simply got a laugh out of the event.

"Anytime." Kane replied. Kale then hopped in behind the two!

"Wow! That was incredible Kane!" Fesh rolled her eyes at her sister's surprise.

"Oh please, I punch people in the face all the time! You punch people in the face just as much!" Kale giggled at that.

"Yes! But I always saw Kane as a softer type! Seeing that just completely remade me think that!" She shrieked, her arms shook from her excitement.

"Hey!" Helix typed, beeping as he added, "I helped too!" followed by a ":(" on his screen. Reaching over his shoulder, Kane gave Helix a gentle pat.

"Of course you did bud, couldn't have scared them off without ya."

Austin Patten

As they moved through the bustling space port, a familiar *whirr* from the many ships either starting up or being turned off was heard all around the place. With each ship leaving there was another zooming in to take the open landing area. People of all species walked throughout the port, filling up the large halls. The port itself was surprisingly clean now that Kane was able to actually look at the place unlike when he arrived. Small bots were scurrying along the floor. They always came in packs of two. One in the front vacuuming, the seconds right behind to scrub the floor clean.

"There's the Jade." Ryko said as everyone stayed close. As they got closer to the ship, the crowds only seemed to get thicker.

"Damn, I see why you wanted to leave sooner." Kane said, feeling more than squashed as he hid to literally rub past people to keep moving. At one point he even had to squish up to Fesh, who had no problems glaring at him for getting too close.

"What? I can't help it." Kane tried to say in defense. Before a bulky looking hellion squished them even closer together. To which Fesh actually hissed at Kane this time. Who moved behind Kale. Kale just found this funny and giggled.

"Don't mind her, she isn't used to guys getting so close to her." Fesh then turned at her sister. Shooting a glare at her. Kale stuck her tongue out in response.

"Careful you two…" Ryko warned. Seeing the tension raise from Fesh. The two looked at Ryko before moving closer,

"Sorry dad." They said. Kale then turned back to see Kane getting stuck in the crowd.

"You guys get the ship started. I'll grab Kane." For a second Ryko looked back to see what she meant by that. Though when he noticed Kane was struggling to push through the crowd he looked back and moved into the ship with Fesh.

Moving swiftly after having plenty of practice in these crowds. Kale got closer and closer to the struggling human. With every person she either slipped or pushed past she eventually got to Kane. Kane quickly reached out for a hand for her. Which she dashed in to grab his hand. Pulling him up to her. Wrapping her arms around him.

"There. Now let's get to the ship silly." She giggled. Helping him as she easily got through the crowd.

"W-wow, you're definitely a lot stronger than you look." Kane commented. Watching her almost effortlessly squeeze or push through others to get to the Jade. Even a hellion moved around her.

"You get used to it Kane. Trust me, one day you'll be just as strong as us!"

Within a few more minutes, Kale got the two on the ship. Kane waited a few seconds as Kale still had him in her arms.

"Uh, Kale?" Kale then looked down at Kane with her arms still around him.

"Yeah?" Kane awkwardly looked around. "You kind of...still have me in your arms." Kale then immediately let go of him.

"Oh! Sorry!" She said, blushing softly. Kane smiled before hugging her for a quick moment.

"Don't worry, and thanks." He said gently before letting go and walked to the seating area. What Kane saw next took him off guard.

"Hello, Mr. Lons!"

Kane's eyes almost bulged out his sockets.

"Dusk?" He exclaimed, shocked. The familiar anvol displayed a smile on his orange screen.

"That's my name!" Without any warning Kane lunged over to hug the robotic ally.

"I-I thought you were done for." Dusk only laughed at Kane's worry.

"Then you greatly underestimate Jok Mr. Lons." When Kane released Dusk from his arms he noticed the arm that Dusk had blown off was still removed.

"Sorry about the arm." Kane apologized, seeing a metal cap sealed around to remove to shield the exposed wires and damage. Dusk only smiled on his screen.

"No need to apologize Mr. Lons. Wouldn't be my first time losing a limb in battle." He chuckled, smirking at the human.

Fesh's voice then yelled out from the cockpit of the Jade,

"Now that you boys are reunited again, sit tight and buckle in." Kane moved by one of the seats to sit down and buckle in. Dusk stood beside Kane.

"Kane and I are ready." Dusk informed Fesh.

"You're not gonna take a seat?" Kane asked, looking at the anvol casually standing in front of him. Dusk merely smirked while pointed down at his feet,

"Magnetic footing Mr. Lons. I should be fine." Dusk replied. Kane tightened his belt and rested his head back.

"If you say so Dusk, just try not to die on us again please." Kane requested, half jokingly.

"Trust me Mr. Lons, I'll try to be more prepared next time. The union had mechs in that battle, if the Jade wasn't already there for us, we would have been obliterated." Dusk said plainly, which only made Kane gulp in his seat.

"Right."

Fesh's voice soon broke in again,

"The Jade is looking good, ready or not this ship is lifting off!" Within seconds Kane heard the hum of the ship coming to life. A few more seconds passed before the ship was in the air! Looking out the window, Kane saw the Jade whipping past several skyscrapers as it glided higher in the air. From above, the cities of Jez almost looked peaceful as Kane watched the people getting smaller and smaller. Kane sighed, knowing the life of peace apparently wasn't wanting him to be a part of it. His attention was suddenly brought to Helix when he felt something nudge his shoulder. Dusk was facing him this time, a X-13 *Fiend*

Burst laser Rifle. The sleek, black rifle was held in both of his hands.

"I'd like you to have this, Mr. Lons, having more powerful firepower is recommended for this mission." Taking the offered weapon, Kane looked at the rifle as he awkwardly fumbled around with it in his hands.

"Hold on now. I've held a few handguns but never something like this." Dusk stood over before bringing his hands back down,

"May I?" Kane was more than happy to hand the rifle back to Dusk. Once the weapon was in his hands, Dusk began to show how to properly hold the rifle.

"The *Fiend* is a common laser burst rifle used by most smugglers and Pirates thanks to its large magazine size and how lightweight it is." Dusk explained, pressing a button to cool the gun. "After long periods of firing laser weapons like this will need to be cooled or you could destroy the rifle in your hands. Press this button when you notice the weapon is becoming incredibly hot or this bar..." He pointed at a currently glowing bar at the side of the rifle.

"...Turns red." Kane nodded, understanding so far.

"Firing the *Fiend*, like any other rifle is quite easy. However, I'd prefer to show when you're not restricted in a seat." Kane chuckled at that.

"Fair enough." Dusk then gave Kane the *Fiend* before pulling out his weapon, a MK2 *Vandal* Plasma Shotgun. The large two barrel shotgun laid in Dusk's hand. Steam emitted from the sides as the anvol cooled the weapon down.

Ignition: Unknown Criminal

"Plasma weapons of this magnitude require frequent cooling, even when not being fired. Even special storage is required when storing the weapon." Kane gulped, feeling both interested and terrified of how that Shotgun must be like in action.

"Anywho, you ready for your first raid Mr. Lons?"

CHAPTER THIRTEEN

"We found them!" Captain Vail bellowed triumphantly in the bridge. Those were the first words Alan heard when the elevator doors opened. The captain didn't even notice the G.L entering as his concentration was fixated on a terminal. Behind the captain, crew throughout the bridge stood in attention. As more and more of the crew noticed that Alan had entered the bridge, it was only a matter of time before Vail noticed as well. One of the crew members beside him tapped his shoulder, to whisper the G.L had come aboard the bridge. Turning back, his eyes suddenly widened as his back shot up with a salute shooting beside his face.

"G.L on deck!!" Alan casually walked onto the bridge,

"At ease everyone." He said. Focusing his attention to the captain. "Seems like some important news has happened." He brought up, gesturing the terminal he's been leaning over.

"Yes of course, please come down sir." Dropping down the small ledge, Alan walked over to the terminal by the crew member and the captain.

Ignition: Unknown Criminal

"You claim that you found them?" Alan asked as he rose a brow at the captain. Captain Vail nodded confidently, looking at the terminal again. The screen displayed several ships shown as different shapes.

"These are ships leaving Jev." The crew member stated, he then typed along the holo-grapphic keyboard to zoom in on a particular ship. The shape was a green triangle just leaving the atmosphere.

"That ship is the Jade sir, the very ship Mr. Lons escaped in." Noticing the G.L's face showing his doubt, the captain was swift to step in,

"We managed to gain the ships serial number from one of the union's soldiers helmet cams. KR-029394-07 to be specific. Which was a reported stolen *Kret* several years ago." Seeming quite satisfied Alan turned to Captain.

"This is excellent, captain, set course to Jev." With a salute Captain Vail barked,

"Yes sir!" The crew on the bridge worked speedily to get the Y-Class moving. Within seconds, the massive ship made a jump.

Both the captain and Alan walked up to the front of the bridge, watching the array of blues, purples and greens flash before their eyes.

"How long till we reach Jev?" Alan asked.

"Minutes, sir. Shouldn't be long by now." Alan squinted, as he never moved his face from the glass.

"Then I'll be seeing you Kane…"

—

After firing the last shot in the magazine, Fay reloaded her standard issue union pistol. With trained speed, she emptied the mag before slapping a fresh one in the weapon. Continuing to fire upon the targets in the range. Axel was right beside her, his rifle in a firm grip as he fired individual shots at the targets displayed in front of him. With each shot he managed to hit a bullseye on each target. Pausing her own shooting, Fay watched as Axel nailed another set of targets.

"Damn! Good shooting Axel." She complimented, seeming actually surprised.

"I learned from the best." He chuckled as he reloaded the rifle. Fay only scoffed,

"Oh please, I taught you basics." Axel however shook his head,

"True, but you helped me a lot more with this weapon than just on the range." He said back. Aiming in as the new set of targets spawned on his lane on the range. Fay on the other hand just finished dispatching her set and had to wait for her set to load in new targets.

"What can I say, it's easier to train on the field. Especially when your life's on the line." While opening fire on his targets, Axel realized what she was referencing,

"You mean on Hazal?" He asked. Fay brought up her weapon as her targets suddenly spawned in.

Swarm formation. Multiple smaller targets started at the end of her lane, though came rushing through quickly.

Ignition: Unknown Criminal

Most of the targets moved side to side at rapid speeds while charging at her! Fay was about to attempt to fight off the swarm of holo-graphic targets with her sidearm, that was until Axel suddenly flicked his rifle on safety and shoved the weapon in her chest.

"Here, I'll use your pistol." Fay shot a confused glare at him. By then her pistol was already out of her hands and was swapped for his rifle. Looking back at the targets rushing towards her, he turned the safety off, putting the weapon on burst fire. She raised the long, black union rifle and began to open fire! Each burst of led smashed pairs of the charging targets! With steady breathing, she quickly pulled the trigger with each burst fired. By the end of the magazine, the last two targets were destroyed. A glowing spark of holographic dust was left of the last of the targets before the effects were removed. Not allowing the simulation on her lane to load another set of targets, Fay turned her lane on stand by mode.

Bringing her attention to Axel, with her pistol now in his hands. He brought up the handheld weapon with ease, watching a triplet of targets making a push as the barrier that they were hiding behind despawned. With his finger aligned with the trigger, he aimed for his first target, the one down in the middle. He pulled the trigger, watching the bullet smash through the holo-graphic circle as it blasted into pieces. The other two were quick to notice their fallen ally and began to move in random directions to avoid getting hit. This began to throw Axel off, as he was trying to aim the pistol properly with the next target. "Damn." He said under breath, soon attempting to fire rapidly at the targets. Since they were getting dangerously close! His only option, or so he thought was to fire blindly at the incoming targets. Each shot however only missed, zooming past the blue circles before they reach the end. With that, a red projection read out the word "Failed" and the simulation ended. Axel sighed, turning back to Fay, who walked up to him.

"Not bad." She said, handing his rifle back to him,

"Though, I know you're more accurate with this." Axel nodded, giving her sidearm back. "Thanks, just saw you needed this more than me during that sim." Fay scoffed,

"Except I wanted the challenge, we were both trained in basic that swapping to our side arm is far more efficient than attempting to reload our primary weapon. Yet, I always notice soldiers seeming to ignore they even have it." Axel thought about it for a few seconds before replying,

"Yeah, you got a point." He brought out his own pistol, hardly remembering the last time he'd even fired the weapon after training. With a smirk she bumped him with her elbow.

"That would explain a lot." She said, as if she read his mind.

Fay's military grade holo-watch soon went off, the call coming from the sergeant. Without hesitation she answered the call,

Ignition: Unknown Criminal

"Corporal Innes, you and Private Vission are needed back in our bunks to suit up ASAP!" The sergeant barked, his voice crackling slightly in the call.

"Understood sir, we're on our way." The sergeant then ended the call and the two were off with a brisk jog.

"Sounded urgent, what do you think?" Axel asked as the pair moved through the various halls of the capital ship.

"You know exactly what I think," Fay said, her speed increasing.

"We found him."

Austin Patten

CHAPTER FOURTEEN

Kane was, for the most part, aware of what this mission was going to be. Though, raiding a U.G.G convoy was not exactly what he had in mind. He had already managed to kill several U.G.G in both defending himself at his apartments and during his escape on Para V. His fingers wrapped around the plasma rifle as he sighed.

"I sense you are distressed Mr. Lons." Dusk stated, still standing by him as the Jade passed the atmosphere of the planet. Fesh could be heard talking to Ryko and Kale in the cockpit, though her voice was muffled from the distance.

"Sorry, still need to get used to...this." Kane said, gesturing the weapon in his hands. The anvol tilted his head, with a puzzled look projected on his face.

"Is there something confusing about the rifle?" He asked, since he believed he was rather clear on how to operate the plasma rifle. A dry chuckle was Kane's response,

"N-no, that's clear. It's more...the fact I'm being hired with the possibility of having to kill again," Kane explained. Dusk rose a finger replying with a digital smile,

Ignition: Unknown Criminal

"A high possibility at that." Kane shot a glare at him. Dusk quickly got the hint that didn't help.

"My apologies." Dusk said. Kane rested his head against the back of the chair.

"You're fine, I should be ok. Just gonna need to keep a level head and get this done." Kane said. Dusk displayed a smirk,

"Don't worry, just like on Para V, as you humans put it, I got your back." Kane smirked back at that,

"Why I'd hope so, we made a pretty decent team back there." Dusk crossed his arms...or well his arm and stump. Though the smirk was still promptly on his screen.

"Well, last time I checked I did manage to carry you through the escape." Kane scoffed,

"Oh please, I totally saved you from that soldier that was laying onto you." Kane playfully shot back.

"Oh yeah, Well I-" Dusk was suddenly interrupted by Fesh's voice shouting from the cockpit,

"You boys need to stop your flexing and buckle in! We're about to make our jump!" Dusk brought his hand down before taking a seat with Kane.

"Well then, I guess you win. For now." Kane removed the smirk on his face after saying,

"Sounds good to me."

Fesh was double checking the coordinates sent by Drazz to the convoy. Ryko spotted the pirates that would be joining them flying behind the Jade. At first it seemed to only be a few squadrons of fighters, which didn't seem much. However, that opinion was changed when two pirate cruisers flew right behind them!

"Wow, it seems Draz really wants this cargo." Ryko stated, his eyes widened at the relatively small-medium size ships following their lead. Fesh didn't see the surprise and shrugged,

"They're only corvettes, show me a destroyer joining us and I may be interested." She scoffed. Ryko still wasn't a fan,

"I get that, though we usually never get back up, let alone this kind." Ryko said back. Fesh looked at Ryko, seeing his concerned expression.

"Hey, everything will be fine Ryko. Just in and out right?" She said. A smile was placed on her face to show her confidence in the words she said. Ryko took in a breath before replying,

"Yeah, you're right."

A transmission was then being hailed to both Ryko and Fesh. Fesh, with one hand on the ship's controls gestured to Ryko to answer the call. He only sighed,

"Just in and out." Then answered the hail. The screen in front of him displayed an anvol, his chassis was damaged, filled with dents occupied by a handful of bullet holes littered along his body. His screen was a dark red, the eyes and mouth displayed in white.

"Ryko? Captain of the Jade?" The anvol asked, raising a digital eye brow. Ryko nodded,

"That's correct." The anvol's face was back on the neutral look,

Ignition: Unknown Criminal

"Understood, I'm known as Tor, I've been ordered to assist you in raiding a particular U.G.G convey." He stated. Ryko gave a smile,

"We appreciate the extra firepower you'll be giving us Tor. Let's try to get our people home safe, sounds good?" He said. The anvol projected a half smile on his face,

"I agree, good luck on your end captain." The transmission then ended.

Fesh smirked at Ryko,

"Always the people guy huh?" Ryko shrugged,

"What? It never hurts to get on the good side on those who are giving you a hand." Fesh shook her head,

"They were ordered to help." It was then Ryko's turn to scoff,

"Yes, but they are still coming. Even then it would be better to get on their good side." Fesh just shrugged,

"Hey, I just fight and fly the ship. Sometimes shoot a few orders but you're the boss." Ryko, then checked the radar, picking up all of the ships that Drazz told them that would be joining them on the mission,

"Alright, everyone is here. Are you ready to make the jump?" Ryko asked. Fesh did a triple check of the coordinates before nodding.

"Let's do this." Ryko began to get the engines ready for the jump, a hum was heard behind them as the components in the engine began to speed up. All that was left was to pull the jump lever in between Ryko and Fesh. Ryko placed his hand on it, bracing himself for the jump.

"W-whoa, Fesh? Do you hear that?" Ryko asked, hearing a muffled crackling in front of the ship. Fesh looked forward,

"Yeah," She said, getting just as worried.

"This is an exit zone, no ship should b-" It all happened so fast! In seconds an enormous U.G.G Capital ship just exited a jump in front of them!! Fesh at a rapid pace, twisted the controls to the left to avoid colliding into the massive vessel.

"Holy hell! That's a U.G.G Capital ship!" Ryko screamed, his eyes widening at the sight! Quickly snapping out of it, he brought his attention down to the sonar, seeing multiple other ships within the U.G.G fleet exting their jump! Before even needing to say the words, Kale was already running back.

"Kane! Get up! We need to mann the rear missiles!" She shouted, hardly giving him anytime before rushing up the ladder!

"W-what? What's going o-" A sudden explosion rocked the ship, almost knocking Dusk out of his seat!

"I suggest you follow her quickly." Dusk said, helping him remove the belts.

"Got it." Kane said, running towards the ladder to climb up.

Kale was already in her seat reloading the missiles. Kane jumped onto his seat, bringing his console online before slamming the headset on his head. Looking up through the glass he could see many fighters. Both U.G.G and pirates flying over the Jade! Each craft bent on destroying each other as they flew along the depths of space! Lasers and heavy bullets flew along the battle before him.

"Kane! I need targets locked now!" Kale shouted in the mic. However, this seemed much more difficult due to the fact there are both allies and enemies in the fight. Kane tried desperately to aim at the *U-4* fighters swooping in on the pirates. Figuring this system quickly as he swiped his fingers along the holo-graphic controls to lock on. Due to the surprising nature of the attack, many of the pirates were ill prepared for the battle. Nearly half of the pirate fighters were decimated by the initial attack. Luckily, a squadron of *U-4's* flew along the rear of the Jade with their attention stuck on three fleeing pirates.

"Kale, get ready to fire! I'm going to get us to assist those fighters over there!" Kane shouted, targeting most of the *U-4's* closing in on the pirates. Kale waited for the second the target lock to go green before pressing her fingers on the joy sticks to launch the missiles at the U.G.G fighters. The two first volloys swooped in fast. Smashing into a pair of *U-4's* getting too close to the pirates. Thankfully the blast from the upcoming explosion only barely scarred the rear of the ally ships. Quickly after the first volley, a second wave of missiles rushed over to the scurrying *U-4's*. Seemingly still unaware of where the first strike came from, the missiles had no issue hitting their targets as well. Three ships tailing the rear of the squadron exploded! The third ship was only partially hit, though it destroyed its left wings. Making it swing in circles before colliding into one of the U.G.G destroyers.

Those destroyers, alongside many of the U.G.G corvettes were pushing the two pirate corvettes that were with the Jade. Both of those rather small ships, especially in comparison to most of the ships in that fleet would hardly stand a chance out there. Both Kane and Kale watched in horror as both pirate corvettes were being pelted with lasers, missiles and ballistics from nearly all of the ships in the U.G.G fleet. However, it didn't seem that those pirates weren't planning on going out without a fight. Both of the corvettes, alongside the remains of the fighters, suddenly made a push of their own against the advancing enemy fleet.

Fesh's voice suddenly cracked through the headset, "Kale, Kane! Defend those corvettes from incoming fighters!" Kane looked up as the Jade moved closer to the pirate fleet. Flying close to get beside both of the corvettes. Both had already sustained heavy damages as fires and hull breaches littered both of the tattered ships. Although, almost every weapon aboard managed to keep firing at the incoming enemy ships. Kane soon spotted several squadrons of *Z-21* U.G.G bombers with an escort of *U-4* fighters moving in from the rear.

"Kane, gotta mark those bombers or those corvettes are done for!" Kale yelled in her mic. Her thumb centimeters away from the button on her control stick.

"Understood!" He said back, both hands moving drastically to aim and lock on the bombers. Once he managed to get at least four lock ons, the targets were then marked on Kale's screen. To which she hardly even read before launching the missiles. Within seconds eight missiles were flying towards the incoming bombers. However, the *U-4* fighters swooped in front of the bombers! Firing their lasers to shoot down the incoming missiles. The lasers were quick to make contact and destroy the missiles before they even came close to the bombers.

"ARUGH!" Kane shouted in stressful frustration, "We can't even get near those bombers with those fighters defending them!" Kane yelled, slamming a fist on his arm rest. Attempting to get another lock on the bombers, however, the fighters kept a line in front and on the sides of the bombers. Continuing to rain a hail of lasers at both the corvettes and the Jade.

"Dusk! The AA gun is armed and ready to go! Give Kale and Kane a hand!" Fesh ordered on the headset.

A minute or so passed before Kane heard an electronic hum above him as the AA gun deployed behind the missile launcher. Then Dusk's voice was heard on the headset,

"AA gun online, what are my orders?" Kale was nearly instant to reply,

"Aim for those *U-4* fighters! We need a clear shot to take down those bombers!" She shouted. Her fingers twitched over the fire button as the squadrons of U.G.G fighters and bombers only got closer to the pirate ships!

Who was already taking massive amounts of damage from the ships in front of them!

"Roger that." Dusk said calmly, followed by firing the ballistic weapon at the fighters. Kane watched as both of the barrels above him fired heavy rounds at the wall of *U-4* fighters! Line in front didn't stand a chance. Ships were exploding and scurrying out of the way as their comrades were being obliterated in front of them. Dusk sat in silence, a digital smirk stuck on his face as he followed fighters attempting to dodge the AA guns firepower. Creating a hole for Kane to lock on the bombers again. Which he did in the moment he saw in the opening. Kale, waited, urgently awaiting for the screen to show the lock on so she may fire her newly reloaded missiles. Her eyes glued to the holo-graphic screen. Then it updated, showing six lock ons on different bombers. She rapidly pressed her fingers on the buttons. Sending twelve missiles at the bombers. *U-4* fighters attempted to dove in to defend the bombers, however Dusk did an excellent job at either destroying or scaring the fighters before they had a chance to get near the missiles! With nothing to defend them, all twelve of the missiles smashed into the squadron of bombers.

Kale whooped in excitement.

"Great work you two! We got em!" Kane sighed with a smile. Watching the remaining fighters pushing back.

The excitement of victory from that battle was quickly lost when Kane spotted one of the corvettes being completely destroyed when a volley of lasers suddenly all collided into the middle of one of the corvettes. Completely severing the ship in half. As the Jade tried to avoid the incoming debris, Kane saw pirates and crew members getting sucked into space.

"Oh my God..." He said in shock. Watching them wiggling and struggling to breathe before becoming limp corpses in the vast darkness of space. The battle only worsened when another series of explosions were heard from the left side. Kane already guessed inside what had happened. Yet he turned his head anyway. To which he saw the remains of the second corvette scattered around the area of the explosion.

"Brace yourselves back there!" Fesh shouted, moving the Jade closer to the debris to use as cover as she turned the ship around. Kane felt the sudden force shooting to his right while sitting back in his seat. Then Kane and Kale's eyes widened at the enormous size of the fleet now facing them. Alongside the giant capital ship, were many corvettes, destroyers and cruisers charging the remaining pirates fighters and the Jade.

"You need to hold them off as I try to get us the hell out of here!" She ordered, making quick, sharp turns to avoid the incoming fire from the U.G.G ships. Heavy lasers and ballistics smashed into the debris Fesh used to protect the Jade. Meanwhile Dusk, Kane and Kale fired everything the Jade had to offer to keep the swarm of fighters off the ships back.

Austin Patten

Sweat was going down both Fesh's and Ryko's faces as they heard muffled missiles and gun fire from the AA gun and the missile launcher firing at the advancing U.G.G forces coming closer.

"It's going to be close..." Ryko said under his breath. Watching the U.G.G ships close in on their blip on the radar. Fesh kept quiet, keeping all of her concentration on flying. As she had to risk getting very close to the debris before making the turn to deter the fighters from getting too close. Which, for the most part, worked effectively. Ryko watched nervously at points the blips from the *U-4's* temporarily moving back.

"W-wow..." He said in amazement. Ryko knew he taught Fesh how to fly. Pretty damn well too. Though these were moves even he doubted he could pull. Yet she was sweating bullets afterwards. As she pushed the ship to an uncomfortably close distance to large chunks of debris before yanking the controls to the side to avoid actually hitting it.

Then, thankfully and finally a transmission was coming through. Ryko sighed, happy to get a sign of something. He wasted no time to answer the call. Draz appeared on his screen! The gwarian giantess looked infuriated! She huffed and stood extremely close to the camera.

"Isss the U.G.G scum in MY bordersss?" She hissed. Her eyes narrowed as he asked the question with venom. Ryko nodded, rather terrified seeing Draz like this.

"Y-yes ma'am. The fleet ambushed us just before we could make our jump. The pirates beside a few fighters

209

are completely destroyed." He said, looking at the sonar to see one of the mentioned fighters disappearing.

"A-and they won't last long out here. Us included!" Draz hissed, cursing in gwarian. Soon hissing orders at her servants.

"Get to these coordinates, you are still to continue your mission!" She ordered darkly. Ryko swallowed down hard, knowing Fesh was already moving toward the sent coordinates, Ryko moved in to ask a question he was more than nervous to ask,

"W-what about the U.G.G fleet??" Drazz then crossed her arms.

"I'll deal with them. Get moving. NOW." The call then suddenly ended.

Fesh pushed the Jade's speeds to its limits, a laser from an incoming U-4 smashed into the side of the ship! Though it didn't do too much damage, the violent shaking was still enough to terrify the whole crew. Except for Dusk. Who simply continued to fire the AA gun at moving fighters.

"Cover is becoming more limited." Dusk stated, shooting down another pair of U-4's attempting to flank their left.

"Just keep it up everyone! We've got new orders from Drazz! We're moving towards new coordinates while she handles the U.G.G fleet!" Ryko informed the three. Preparing the ship to make a jump the moment Fesh gets to the coordinates. Kane was feeling the worry and stress hitting him hard now, the same was felt for Kale as they both continued to take down more of the seemingly endless amounts of U.G.G fighters.

A sudden blast launching towards one of the U.G.G's corvettes took the whole crew of the Jade off guard! The massive laser crashed right into the bridge of the corvette, completely destroying the vessel in one hit! Fesh and Ryko saw a huge pirate fleet moving towards them! Being led by a battleship! Which was the very ship that took down that corvette! Soon enough, the U.G.G refocused their attention to the much larger incoming threat opening fire on them.

"This is our moment." Fesh said, finally saying something. She sighed, with her grip tightening on the controls as she was getting closer.

"You make that jump the second we get the jump point." She ordered, sounding more dark in her voice then she intended. Ryko, was more than ok with it due to the current situation.

"You got it, I'm all ready to go." He said confidently, his hand on the switch.

As they flew closer to the point to jump, both Ryko and Fesh watched as both fleets only pushed further towards each other! Fighters on both sides had already collided, beginning many dogfights against each other. The numbers seemed to even for the most part to tell would be victorious. Though one thing that definitely played in the union's favor was that capital ship. Even with the rather large battleship under the pirates command, the capital ship was still far larger in comparison. Ryko watched as they

had to only flay past the battle. The muffled battle getting
farther away. However, Ryko spotted a few ships from the
fleet departing to join the Jade. This time a destroyer and
two additional corvettes.

"Looks like you'll be seeing your destroyer after
all." Ryko said, just before flipping the switch as he noticed
Fesh got to the jump point.

Now in the jump to the new coordinates, the crew
sighed, sitting back in their seats.

"That...was intense." Kane said to break the silence
after everyone collectively sighed.

"Yeah, no kidding." Ryko replied, rubbing the sweat
off his face.

"I can't believe we lost those pirates so easily."
Kane added, feeling terrible. The image of all those people
helplessly being sucked into the vacuum of space hitting
him hard. Followed by the guilt of not attempting to help.

Could they have boarded?
Tried to evacuate the survivors?
No.

Kane was aware of the reality of that situation. They
would've never stood a chance trying to dock with that
entire fleeting gunning after them. In fact they were lucky
to be alive at all after that. Kale broke his trail of thought,

"Please don't feel bad Kane. We were too
outnumbered." She said, though the choked up tone of
voice made it hard to believe she even believed her own
words. Fesh was quick to add,

"No, she's right. That fleet ambushed us. With the little firepower we had, the chances of us doing much to that fleet were slim." Kane nodded, even though no one could see him doing so.

"It...It just happened too fast." He croaked. Feeling a few tears fall down his face. Upon hearing Kane crying softly, Kale jumped down from her seat. Kane looked back to see her offering a soft smile before opening her arms. Lunging out of his seat, Kane wrapped his arms around her in a hug. The sudden speed of this action took a minute for her to process before she brought her own arms around her.

"Hey, it's ok Kane." She said softly, keeping her arms around him. She sometimes forgot how rarely he saw combat before these past few days. The horrors of battle were still something he needed to adjust too, and that's not something normal people like him just got used too.

"Thanks" He sniffed in a muffled voice, his head resting on her shoulder. "It means more than you think." He said. Kale sighed,

"It's cool, we all know this is still new to you. There's no shame in crying after an intense battle like that." She said gently.

Eventually, Kane would let go. He wiped his face with his sleeve,

"I'm sorry, getting your shirt dirty." Kale only laughed with a scoff,

"Please, the shirt is the last thing I'm worried about." Even Kane quickly reliazed how stupid that was and chuckled.

"Yeah, no that makes sense." Kale then jumped a little closer with her hands behind her back,

"So, are we ok?" She asked kindly. Kane smiled lightly, nodding.

"Yeah, I'm better. Thanks to you." He said, unaware of the blush that appeared on Kale's face since he turned around to sit back in his chair. Kale was silent for a few seconds as she got back to her own seat. Forcing herself to attempt to stop blushing. Yet, her face...and emotions wanted to say otherwise. She sighed, at least grateful no one could see her like this.

Fesh and Ryko sat in silence. Both feeling the same things in that they were both shocked that they managed to get out of there in one piece. Alive to be specific.

"That was some incredible flying you did back there." Ryko said, sounding awfully proud of her. At first, Fesh blushed a little before turning her head away,

"Shut up, of course it was decent. I wouldn't let us die." She scoffed. Ryko chuckled,

"Of course, I wouldn't wanna hear it any other way." He said back. "Besides, I can't get all the credit, the three back there did an excellent job keeping us covered. I'm amazed how little damage we took." Fesh added. Ryko muted his mic before replying,

"True, then again they were clearly ordered to concentrate their efforts more so on the pirates then us." He said solemnly. Knowing only a few fighters managed to escape alongside the Jade. Fesh did the same,

"Yeah." Fesh said, sounding sad in her voice as well. "Honestly I agree with Kane. I wish we could have done more to help." She said, though before her dad could try to comfort her she quickly added,

"I know there was nothing we could have done. Realistically we got the best case scenario."

"May I join?" Dusk suddenly broke in. The two looked at the anvol. Fesh answered,

"Actually we were kind of talking in private, how about you go check on Jok? I'm sure he's still hiding in his office." She said with her arms crossed. Though Dusk on the other hand thought it was a brilliant idea,

"Of course! Thank you Fesh!" He said cheerfully, a smile displayed on his screen before he exited.

Dusk walked up Jok's office door, knocking the door gently.

"Is it over?" his muffled voice asked on the other side.

"Why yes! We are currently in the jump as we speak!" Dusk answered in that same happy tone. After a minute or so, the doors opened. As Dusk entered, he noticed how messy the inside was. Papers, and other office and medical supplies laid strewn all over the floor.

"Wow, it's filthy Dr. Jok." Dusk stated, looking all over the mess. The large hellion huffed,

"Thanks for noticing. You can thank Fesh for this. Her insane flying managed to trash my workspace again." He grumbled, bending over to start cleaning.

"Her "Insane" flying saved our lives." Dusk said back. Jok nodded as he picked up a handful of papers,

"Yeah, I was watching the whole thing on my monitors." He said, gesturing to the four small monitors at the coroner of his office One face the front of the ship, the other the rear. While the last two showed different angles of the inside of the ship. Though the visual was decent quality there seemed to have been zero audio.

Shame. Dusk thought.

"Besides, you managed to take down what seemed thirty or more of those wretched union fighters in the sky." Jok shot back.

"And with one hand!" Dusk kept the smile on his screen as he rubbed the back of his head.

"Oh please, it was nothing." Dusk said. Though Jok thought otherwise,

"Oh it was something. Everyone played an incredible part in that. Even Fesh. Well…" Jok said with a nervous scratch of his arm, "Everyone but me." He said shamefully, going back to cleaning the mess. Dusk paused for a minute to think.

"Well, now that's not true." He said. Jok chuckled,

"Well thank you, though I know I was rather useless in that encounter." However, Dusk wasn't planning on giving up. He walked right in front of the hellion, his larger appearance not bothering him at all.

"What would have happened if an explosion much larger struck this ship right now?" He asked, stepping even closer to the doctor. Jok raised a brow,

Austin Patten

"Is this a trick question?" The anvol tilted his head, his expression seeming serious,

"Did it sound like a trick?" He asked back. Jok then tried to answer,

"I'd...try to get to them, to save them." He said nervously. Dusk then returned to his smile,

"Exactly! We need you to stay safe in your office during combat, because if YOU are the one who is damaged during the fight. Well...I'm sure that speaks for itself." He explained. Jok smiled at the explanation, feeling his confidence return.

"Huh. Thank you Dusk." He said in his deep voice, patting the anvol on his shoulder.

"Anytime doctor. Now, we have a raid to attend too."

CHAPTER FIFTEEN

Alan, alongside Captain Vail, watched the battle unfold over Jev. Other than some squadrons of fighters and bombers, followed by a few corvettes, casualties had been low. However, the size of this pirate fleet was still concerning. Alan found the frustration of the situation only worsening when he watched the ship Kane escaped on make a jump while the pirate fleet forced their attention away.

"Orders sir?" Vail asked, his hands still behind his back. His head now facing the G.L. Alan watched the space battle continue. In front of the capital ship, another corvette was taking heavy damage and was attempting to pull back while a pair of destroyers provided covering fire. As well as a few cruisers followed by several other corvettes pushed the right side of the pirate fleet. The ships peppered the pirate fleet with their firepower as they assaulted the side.

"Are the 1st and 2nd assault divisions ready?" Alan asked, his eyes still watching the space battle before them.

His eyes, trailing towards the few defence platforms that were orbiting the planet. Vail nodded,

"Yes sir, as well as the 3rd and 4th nearly ready to go on your command." Vail replied.

"Perfect, contact Draz." He ordered suddenly. Though taken off by the order, the captain knew better than to question,

"Of course sir." He said, before barking orders at one of the communication officers.

"Put the call on the main screen." Alan added. The transmission was answered in seconds as the whole crew saw the gigantic gwarain standing in front of the camera. Some of them gasped at the sight of her! Most of them clearly never seen a gwarian giantess before. The captain was fast to shut them up and get the crew back to order. Draz hissed as he sat on her massive throne,

"You've got ssssome nerve to come onto MY ssssystem Alan." Alan scoffed,

"And you got some nerve to be harbouring rebels Draz." That only made the large gwarian hiss again, her fist suddenly slamming on her armrest. Scaring a few of the servants below her.

"Allow me to do this quick and easy so your simple union brain can understand it. GET. OUT. NOW." She spat.

Alan however only crossed his arm, his eyes narrowing down.

"You know, I don't think I will." He started, giving the signal to the captain.

"In fact…" Vail was heard giving the order in his wireless headset,

Ignition: Unknown Criminal

"The light is green, go go go!" He ordered. Making the gwarin giantess's eyes widen.

"...The amount of pain and suffering I'm going to make you and this world feel for spitting in not only my face. But the face of the United Galactic Government will be beyond words you could even imagine." He said darkly. The look of shock was then replaced with rage,

"You send a single soldier on my world and I'll-" Alan waved his hand, signaling the call to be cut.

"Captain, send in four cruisers to deal with those platforms. I want them gone before Draz can have time to notice the transports." Captain saluted before replying,

"Yes Sir!"

"Get moving!" The major of the 1st assault battalion shouted! Followed by collective orders from different sergeants across the squads within each platoon. Hundreds of soldiers, tanks, vehicles, robots and mechs were marching onto their transports to begin their attack on Jev. Fay stood beside the fellow soldiers of her squad. Being assigned to the 6th assault battalion and already aware of her orders, she would only watch as the valiant soldiers of the U.G.G were loading up. Troops and smaller vehicles were placed in *Falcons*. While mechs and tanks were to be transported with much larger *Condors*. Something that stuck out to Fay was the variation of Mechs that were being deployed in the assault. While she was more used to fighting alongside the more common *Sentry*. For the first time, she had been able to see much more heavy and frontline mechs and machines. The massive moving wall known as the *Escort* grabbed her attention first! This enormous robot stood up to two stories tall! Being the only robot to stand up to the roof of the capital ships hangar bay! Fay heard orders being shouted to the various crew members to get out of the way as five of these titans stomped towards their transports. People scattered to the other ends of the hanger, watching in shock and awe as the Escorts walked under each of the transports. Their legs needed to retract before huge clamps to hold off the top of each robot. Once they were loaded, Fay spotted a squad of *AA MK2* and *Nemesis* mechs moving towards their transports.

The *AA MK2* Mechs rolled onto the condors with large tracks. While the *Nemesis* walked on four legs. Armed with heavy, long-range laser cannons the *Nemesis* looked like a horrifying mech to be up against. That was not to discredit the power of the *AA MK2* mech either, even if it was restricted to only attacking air targets, with its large machine guns and built-in missile launchers the *AA MK2* was a devastating mech for enemy air support!

Fay gave a salute when she watched the doors of the *Falcons* and *Condors* closed. The other soldiers and crew members quickly did the same, watching the engines burst to life before lifting the many ships out of the massive vessel.

Ignition: Unknown Criminal

"Give 'em hell," Axel said softly. With his salute crisp and solid beside his face. Once the ships had exited the hanger bay, orders were given out once again and people were back to work. Though Fay walked up to the energy field, the very thing kept her and everyone aboard the hanger safe from being thrown into the vacuum of space. When she stood right in front of the field, she looked down. Watching the transports rush towards the planet's surface. The defence platforms were all but destroyed as four cruisers peppered the defences with a hail of lasers to keep the transports protected, even from incoming pirate ships. The Sergeant had dismissed everyone till further orders were given. Walking up to the corporeal, he stood beside her. Seeing the same view as her. Then, soon enough the ships were out of sight as they began their attack.

"Hard to believe that the neutral worlds were this organized. And powerful." Fay said, bringing her eyes to look at the smouldering remains of the defence platforms. Most of the debris has either been obliterated from additional explosions or were crashing down on the surface. Surely about to cause massive damage to the scum that lived below.

"This is rare." The sergeant spoke in his deep yet calming voice. "Most neutral worlds are a mess, full of chaos and destruction." He explained, getting faint memories of the battles he fought on those worlds.

"Jev, has a capable leader under it. An equally rare one at that." He said, looking down at Fay.

"Oh? Who's that?" Fay asked, crossing her arms. "A gwarian giantess known as Draz." Fay's eyes nearly bulged out of her sockets.

"A gwarian giantess?" I thought they went into hiding!" She exclaimed. Starting to become fearful for the soldiers on the planet surface. The sergeant nodded,

"Most of them did after a war that almost brought them to extinction." The sergeant explained, "Draz however, with her pride, didn't allow herself to attempt to hide. Instead, she forged something new under her. This." He said, gesturing the planet.

"The number of allies she has is completely unknown to us. Though, even with the pirates and smugglers under her directly, even right now she has proven to be a rather powerful enemy to us." Fay stared down at Jev, still finding it hard to believe a gwarian giantess was down there. The largest, most terrifying breed of gwarians. Like practically everyone stationed on this entire fleet, she had never seen one in person. Only in either texts or online. Knowing how enormous they could get alongside the equal intelligence of any other gwarian made them horrifying to fight against.

"And we are only sending two battalions for the initial assault?" Fay asked, concerned for those in the battle on the ground. The sergeant had no answer for her question,

"The G.L is more than aware of his orders. Keep in mind this is only the initial attack, the 3rd and 4th battalions will be sent in to assist the moment the order is given." He said.

Ignition: Unknown Criminal

Silence brewed between the two for a moment, then Fay said,

"Hard believe after chasing down one man, we would be fighting a battle with one of the most powerful neutral worlds in the verse." The sergeant was able to reply fast, since he had been thinking the same thing during their silence,

"The G.L is most likely thinking he could kill two birds with one stone. Due to the size of the fleet, he brought with him. He was expecting to be having to fight rebels, yet he found something far more valuable to him." The sergeant said. Hearing that surprised Fay as she turned to the sergeant with a confused look on her face.

"He values taking down pirates more than rebels?" She asked.

"I can't exactly know what he's thinking. I'm only an old soldier. Though through the many battles I survived. I tell you without a doubt it's a hell of a lot more difficult to take down a group of pirates than a squad of rebels. The way they take on combat is far more...brutal and aggressive than your average soldiers. " The sergeant explained further. Fay then looked down,

"Oh, I see." She said. The sergeant crossed his arms,

"Oh you will. I just hope you'll be ready when the time comes. For both of our sake."

Alan continued to watch the raging battle in space continue. Ships from fighters to corvettes charged, flanked and attacked to the best of their abilities. Alan was surprised how even this battle was becoming. Especially with more pirate ships jumping in to reinforce the defence.

"Two more pirate destroyers have entered the battle sir!" One of the bridge crew bellowed. Captain Vail watched as the two ships flew towards a formation of pirate corvettes attempting to attack the left of Alan's fleet. However, the G.L was able to see this clearly as he spoke his next order,

"Captain, have the Capital ship's *Arrowheads* target those incoming destroyers." Alan ordered,

"We shouldn't afford losing additional ships on our weakest side." Captain Vail immediately ordered the weapons officers to focus all *Arrowheads* to concentrate on the added destroyers.

Arrowheads.

Deadly, long-range cannons placed on either larger ships that carry the extra room for more specific weaponry or medium ships specialized in long-range combat. With vessels as enormous as U.G.G Capital ships, they could carry up to nine *Arrowheads*. Since they have to be installed on the rear of the massive ship to keep them protected. With how huge each cannon was, they required large groups of space between each.

Ignition: Unknown Criminal

Captain Vail has specifically ordered two *Arrowheads* to take down the incoming destroyers. Alan only kept his attention on the two vessels he ordered to destroy. Watching as they flew closer to the fleet of pirates. Then, after a few minutes of the *Arrowheads* charging up, two massive purple lasers came soaring past the capital ship. Both the captain and Alan eyed the two enormous lines of lasers got closer towards their target. From there it was seconds before both pirate destroyers were obliterated with a giant explosion. While one of the destroyers was completely decimated by the impact. One managed to have the front half intact. Due to the laser hitting the rear of the ship. Alan watched as some of the ship's escape pods launched. His lips twitched in frustration, knowing there were now survivors. However, he quickly suppressed those feelings, as he was pleased that the ships were gone. Though, he looked back where the ships would exited from.

"Captain, designate at least four *Arrowheads* and if possible some additional ships to keep watch of that area of space. We must not allow the pirates to claim reinforcements. This battle is already even as it is." Alan ordered.

"Of course sir," The captain responded.

Alan then brought his attention to Jev. The homeworld of Draz's pirate operation. Alan had then considered if she would have as strong opposition on the ground as she does in space.

"Have the forces on the ground established communication yet?" Alan asked. Captain Vail kept his eyes on the space battle when he replied,

"Not yet sir." Alan noticed at the corner of his eye another pirate corvette being destroyed by a handful of U.G.G Bombers.

"Are the 3rd and 4th battalions ready to launch?" He asked, wanting to send reinforcements immediately. When the first battalions land on a hostile world, they would have to destroy any enemies at the landing zone. Then set up communications as soon as possible for the next wave to land. Alan had expected to be contacted by now.

"Yes sir! The 5th and 6th battalions should be ready soon as well." He added.

"Excellent, send them in. Orders are to assist friendlies on the ground and then establish communications." With another salute, Captain Vail was quick to get to work.

Alan watched as the hundreds of ships soared towards the surface. With every soldier, mech and robot aboard, Alan watched them all move towards Jev to fight for the U.G.G. The G.L had only hoped he wasn't too late to assist those already fighting.

"Inform me as soon as the next battalions are ready, even soldiers that were originally sent to assist with capturing Kane." He ordered.

"Sir?" Vail asked, seeming confused.

"What about the fugitive?" With his eyes glued to the planet, he answered,

"If he truly is working for Draz, it'll only be a matter of time before she calls for him to help." The captain only saulted at his reply.

"Understood sir! They will be informed immediately!" With that, while the captain was barking additional orders, Alan brought his attention back to the space battle before him.

CHAPTER

SIXTEEN

The Jade, followed by the accompanying fleet soon exited their jump. Everyone knew they had to work fast. The Jade was first to move towards the unsuspecting U.G.G convoy. Which consisted of massive cargo ships and a handful of corvettes and a destroyer guarding it. Ryko was swift to begin a transmission going with the additional pirate ships. The second the connection was established Fesh began barking orders,

"Arlight! This is a smash and grab! Give us cover so we can get that cargo!" After hearing a collective reply of

"Yes ma'am!" She slammed the pedal to the metal. Sending the Jade in full speed towards the largest cargo ship. A destroyer and the two corvettes deployed fighter craft that followed close by. While the small-medium ships engaged the ill prepared enemy corvettes, The fighters soon soared past the Jade to open fire at the cargo ship, specifically the ship's engines, attempting to disable the jump drive.

Fesh then focused her next of orders on the *BruteShot,* the closest corvette,

Ignition: Unknown Criminal

"Deploy three dropships to assist us with raiding the cargo ship! We may need some backup in there!" The captain, another gwarian nodded with a grin.

"Already thought you'd need the hand Fesh." He said. Ryko then spotted three pirate dropships exiting the corvette.

"Thank you, let's do this." She said bringing the Jade towards the cargo ships hangar bay.

"You boys and girls better be ready back there! This is gonna get rough!" Fesh shouted out back.

Kane, Dusk and Kale checked their weapons. Helix deployed his new set of weapons, which included a plasma gun, stun gun and an EMP launcher.

"Guess we're gonna see these new upgrades in action, huh?" Kane said. Helix displayed a ";)" Before typing,

"You wouldn't expect me to come into battle unprepared would ya?" Which made the three chuckle. Kane patted the weaponized cybel,

"Of course not bud!"

With Kane's plasma rifle, Dusk's shotgun, the two turned to Kale, curious what she was carrying for the upcoming conflict. The gwarian soon pulled out two heavy magnums.

"Thought these bad boys would come in handy." She said with a smirk with those massive hand held weapons in her hands! Kane and Dusk exchanged glances for a second before looking back at her. Kale looked at the two that glanced towards her.

"What?" She asked. Dusk chuckled before standing by the door.

"Just please don't dislocate your shoulders with those please." Kale only stuck out her tongue.

"I'll be fine!" She hissed back playfully. Kane only shook his head with a grin,

"You better."

After a muffled explosion followed by some violent shaking, the three heard Ryko this time,

"We've entered the hangar bay!" he shouted! The sound of the Jade's energy gun lighting up any soldiers attempting to shoot the Jade down.

"That's our cue." Dusk said calmly, pressing the button to open the door before jumping out. Kane already heard the heavy BANG from the anvol's shotgun. He jumped down as well, landing right beside Kale. To his left he spotted a union soldier blown in half laying in front of Dusk. A laser zipped past Kane from a squad of incoming union soldiers rushing the right side! Each soldier dashed towards the nearest pieces of cover, their choice being the debris of a destroyed U-4 fighter. Within their new positions, they began to open fire on the three. Forcing them all to duck for cover as well. Kane spotted a handful of scattered crates, Kale was right beside him. While Dusk was much further in the hanger bay, using a destroyed chunk of metal as a shield in one hand with his *Vandal* slung on his back. The shield managed to deflect every shot from the squad of Union soldiers as he pushed towards them.

Kale then spotted another squad coming up from an elevator. However, they were all shot down by one of the squads of pirates that deployed from the two dropships. A total of four squads of pirates joined the fight from the dropships. Two of which formed defensive positions around their specific dropship. While one moved in to assist Dusk with his offensive push, the other ran to Kane and Kale, taking cover by the crates. Six pirates lined up in front of the two, laying suppressing fire upon the additional union forces in the hangar. Though, as Kane noticed even more soldiers pouring into the hanger bay, he knew they wouldn't be able to hold this position for long, even with the additional forces to assist them. Pulling out his holo-watch he began a transmission with Fesh,

"My ship is dead ahead from my position, but where's Draz's cargo?" He bellowed, trying to keep up with the loud gun and laser fire behind him.

"The cargo is located in the cargo bay to the left of the hangar bay!" Fesh replied while concentrating her firepower on large doors opening on each side of the hangar bay opening.

They were sending in mechs.

"Oh Shi-Ryko! I need shields on full power! We got *AA Mk2's!*" She shouted, Kane heard as the transmission was still live. Muting Fesh as she was barking further orders, he focused communication on Dusk while Kale and the squad of pirates fired upon the additional infantry that joined the mechs.

"Dusk! Watch yourself! Mechs incoming!" He yelled. Though, even if Kane didn't see the anvol's face, he knew a grin was plastered on his digital face as he pushed forward with the pirates accompanying him.

"I appreciate the heads up." He replied simply, cooling his *Vandal* before he noticed the massive tracks drive in front of him. Yet, unlike the pirates behind him, instead of scuttling away from the enormous machine he charged towards it! When the pirates noticed the anvol was actually taking the charge to the union mech, the squad leader suddenly made a call,

"Cover that insane anvol!" She ordered, pushing towards a fallen destroyed robot with her *feind* tight in her grip. Her fellow pirates were half a second hesitant before catching up. Firing their weapons at the infantry that accompanied the *AA Mk2*. Forcing the union soldiers to use the massive machine as protection while a few fell from the sudden spray of lasers and bullets. For a few minutes, it seemed the six pirates managed to keep the soldiers pinned.

Until a squad of *Enforcers* rushed into the fray.

Enforcers were heavily armored union soldiers used in the front lines of battle alongside the normal frontline soldier. Carrying an assortment of heavy machine/laser guns to rocket launchers and even energy shields. Unfortunately for the squad of pirates trying to cover Dusk, Three of the five held the front with the two handed energy shields. Easily soaking up the firepower being used by the pirates. While the other two carried large laser weapons.

Ignition: Unknown Criminal

One of the *enforcers* barked something through his communicator. The union soldiers soon emerged from the *AA Mk2* to join the *enforcers*. Once they quickly assembled, the squad leader of pirates realized they were going to charge! Seeing how they stayed hidden behind the three energy shields.

"Get your bayonets at the ready!" She barked, pressing a button on the side of her *fiend*, watching a green blade form under the barrel of her weapon. Each pirate copied the same action as blades of different colors were deployed. One of the pirates then took an *Orb*. *Orbs* were small hand sized robots capable of deploying shields up to a person's chest in front of them. Tossing the *orb* in front of the squad, the small metal ball deployed two small wheels on each side before deploying the shield in front of it.

"Stay low, we won't stand a chance till we get close to those bastards!" She shouted as she jumped over her cover to duck behind the *orb's* shield. The rest followed close by, some firing blindly over the shield. Once the pirates were in position the pirate that deployed the *orb* gave the order for the robot to move the second the squad leader barked the call to charge! Staying at a couch, the pirates soon ran towards the union soldiers. Shouting, voices filled with rage as the six pirates braced themselves for close quarters combat.

An explosion brought Kane's attention to the *AA Mk2* Dusk rushed at. Kane noticed one of the tracks blown off with a trail of fire as the anvol climbed onto the titanic mech! Kane's attention soon moved away from the battle on the other side to his own. He spotted Kale and the pirates continued to fire upon the union soldiers pushing on their end. Soon enough, *enforcers* were spotted. However, only a few of them luckily. Though each still carried heavy laser guns. Spraying an array of blue lasers at the pirates and Kale! Forcing them to get down. Even Kane had to stay hidden behind his crates as lasers smashed onto his cover! Helix was still beside him, awaiting for a command. Since he was just firing when he could on the other side of the crate.

Looking around frantically, Kane tried to think of something quickly. Kale and the pirates were still pinned. One of the pirates even tried to fire his smg blindly only for it to get shot out of his hands! Kane knew without even having to look that those soldiers were using this to their advantage to push forward. Turning back to Helix he said,

"Alright bud, this may be risky. But it's now or never. I need you to find a way to take down those *enforcers*." Helix kept his screen blank for a second as he scanned the hangar bay, searching for solutions. Then he spotted a vent. Bring his screen back to Kane, he typed his plan,

"You're going to need to cover me. The vent should allow me to flank the union forces." Kane looked behind Helix, seeing the vent he was referring too.

"Alright, I'll let Kale and the others know." Moving up to the side of his crate behind Kale, Kane shouted,

Ignition: Unknown Criminal

"We need to cover Helix! He can flank the
enforcers!" Kale then looked at the human with a worried
expression,

"How? They got us completely pinned down!" She
yelled back. "We can hardly even fire blindly without
losing our weaponssss!" Kane had to be quick, at the corner
of his eye saw the *enforcers* closing in on their position! He
knew everyone else was far too busy fighting other soldiers
or defenses to assist them.

"We have to anyway! Sacrifice a weapon! All of
you if you have too but we have to fight back now!! It's
that or we die here!" Kane bellowed, already firing his
fiend from his cover. The pirates didn't hesitate, they all
knew Kane was right. Even the one who lost his primary
took his pistol and started to fire over his head! Kale was
quick to join as well, firing one of her magnums to her
right. The combined firing, even if inaccurate, manages to
kill one of the *enforcers* from one of the lasers hitting the
weak point at his neck. Other soldiers were either shot as
well or fled into cover.

Helix didn't waste any more time. The second the
enforcer hit the ground he flew towards the vent. The weak
metal broke instantly when the cybel smashed into it.
Soaring through the straight tube of metal, Helix was
speedy to notice the union forces unaware of his position.
Running through the vent again, his plasma gun fully
charged, he opened fire on the remaining *enforcers*! One of
which dropped quickly as he was pelted with hot plasma.

The other turned around, aiming his laser gun at the cybel! However, before she could pull the trigger, a burst of laser bolts shot through her head! The very burst came from Kane, who peeked to get the accurate shot.

"*Enforcers* down! Everyone up!" One of the pirates shouted, with a laser pistol in his hand due to his rifle being destroyed. Most of the pirates lost their primaries except for two, who carried *rift* carbines. The rest had to use pistols. That is, expect for the one who now lost both of his weapons. So he had to stay down with nothing but a dagger in his hand.

Now that the enforcers were down, Kane was able to concentrate on the task at hand, the cargo, then his ship. To his left he spotted the entrance to the cargo bay Fesh mentioned. Though there was very little cover from his position to that door. Helix soon popped in front of Kane, giving him a jumpscare as his head bounced back. Though Helix typed,

"Mission complete. :)". Getting over the sudden scare, a plan started to formulate in Kane's mind. Looking over to the pirates he saw that nearly all of them, including Kale were thick in combat. All except for the one armed with nothing but his dagger. Kale shouted while waving him over,

"Come over here!" Though rather confused why he was chosen, he quickly moved towards Kane to join his cover.

"You and I are gonna get Draz's cargo. You're gonna need to stay low and keep them suppressed." Kane said.

Ignition: Unknown Criminal

"With what exactly?" The lykoi pirate spat. Gesturing his melee weapon. Kane only replied by handing his *fiend* over.

"I learned I prefer handhelds anyway." He said, patting the *Lance* that Dusk gave him in his holster.

"Works for me." The pirate chuckled, more than pleased to have an actual rifle in his hands.

"Alright." Kane said, pulling the laser pistol out, clutching it with both hands. "Then you and Helix are with me." He said, bracing himself before making the call.

"Lets go!" The pirate and Helix were close to Kane as they sprinted through the open area of the hangar bay. All three fired their weapons at the union soldiers, forcing them to get into cover. Buying them more time to run.

Due to the speed they were making, it took roughly a few minutes to reach the door. Though to the three it felt like hours. The pirate found a medium sized crate and quickly dragged it over for cover as he opened fire at the union soldiers at the new angle. Helix was already at work to hack the door controls. Kane was relieved to see the speed everyone was working at as he joined the pirates in fighting the union soldiers trying to concentrate on them. Kale also spotted this, trying to fire at those attempting to stop Kane. Two heavy shots from her magnum smashed into one of the union soldier's chest! Blowing two large holes into her before her body slammed onto the metal floor! Kane kept his shots to careful controlled shooting. Firing only when one of the soldiers tried to peak from their cover. One of his shots slammed into the gut of a soldier. The pirates kept his *fiend* on burst fire. Keeping his focus more on suppression then actually hitting the soldiers.

"How much longer?" The pirate asked, cooling the *fiend* down as he ducked under the crate.

"Helix should be done soon, who knows how strong union security is." Kane replied, reloading his lance as well while bullets rippled the crate the pair was using as cover.

As if on cue, Helix unlocked the door seconds after Kane's reply. Practically jumping onto his feet Kane sprinted inside the cargo bay. The lykoi stayed close, firing a burst of lasers behind him. They were led inside a massive room, filled with rows and rows of cargo. Boxes, crates, cages and other packaging material were placed neatly along the many shelves organized into large rows.

"So, what does Draz's cargo look like exactly?" The pirates asked, looking up at the hundreds of crates lined up, staring down at the three.

"Good question." Kane said, bringing up his holo-watch to contact Fesh,

"Fesh, we reached the cargo bay, any idea what we're looking for?" Ryko was quick to respond, though laserfire was heard in the background,

"There should be two small crates by the third row to your left. You want the yellow crates with the Xhell Corp logo on it." He answered, soon ending the call right after.

"You heard him, let's move." Kane said, holstering his *Lance*. Helix took point, then Kane and the pirate moved closely behind as they jogged past the rows. Since it was only three rows away, thankfully they didn't have to move far. Once they reached the specified row, they moved towards it.

"There!" The pirate said, jogging towards the yellow crates stacked on top of each other. Kane caught up to the lykoi, looking down to see the Xhell corp logo.

"Perfect." Kane said, grabbed the bottom crate. Lifting both of the crates.

"Time to leave, who knows how things are holding up in the hangar bay." He said, letting the pirate lead the way.

Though, before the pirate could get to the door, he was suddenly attacked by an anvol jumping down in front of him! The robotic foe held an energy blade. A serious face was displayed on her dark blue screen.

"Halt! You are in possession of U.G.G property! Return it or be properly destroyed!" The female voice boomed in the cargo bay. Placing the crates down, Kane was placing a hand on his *Lance*. The pirate already had his sights on the anvol. Helix flew beside Kane, with his plasma gun deployed. The anvol noticed this aggressive reaction as a digital brow rose,

"So, you fools choose to fight? So be it." She said, suddenly lunging towards them. Both Kane and the pirate started to open fire at the anvol. But she was quick. She dodged side to side, hardly being touched by the incoming laser fire! In seconds she jumped over the pirate. Her blades in hands as she prepared to strike. Though he barely managed to dodge to the right. Missing the blades that smashed onto the metal floor! His back slammed into the wall of a row of cargo. The anvol saw that she missed the pirate, turning to face him, her face showing a rather irritated expression. Before she could attempt to attack the fallen pirate, Kane fired three shots into her back. Making the anvol face Kane now. Once turned, she easily avoided the other shots he fired at her. When pushed into a full sprint towards the human. With her left arm, she swung the energy blade at Kane. Who flung himself back. Watching the blade miss his face by inches, the warmth touching his upper body as the energy blade flew past him. He then tried to lift the *Lance* at the anvols face. However, the anvol predicted this as she grabbed his arm half way.

"Good try pirate filth." She scoffed, beginning to crush his arm in her hand. Kane screamed as the cool, metal digits pressed down on his arm. Before any substantial damage could've been done, Helix soared at full speed into the anvol's face. Kane heard a heavy smash as Helix cracked the anvol's screen, creating a large dent in front of her. The anvol's grip loosened, giving the opportunity for him to yank his arm free.

The anvol stepped back away a few more steps before regaining her balance. Her damaged face looking up, the glitching image attempting to convey an angered expression. Her hand clutched her energy blade tightly. The pirate got back to his feet, lifting the laser rifle towards the anvol. While Kane and Helix faced the anvol, *lance* raised and plasma gun charged up.

"I recommend you shut down and let up pass you piece of trash." The pirate spat, his finger pressed on the trigger.

"At least you may be able to live."

The anvol chuckled however. Her voice became as distorted and glitchy as her digital face.

"If you think I'll let up that easily then you're all as foolish as you look!" She sneered, watching them through her damaged vision. Though before anyone could make a move, she darted to the closest, the pirate. He pulled the trigger to send a burst of lasers towards her. Only for them to smash into some cargo behind her. He didn't get a chance to fire again as the *fiend* was sliced in half. Turning the laser rifle into junk in his hands. The pirate couldn't even process what had happened to his weapon before seeing the blue energy blade slide towards his chest.

Kane had already begun his sprint before the pirate's weapon was destroyed. He was out of options. Running towards danger with nothing but a small energy dagger.

The *Lance* was empty.

"Now Helix!" Kane shouted. The cybel flew past Kane, sending a barrage of plasma at the anvol! Most of those rounds of hot plasma plowed into the anvol's chassis. Causing her to stumble back again as she dropped her energy blade. Large black streaming holes were present all around her. One of these was on her chest, exposing her core. An anvol's core was extremely important, as the core not only kept the anvol connection with *Optix* live, the A.I that controlled all of the anvol, it controlled most major functions of all anvol.

This was Kane's opportunity, now or never. He lunged after her, energy dagger in both hands as he forced the blade into the exposure of her chest. However, the anvol was now becoming desperate. She swiftly brought a robotic fist to his gut. Stopping Kane in his tracks. Winded, dizzy and forced to hold his stomach. Kane looked up as the anvol suddenly smashed her foot in his face. In an instant Kane was back first on the solid floor! He gasped as more air was shot out of him.

"P-p-pathetic." The anvol scoffed. Walking towards Kane, lifting her mechanical foot over him. A glitchy grin on her face. Helix attempted to charge the anvol again due to both his EMP and plasma guns needing to charge up. The anvol however was prepared for the cybel this time. Looking at Helix flying towards her, she slapped the cybel away. Sending Helix into a crate. This was the split second Kane needed for his second chance. Without any warning or hesitation he took the energy blade with both hands and lunged towards her chest. The anvol wasn't even able to let out a scream before her core was abruptly devastated by the blade piercing the weak core and its components. Within seconds the anvol became limp, her body collapsing on the ground.

Kane sighed, clutching his damaged arm as the adrenaline began to wear off a little and he began to notice the pain again.

Ignition: Unknown Criminal

"Ah, damn." He then looked back at the pirate, who was getting back to his feet. He was catching his own breath before walking back to Kane.

"Wow, you're more of a fighter then I took you for." He said, offering a grin,

"Thanks." Though wincing in pain, Kane returned a smile.

"No worries." The lykoi rose a brow as he noticed Kane' arm. The outline of bruising where the anvol attempted to crush his arm was a dark purple.

"You gonna be alright?" The lykoi pirate asked, seeming concerned. Though Kane nodded,

"I'll live." he replied simply.

"You may need to carry the cargo now." He said. The pirate only replied by shooting a look that said,

"You think?".

Kane then realized how quiet it was. The muffled sounds of combat were no longer heard on the other end of the door. The pirate and Kane looked at each other.

"Hey, if we die now. I'd rather do it out there then in here." the pirate said sternly. His grip tightening on the crates. He held one in each hand. Ready wield them as blunt weapons if needed.

"Works for me. Hey, I never got your name, I'm Kane." He said, finally introducing himself.

"Tarrus." The lykoi answered. "Now, you gonna open that door or what?" Tarrus said with a smirk, ready for whatever that door has to offer.

"Alright, Helix, lets see what's on the other side."
He said, clutching his energy dagger with his good hand.

In a minute or so the door opened.

"Kane! There you are!" Kale shouted. Her
magnums now holstered as she ran towards him. The
amount of the relief that washed over him was like a tidal
wave. Though he had to raise his hands up to avoid
accidentally stabbing the sprinting gwarian going for a hug.
Kale soon wrapped her arms around the humans as a wide
smile was on her face.

"We were so worried! We couldn't open the door!"
She exclaimed.

"That would be because of her." Kane replied.
Pointing at the dead anvol laying on the ground. Kale
looked over to see the broken anvol on the floor.

"You guys got attacked by an anvol?" She yelled,
soon seeing Kane's arm. The bruised hand print easily
caught her attention. He felt his injured arm being carefully
grabbed by Kale's hands. He carefully brought down the
other as well.

"Are you ok?" She asked, noticing the bruises and
scrapes on Kane's face too. Though he nodded,

"Yeah, I'm alright. Who knew anvols would be
such excellent opponents." He tried to joke. Tarrus rolled
his eyes with a grin. Kale still seemed worried as she
observed the injuries on Kane. Kane placed his hands on
her shoulders,

"Hey, I'm fine, really." He assured her, though she
only showed a weak smile and nodded,

"O-ok. If you say so."

Ignition: Unknown Criminal

Kale then led them out to the hangar bay. To which Kane saw was scattered with the remains of battle. The first thing he noticed was the destroyed *AA Mk2* Mechs. Both of them were blown to pieces where they once stood. Dusk stood by the one he had taken down. Though he was assisting the last pirate in his accompanying squad.

"We had taken a lot of casualties to take this hangar bay. If Dusk hadn't taken out the first AA so Fesh could focus on the other, you probably would've been welcomed with some less friendly faces." She explained. The squad that was with Kale was still alive. Sitting on the crates they were fighting on. Tarrus smiled at this, seeing one of the pirates punch his shoulder.

"Tarrus, you tough son of bitch! I couldn't believe my eyes when I saw you sprinting out there like that!" He exclaimed. Tarrus chuckled before returning with a hard hug, making the man's back crack.

"It's good to see you Verv."

Kale then mentioned Kane's ship.

"I hope you brought the keys with you. I didn't realize how old school your ship was," She chuckled, crossing her arms. Kane couldn't help but smile widely at his ship.

"Trust me, she's way tougher than she looks." He assured her. Pressing a button on his belt. They watched as the door began to come down. The door however was quite slow. Kale smirked as she turned to face Kane, who blushed a little.

Austin Patten

"H-hold on." He then gestured to Helix to come closer,

"Hey bud, could you get Gwen back online real quick?" He whispered. Hoping the smirking gwarian wouldn't be able to hear. Helix then flew into the opening into the ship. Going straight for Gwen's core and powering her back up. In a minute or so she was online, powering up the rest of the ship.

A beep came from Kane's holo-watch, just after Helix returned. A sigh came from Kane as he read a message from a familiar ship board A.I:

Hello Kane, It's good to see you again.

"Good to see you too Gwen." He said. Extremely happy to say that name again. The door then came down, Kane waved Kale to follow as he led her into the ship.

The first thing Kale noticed was how small the interior was. For how huge the ship itself was she was expecting more. They were in a hall. The door at the end led to the bridge, while the rest led to Kane quarters, the kitchen, washroom, living area and lastly the cargo bay. The largest area by far. Since there was currently no cargo onboard it seemed so open. Just a massive room of metal. Connected at the end of the cargo bay was the engines that hummed as they booted up. The washroom, living area and kitchen were as small as she expected. This ship had enough room to store possibly three crew members at most.

Though Kane's quarters were larger than she expected. To the left were bunk beds. Given how messy the top bunk was, she assumed that was Kane's. Beside the bunks was a bookshelf. Filled with pictures of planets.

They all looked beautiful. On the third shelf Kale spotted the camera that probably took the photos. There were also books and other valuables lined up along the bookshelf. On the right side was the closet, though she doubted he had a large assortment of clothing. So next was the dresser. Which had another set of tools and mechanical parts laying around. Kane chuckled as he walked up to them.

"Ah, these were some spare parts for Helix. Guess they aren't too useful now. Huh buddy?" He asked the cybel flying close by. He only projected a " :) ". Since it was physically impossible for him to shrug.

The pictures however, grabbed Kale's attention more than simply spare parts laying around. She noticed each one showed Kane with another human. A female one.

"Who's this?" Kale asked, picking up one of the frames. Kane placed the part down, stepping behind her. His smile quickly dissolved into a frown.

"That was Emily." He answered downheartedly. Soon looking away from the photo. Placing the frame down, she turned back to Kane.

"...Was?" Though he was already at the door.

"Another time Kale. Let's head to the bridge. You can meet Gwen." He said with a half smile. She then nodded,

"OK!" Following him, Kale watched Kane type the password on the keypad to the bridge. Now that was old. She has never seen a ship require a passcode. It was always a scan of sorts.

After a beep, followed by the red light turning green, the door opened. Kale was right behind Kane when she entered. The bridge was actually a decent size. Easily able to fit up to three or even four people. The captain's chair was a little worn. Yet the other chairs seemed to be in good condition.

"One man crew I see." She said, observing everything in the bridge. Seeing how clean the place was.

"It works for simple cargo work." He said with a shrug. "But I have Helix!" He said, gesturing to the little cybel. Who typed, "Yeah!" Kale nodded with a giggle,

"Ok that's true. You do have Helix." Kane then rubbed the back of his head, "Even though this was good for cargo runs, I don't know if it's as good with taking on the U.G.G" He said.

As if he was listening through Kane's open mic, Dusk suddenly chimed in,

"If you require some additional crew I can happily assist." Kane shot a surprised look at his holo-watch.

"Um, sure! That would be great Dusk!" Kane replied. However Fesh was nearly instant to shout at the human!

"You trying to take my people Kane?!" Her voice boomed through the holo-watch, "U-uh…" Kane tried to say, unsure of how to answer. Thankfully Ryko came to rescue,

"Don't mind her Kane, you can have Dusk for the ride back to Jez." He said, chuckling as Fesh grumbled under her breath before disconnecting.

Turning back to Kale, she only shrugged.

"I guess we're good then." She said. Taking a seat in one of the chairs. Kane rose a brow,

"What are you doing?" He asked, watching her already to get to work. As older ships were much easier to understand.

"Well, there's still an extra seat. I can stay too." She said softly, not turning to face Kane as she worked. Kane however soon walked over to her to place a hand on her shoulder.

"Dusk and I will be more than enough." He said gently. Watching her composure drop from the word.

"But-" Kane was quick to add before she could protest,

"Plus, I'm sure your sister is already upset that I had taken Dusk. I'm sure she'd actually kill me if I took her sister." Kale sighed, nodding.

"Yeah, your right." she said, getting up from the chair. "It's just after seeing you surviving the fight with that anvol...I thought." She tried to say, soon feeling the human wrap his arms around her.

"Hey, I'm fine. And I'll be fine out there." He said. Letting her go with a grin. "Besides, I know you have my back." This time Kale fired a smirk at him,

"You know it!" Kane then giggled,

"Good, I'll see you out there." He said, watching her leave.

As Kane was checking up on everything with Gwen and the ship, he heard a set of footsteps entering the ship.

Getting up from the captain's chair, he turned, expecting Dusk.

"Hey Dusk, I'm gonna need you to-" Kane suddenly stopped, seeing Tarrus standing beside him. The lykoi's arms were crossed as he grinned at Kane, who noticed his fourth new weapon slung to his back,

"Good to see you again." Kane returned with a half laugh. "I can say the same, just unexpected to see you again." He said back.

"You here to join my crew now?" Tarrus chuckled, walking up to Kane to pat him on his back.

"You saved my life back there Kane, normally I'd owe you my life in return. Though, if being a temporary crew member is enough for you I'll take it." He answered. Kane tilted his head. Even shaking his head,

"Whoa, hold on. We both helped each other back there." Kane shot back. Though the Lykoi didn't budge,

"Perhaps, but I still feel like you are owed. So, I'm going to pay." He said plainly, yet carried the same grin on his face. Kane knew time was short in this hangar, so instead of wasting time trying to argue, he accepted the pirates help.

"Alright Tarrus, your in. Welcome to my ship." He said.

Walking back in the bridge, both Tarrus and Dusk followed Kane.

"Dusk you'll be on engines and communications. Since I expect a lot of talk to happen once we return to Jev. Plus, those engines are gonna need to be monitored for the upcoming battle. Tarrus, she may not have much, but you're gonna be on weapons." He said. While Dusk offered a salute, Tarrus still took a seat, but turned back to Kane.

"And what will you and the cybel be doing?" He asked, clearly trying not to sound harsh, but was wanting to know regardless.

"I'll be piloting us. While Helix will be on repairs since I expect we'll need them. Then lastly Gwen will provide tactical guidance, not her strongest suit by almost any means. Though I want to put full capacity on that, so that's why the main functions of the ship will be up to us." He explained, Pressing a button on his chair. In a matter of seconds a small control stick and console was deployed over his lap from the chair.

"Any questions?" He asked, looking over at the two. Dusk answered, "All clear for me Mr. Lons." Tarrus offered a smile this time before shaking his head,

"All good over here." Kane smiled, looking up before saying his first order to Gwen,

"Gwen, it's time for us to leave. Bring piloting control to me so I may bring us to the nearby pirate fleet."

In a few minutes, the engines were humming louder, Kane retracted the landing gear as the ship hovered. Then, carefully he turned the long ship to the exit of the hangar bay. Sighing with relief that the other ships had already left, he moved his ship out.

CHAPTER SEVENTEEN

The space battle over Jev was almost as chaotic as the invasion on the ground. Communications to the ground were established within fifteen minutes of the next wave of battalions being sent in. Though the feed was distorted. The comm tower was set up quickly. So only two cameras were placed at the moment. Alan stood by the monitors the feed was being displayed too.

Gun and laser fire filled large portions of the feed, union soldiers forced into using their vehicles and mechs as cover. Even the dropships had to stay to help the soldiers survive. Spraying a barrage of lasers down at the incoming pirates. Yet their numbers seemed endless. Tanks and mechs were soon in combat with not only the infantry but other pirates mechs being deployed in their area. From the two angles Alan could see, one thing was clear.

His soldiers were surrounded.

Pinned, unable to do much more than hold their position. However, as Alan watched half a platoon of soldiers get mowed down by a pirate *sentry*. He knew he would need to act quickly. The other battalions were still getting prepared to drop. So reinforcements weren't an option at the moment.

Ignition: Unknown Criminal

"Captain, you're in command of the fleet, stay on the offensive. We can't allow the pirates to send additional troops from their ships." Alan ordered. With salute the Captain got to work. Bringing his attention to the crew member working by the monitors he asked,

"We have communications to give orders?" The gwarian nodded, handing over a headset to the G.L.

"It may be as distorted as the video feed. But it works sir." She added, watching Alan put the headset on.

"Just say the word." The crew member said, hovering her finger over the communication button. Press to talk communications were hardly used. Through it allowed any secret information to be easily unable to be heard as long as the user let go of the button to talk. It was old, but effective. Alan nodded,

"Go." The crew member then pressed and held the button for him.

"This is Galactic Leader Alan speaking, is anyone reading?" He asked, looking at the first screen, which not only showed the battle but the communications terminal placed by the comm tower. When the light turned blue, indicating someone was trying to reach them, Alan waited a few minutes before a soldier noticed and took the headset.

"H-zz-llo..?? I- his...ap-tin--zzzt..al?" The male voice asked. Alan didn't flinch, even though it was more than distorted, he was able to get the general idea of the question.

"Negative, this is the Galactic leader. Who am I speaking too?" he asked calmly. Watching a burst of laser brush past the soldier's helmet.

"Ma--ZZZT--or...How-zttt..W--zzz...aken-h-heav---t zzz...N-ed...up…-Ztt-ow!" The soldier shouted. Still sounding horrible, the sounds of combat hardly helped. Though Alan was able to get the important information,

"Major Howard, I need you to have your remaining mechs push forward. Allow them to destroy the swarm of infantry while your troops and vehicles cover them from enemy mechs. Do you understand?" He ordered. Awaiting his reply.

Howard however, had to duck under for cover. Pulling out a standard union laser pistol as two pirates jumped over an opening in his defenses! One of the pirates carried a hatchet. A barbaric looking melee weapon, while the other was going in with his fists and a rock! Howard was swift though, quickly raising his weapon to fire a red bolt in the first pirates chest. The other seemed shocked, though enraged soon after. Yelling something Alan couldn't quite catch before getting two lasers shot through him. One in the stomach, the other in the head.

After dispatching the two pirates, Howard picked the headset back up.

"-es...I---zztt-re--...ou..ech….Mov--zztttttzz..." From there it was only static. Alan nodded to the crew member. She immediately removed her finger from the button. Getting back to work as Alan returned the head set.

"You think they got the orders sir?" She asked, watching the screens. Alan was silent, keeping his attention

Ignition: Unknown Criminal

on the screens. Watching the major remove the headset and move out of view. As continuous firepower reigned across the distorted battlefield, Alan felt powerless. Being unable to further assist with troops or give orders for the moment. An explosion from one of the pirate's mechs destroyed one of the cameras, the other was partly disconnected from the comm tower. Hanging upside down by its wires. Alan had braced himself for what he was about to witness. Union soldiers were being demolished by more pirates making a push on their defenses. Though, as vicious as the pirates were on their offensive, the union soldiers were not backing down. Every soldier the camera spotted showed nothing but a fight to the death. No one ran, regardless how desperate the battle was becoming.

However, Alan suddenly noticed that there were no mechs in view. Though he couldn't tell if that was because of simply where the camera was angled or if Howard actually managed to get his mechs moving. Tanks and other vehicles soon came into view, rolling onto the grassy plains of Jev. Opening fire with heavy cannons, laser fire and missiles at the incoming pirate forces. As the union soldiers used this opportunity to regroup, more specialized infantry joined into the camera's views. More specifically a platoon of *Enforcers*. The first row carried heavy energy shields, deflecting small arms fire while absorbing most laser fire. While the *enforcers* behind held massive laser guns, holding them with two hands as they provided suppressing fire at the pirates. Forcing them to duck for cover.

Alongside the *enforcers* were a few squads of *rocket* troopers. A squad of three union soldiers equipped with heavy armor and carrying large *bison* rocket launchers. Every one of these *rocket* troopers were concentrating their fire on certain targets. Though Alan couldn't exactly see who those targets were, he assumed it wasn't simply infantry as each *rocket* trooper took a few minutes to align themselves before firing.

Alan's attention on the screen was suddenly interrupted when he felt a violent shaking across the bridge. Alan held his balance by holding onto the crew members chair. In a matter of seconds the shaking ceased. With a tight grip on the crew members chair, he turned to see what happened to his ship.

"We took a direct hit from an laser battery from the pirate's *battleship*!" One of the crew members shouted! Answering the question for Alan. Standing up straight, he moved up the stairs to meet with the captain.

"Report." Captain Vale looked back at Alan, his face staying calm, yet serious when he said,

"The pirates are becoming bold sir. Most of their fleet has been on the offensive now." Alan looked out from the bridge. Watching the battle unfold, the first thing he noticed was how much closer the pirate *corvettes* were getting. As union ships fired towards the incoming ships, Alan spotted the additional Flak guns they carried. Shooting any missiles, gun, or laser fire coming their way.

"Those *swarm corvettes* are going to be picking at our frontline ships. Most likely in an attempt to provide cover for the *destroyers* and *cruisers*." Captain Vale guessed. Watching the union ships struggle to take down the *swarm corvettes* that are using the little firepower they have to inflict damage on the union fleet. It seemed that they carried ballistic weaponry.

Cheaper, expendable ordnance. Smart.

Alan was becoming less and less fond of this as the battle continued, he knew this was slowly turning into the pirates favor. Possibly the same was happening on the ground. The union ships he had we're the only one's available. Then he only had two more battalions of troops to send into battle.

One of the swarm corvettes exploded as a squadron of union bombers made a successful run. *U-4's* soared towards them to provide cover from advancing pirate fighters. Alan watched as they slid past the debris of the *corvettes* to assist their vulnerable allies. His eyes then scanned the entrance of pirate reinforcements emerging from. Even with the *Arrowheads* firing upon the extra ships. The pirates were still coming through. Alan bit his lip. He was clearly unaware of how many forces Draz had under her command. Plus her allies, running pirate and smuggler operations, surely paid off well. In more ways than one. He also noticed as the numbers increased with each jump, the Arrowheads were having difficulties taking them all down. Alan even saw ships managing to regroup with the fleet before the *Arrowheads* had time to recharge.

Not good.

Austin Patten

At this pace, Alan knew the pirates would gain the opportunity to overwhelm the union fleet. Looking closely at the battle before him, Alan spotted the *corvettes* on each side pounding firepower at each other. The union corvettes were more focused on lasers, while the pirates defense. Creating an even playing field. As he watched, Alan heard Captain Vale bark orders to send in some *destroyers* to assist on destroying the *swarm corvettes*. Soon, four of those larger vessels flew behind them, firing their more varied array of weaponry. Though *standard union destroyers* held plenty of flaks and A.A guns. Keeping them well protected from enemy fighters. Yet they also had *Autocannons* on the sides of the ships. Large barrels firing a spray of heavy projectiles at their targets. Alan watched as one of the *destroyers* managed to aim most of its *autocannons* at a flanking *swarm corvette*. The sudden shower of bullets smashing through the ships all in seconds. Finishing off with an explosion! With the assistance of the *destroyers*. Alan saw as the *swarm corvettes* were being picked off.

Then Alan was suddenly interrupted by an explosion from one of the *destroyers*. A barrage of lasers rapidly pushed towards the vessel, colliding with such sudden speed, the crew inside never stood a chance to react. When the *destroyer* exploded, the debris crashed into nearby union ships. Damaging one of the *destroyers* while nearly destroying a *corvette*. The small vessel retreated, as it only had its engines, life support and a single AA gun remaining. As the crew would try to make repairs, the heavily damaged *corvette* may at least assist with defense within the fleet.

"Captain," Alan started, his eyes facing the capital of the pirate fleet. "What are the chances of hitting that *battleship* with our Arrowheads from our current distance?" He asked. Captain Vail then looked at the same ship, the largest in the pirate fleet. Armed with powerful weaponry, most of it was surely stolen from other factions.

"If it weren't for the number of ships in the way I'd say painless." Vail replied. He was correct, the pirate fleet had made a wall of ships to block off any long range attacks.

"Hmmm…" The GL thought, observing the wall of mainly cruisers. Carrying long range rail guns to assist the attacking fleet. Alan watched as they pelted the union ships with each shot. His own *cruisers* were already returning fire with lasers. However, Alan saw that they would need some assistance to break through that wall.

"Captain, target every *arrowhead* to fire in the center of those *cruisers*. Once destroyed, target that *battleship* in the opening." He ordered, glaring at that wall of cruisers, trying to protect their leadership.

"Want the *cruisers* to fire at any ships attempting to reseal the hole in their defenses?" The captain asked, offering assistance. Alan thought for a second before accepting,

Austin Patten

"Yes, that sounds perfect." With an accomplished smile on his face, hearing such words from the G.L, he gave the order for the *arrowheads.*

After a brief moment for the *arrowheads* to charge up, Alan and the captain watched the array of large, purple lasers smash into the center of the wall of ships. Tearing a large hole through the defenses. A total of six *cruisers* were completely decimated. Nothing but the debris and scrap remained once the explosion had ended. *Cruisers* that happened to be nearby had taken massive amounts of damage from the large chunks of debris slamming into them. Others were more fortunate as they were able to escape the incoming debris, having only the edges scrap along their hull. Several pirate fighters exiting the *cruiser's* hangars had to zip past the moving debris. Some of which crashed into the huge chunks of metal.

"You may target the *battleship* captain." Alan said, seeing the bridge facing him. It was a wise call on the captain's end to order the *cruisers* to protect that opening. Both the *cruisers* but also *destroyers* from the front of the fleet tried to fly into it to reseal the defenses. It was surprising to the G.L. Yet, he couldn't help but smirk as he watched the ships desperately run into the union's cruisers firepower. From fighters to *cruisers*, they were all being destroyed by the near constant firing from every union cruiser in Alan's fleet. Then, Alan heard the *arrowheads* fire again. The bright long lasers pouncing onto the bridge of the *battleship*! Alan sighed at the sight, watching the largest ship within the pirate fleet brighten up with an

261

enormous explosion! Devastating the *cruisers* trying to defend it!

Patting the Captain's shoulder Alan said,

"Great work Captain, any word on the 5th and 6th battalion? Our forces on the ground could use a victory like this." Turning to his crew member assigned to give him the word. The human shot a thumbs up.

"They are ready to go sir, just give the word." Captain Vail said, his finger on his communicator. But Alan looked at the Captain,

"That won't be necessary." He said, a grin forming on his half mechanical face.

"I'll give the order personally." The Captain rose a brow. "Are you going to face Draz and her forces?" He asked, unsure. Alan nodded, his grin becoming serious again before he turned to walk to the exit.

"You'll be in command of the fleet while I'm gone." He said. Captain Vail stood there for a moment before he spun around, about to protest. Though Alan already pressed the button on the elevator.

"Good luck." Alan said as the doors closed. "I'll contact you shortly." Then the doors closed, and the bridge was silent other the sounds of the crew members working. One of which rose her head.

"Orders sir?"

Fay had double checked everything. Rifle, sidearm, armor. Even checked her pouches for extra ammunition. After a perfect count, she placed her helmet on, the clear visor was clean. Giving her clear vision for the battle to come. She sighed, strapping the helmet on tightly. She watched as countless fellow soldiers did the same. Everyone felt it, the silent unease before dropping into battle. No one knew what the current situation was down there. Thoughts of the situation made most of the soldiers tense. Since the moment the battalion was ready to go they were called in.

"You alright?" Axel asked, holstering his rifle as he stood beside her. The rest of the squad ready to go.

"Yeah." She said plainly. Watching the rest of the soldiers stand in formation alongside each other. Mechs, tanks and other ground vehicles were also appearing in the massive hangar. When the first set of transports landed on the ground Fay noticed no one was actually entering them.

"What's going on sir?" Fay turned to the sergeant. Who kept his position, standing at attention along with every other soldier in the battalion.

"Your guess is as good as mine corporal." He answered simply. With that Fay brought her face forward. The position she faced with the battalion was the exit/entrance of the hangar bay. Everyone spotted the five cruisers firing their ordinance to protect the opening for the transports. Every one of the soldiers depended on the success of those ships to keep them alive to reach the planet's surface. That was something Fay couldn't stand about assaulting a world. The risk of simply trying to get to the planet. Time and time again, thousands of fully trained soldiers would die from within a transport before they could even join the battle. It was a sad way to go, and it was a death Fay would fear often. A death like that was out of her control. The Major of the battalions then suddenly barked,

"Galactic Leader! Attention!"

With near perfect unity, every soldier saluted. Crisp and clean. All eyes were straight. Even though the soldiers couldn't watch the G.L walk closer. They could surely hear him. The hard slap of his boots hitting the metal floor. Then, there he was. Standing by the entrance of one of the transports. Alan wore light combat armor. The kind of gear that scouts would get. Offering much more flexibility but lacking in much protection.

"Hello everyone." He began. Taking a moment to look at every single person before him. From humans, gwarians, lykoi, anvol and even hellions. Each of these soldiers would die for him and the U.G.G as a whole. Fay included as she tried to straighten her back further when Alan spotted her and the rest of the squad.

"You are all already aware of who I am. So I'd rather skip an introduction. I may not need to state this, but we are the last of the available troops we can send on the planet's surface. I had expected Jev to be a well-protected world. However, the level of resistance we've seen in a neutral world is staggering to say the least." He stated. Fay was shocked by what she was hearing, though more she tuned in on him saying "we".

"Many have already died trying to achieve our objective on this world. Some of you think I plan to take the world from the pirates. As much as I'd love too. We all know it'll take far more resources and troops to handle such a task." He then shook his head,

"No, we are going to cut off the head of this little operation. Our target is Draz herself." Though everyone wore helmets, Alan could feel the worry in the room. None of these people have even seen a gwarian giantess, let alone tried to kill one.

"It will be difficult, trust me. I understand, since I'll be accompanying you all in this mission." Alan said, patting the *Hize* Handcannon. Even the major was surprised by Alan. It was rare for a G.L to be seen in combat. Now these soldiers were about to see one in action. Though to a few, this made sense, since Alan was once a grunt on the battlefield as well. Making such a bold move would only boost morale. And surely it did. As Alan could swear he could see the smiles through his soldiers' helmets.

"Together, we will destroy Draz from this world, cripple the pirate operations. Then one day return to finish this planet. However this will only work if I can count on each and every one of you to fight! FIght with me. Fight with your fellow soldiers to victory! For the U.G.G! For our families watching and working every day so we may get one step closer to unification!" Then the hangar roared with cheers.

Ignition: Unknown Criminal

"Step closer to unification!" Everyone yelled in union. Soon, Alan gave the signal to the major who began to give orders to troops and vehicles to load up. Once Fay and her squad was called up. They marched into one of the smaller drop ships, a *Falcon*. These dropships were quick, yet weak. Armed with small laser cannons and with enough capacity to carry up to three squads of soldiers. Fay sat down, strapping herself in as the rest of the soldiers got inside the transport. Once everyone was seated, the doors closed. From there, they waited. Waited for the pilots call to launch.

"Brace yourselves everyone. Just got word from some other pilots, it's gonna get rough down there." The pilot advised, tightening her grip on the ship's controls. Fay only took hold of the seat straps. Breathing in and out. One way or another, or at least to the best of her abilities, she was ready to face hell on that planet.

CHAPTER EIGHTEEN

"For such an old ship, I have to admit. She flies a lot better than the ships I've driven under Draz." Tarrus said, a smile came onto his face as he watched how smoothly Kane's cargoship got into the jump.

"Thanks, I keep her and Gwen in the best condition I can afford." Kane stated, patting his chair. "My ship may not be the prettiest on any scale, but she's practical. Tough as a *corvette* and nimble as a fighter." He explained, sitting back in his seat as they continued the jump.

"Your ship is rather impressive, however, how do think she will fare in battle?" Dusk then asked, checking on the ship's engines, which were all working optimally. Though simple and rather minor at the moment, the Anvol took his assigned tasks seriously. Consistently checking his monitors for a transmission or for any sign of error with the engines. Tarrus, who was reading, checked the status of the few weapons the ship had on board, replied,

"It carries rather standard weaponry for a cargo ship. So, not much. But I've discovered to never underestimate coil guns." Dusk rose a digital brow at that,

"Your ship is carrying only kinetic weaponry?" He asked, seeming unsure of their survival once they exit the jump.

Ignition: Unknown Criminal

"Yes," Kane replied simply, "I never relied on combat in my work. Though, it was standard for doing cargo work outside the inner colonies to have our ships armed." He explained, looking at a monitor to see how long till they will need to exit the jump. It wasn't long. He sighed, clenching his fists tightly on the ship's controls.

"We're getting close, everyone better be ready." Kane stated, bracing himself to exit the jump. Both Tarrus and Dusk nodded in response. Then Dusk heard a beeping from one of his terminals.

"We have an incoming transmission from the Jade." Dusk announced. Answering the call. Fesh's face was soon seen on one of Dusk's and Kane's monitors.

"How's the ship feeling, boys?" She asked, her attention soon back on the direction of the Jade. As they were right behind them in the jump.

"Feels good Fesh, I'm grateful that the U.G.G didn't damage her." Kane said, a smile on his face as the lykoi chuckled.

"That's good, I could imagine the worry you may have had for her. If those bastards did anything to the Jade. I'd burn down the shipyard they tried to take it too…"

Kane replied with just a nod

"Anyway, just got new orders from Draz. It's been an all out battle on both the ground and in space of Jev. We've been ordered to assist in taking down another set of transport ships coming in to reinforce U.G.G ground forces.

From the sounds of it, They have the upper hand for now." Fesh informed him.

"...but?" Kane asked, seeing the shift in the expression of her face.

"The battle is going well on the ground, but in space, not so much. Draz told me they lost their *battleship*, alongside many of their others in the defending fleet. Other pirates and smugglers are jumping to assist but it's been a bloodbath out there. Just...be careful, alright?" Fesh said, bringing her eyes to face the screen for a few seconds. Kane sighed, hearing the news of the battle in space. He expected to be bad. Though he wasn't ready to hear that. From the looks of it when they left the *battleship* seemed like their best option. Now it's gone. Though he replied,

"Yeah, you too."

Then the transmission ended. However, before he could fully decide his next move, another transmission was coming in.

"Uh...we have another transmission. From the U.G.G capital ship!" Dusk shouted, seeming surprised that the enemy would bother to communicate with them.

"Put it through." He said, admittedly a little interested on what this may be about. Though he was more terrified than anything. As the call was answered, he was greeted with a U.G.G captain. Standing tall with his hands behind his back. His face stern, eyes staring right into Kane. Sounds of muffled weapon fire surrounded the caption from the massive capital ship.

"Kane Lons…" The captain started, his eyes squinting for a moment. "...I'm Vale, Captain of the Hollan, a U.G.G Capital ship." He stated. Kane straightened himself in his seat.

"Hello, what can I do for you captain?" He asked, honestly quite unsure how to respond. Captain Vail kept his face serious, his gaze on Kane.

"I'm here to give you an opportunity." He stated, pulling out a holo-gram of Kane, alongside the crimes he committed against the U.G.G. Supposedly that is. The list wasn't long, but the severity of each crime would be enough for a death sentence. "Kane, I'm aware that you are returning to Jev, most likely to assist the other pirates. However, you have another option. You can redeem yourself. To simply put it, you can join us." He said. Tarrus immediately turned around in his seat. Watching Kane closely. Waiting to hear his answer to the captain's offer. His hand on the holster of his pistol. Kane swallowed, surprised to hear such a sudden and alluring offer before him.

"Why are you offering this to me?" Kane asked. Trying to find any sort of sign that the officer was lying or if he was actually telling the truth. However the captain had quite the poker face.

"Even if you have had an affair with the rebels. You are still a valuable asset to the U.G.G. Being one of the most impressive cargo pilots in the outer worlds...." Vale explained. Before Kane could reply he noticed the glare from Tarrus.

"Kane, I swear if you-"

"Oh shush Tarrus." Dusk said calmly, continuing to work on his terminal.

"W-what? How are you so calm about this?" Tarrus erupted, pulling his pistol out.

"Easy." Dusk said plainly, showing a smile to the irritated Lykoi. "Kane couldn't betray us even if he wanted. It's a two on one situation." Kane widened his eyes, hearing the two talk as if he already made a choice.

"W-whoa guys I-" But he was interrupted by Helix, who soared in front of him. Preparing his weapons if either Dusk or Tarrus dared to make a move. The captain managed to sneak in a grin while Kane was looking at Tarrus and Helix eye each other. Silently daring the other to make a move.

"Don't tell me you saved my life just to deal with it yourself." Tarrus said, soon feeling despondent after the initial anger tamed down. Kane looked back at the captain. Seeing his face still the same as he awaited an answer. Kane knew what he had to say. He wiped the sweat forming on his forehead.

"No." He answered. A twitch came from the captain.

"Excuse me?" He asked, trying to sound calm but a twinge of irritation was heard. Kane shook his head, leaning in to the monitor.

"No. That's my answer. The U.G.G has taken nearly everything from me. Including my life." He said darkly. Staring at the captain this time. Who only sighed.

"Very well. I tried to be civil with you Mr. Lons." Kane only scoffed,

Ignition: Unknown Criminal

"I'll see you on the battlefield." Then waved his hand for dusk to end the call. There was a moment of silence. Tarrus holstered his weapon and turned to Kane.

"I'm...sorry about that. Honestly thought you were gonna side with them." He said shamefully, his ears drooped as he looked at the human.

"I don't blame you. I'd probably act the same way if I were in your position. Though, with the fact that they were only gonna torture me for information I don't have and with Dusk's lovely reminder. I knew my discussion rather quickly." He said. Dusk couldn't help but chuckle.

"Oh Kane. I knew the probability of us needing to eliminate you was only fourteen percent." Dusk turned to show his joyful expression of the outcome. Helix soon calmed down, retracting his weapons and landing on Kane's shoulder. Who gave a nervous chuckle.

"Only fourteen huh?" He asked, surprised it was even that high. Though the Anvol nodded, Kane still found that hard to believe.

However before everyone could fully calm down from that situation, Gwen sent a message to Kane's holo-watch.

Kane. We have a major problem. I believe the U.G.G are attempting to remotely hack the ship. Me specifically.

"What?" Kane suddenly shouted. Finishing reading the message. Tarrus shot out of his seat, ready for anything. Dusk looked at Kane with a puzzled expression.

"Can you fight it off?" Kane asked, awaiting Gwen's response. Which came soon,

Temporally, they are more advanced than the firewalls and defenses I have at my disposal. I estimate I have ten minutes tops.

"Alright, transfer everything to manual control. Quickly!" Kane said hurriedly. Tarrus seemed quite confused again, so Dusk looked at the Lykoi with a serious look on his digital face.

"I'd recommend you locate any EVA suits. There's a high probability that the U.G.G will attempt to shut down life support once they have complete control of the ship board AI." Dusk advised. Tarrus only nodded, turning to Kane as he got out of his seat. Kane however still seemed hopeful that he can still keep control of his ship and Gwen. Watching his terminals as more and more control of the ship was given to him. Though Dusk brought his attention to Kane as Tarrus rushed past him.

"You should join him Mr. Lons. I believe your A.I won't be able to hold them off for much longer." Dusk said, watching Kane bring his eyes up to the Anvol. His gaze filled with worry, doubt. Dusk analyzed swiftly, preparing a proper response to the silent reply, which read "No." Though Dusk had suspected this answer. He pushed again,

"Now. You have only a few minutes. Possibly even seconds." He watched Kane struggle to decide, the pressure, the little time was getting to him. Dusk however was a stone, unmoving in the situation. His face stern, calm.

Ignition: Unknown Criminal

"Please. " He pleaded. Hearing the ship crackle as Gwen was losing control. Kane then sighed, getting off his chair. Heading out the door to meet Tarrus. Dusk then moved to Kane's terminals, preparing to get the ship out of the jump. While he waited, he received a new message. Opening it, he read it was from Gwen, the message read:

Thank you.

A smile came onto the Anvol's face.

"Of course."

As Kane rushed through the halls, he saw the door to his quarters was open. Moving towards the open door, he watched Tarrus putting on one of the Eva suits.

"About time you got here!" He shouted, tossing the other suit to Kane. Who immediately started putting it on. Working much more smoothly then Tarrus, who seemed to be struggling to make the EVA fit!

"Why must you humans be so small?" He grunted.

"Are you serious? It's the largest one I have!" Kane replied. Getting his helmet secured, he then quickly walked up to Tarrus. "Stop struggling, let me help!" He yelled, watching the lykoi stop so he could see what the problem was. The chest seemed to be rather large. However, when Kane patted his chest. Getting a growl from the lykoi, he noticed it was mainly his fur!

"You need to tuck that in now!" Kane yelled. "What are you-" Kane then shouted again, interrupting Tarrus's attempt to argue. "Now I said!" The lykoi then shifted his hands down his fur. Trying to make it skin tight as Kane moved the suit over his body.

"Time's running out! Gwen is no longer responding to me!" Dusk warned. Knowing they were down to seconds to get their EVA's secured. Kane stepped up his speed and Tarrus soon followed. Soon, they finished with his body, Kane grabbed the helmet and handed it over to Tarrus.

"Get this on and meet me at the bridge." Kane instructed. Dashing out the door before Tarrus could respond. Now in his bulky EVA suit, traversing the hall of his ship became much more difficult. Matters soon got worse as he felt the ship beginning to shake from exiting the jump. Dusk must have exited the jump. Meaning they were at Jev.

"Mr. Lons! We have arrived!" Dusk shouted from the bridge. Taking the controls of the ship. After a rushed, bumpy trip down the hall, Kane reached the bridge. As they entered the massive space battle, Kane saw other pirate ships exiting a jump. However, Dusk veered the ship to the side as an enormous purple laser flew towards them. The gigantic projectile missed the ship, slamming into a pirate *corvette* right behind. The explosion from the vessel rocked Kane's ship violently. Knocking Kane on the hard floor, as Dusk continued to steer the ship away from the U.G.G's incoming fire. Feeling the weight from the sudden turning press down on his fallen body, Kane gasped for air. Waiting for the artificial gravity to loosen before getting back on his feet. Seeing how Dusk was actually doing a good job keeping them alive, Kane decided not to kick him out of the chair. Instead, he moved towards the communications terminal. Dusk on the other hand, heard Tarrus coming to the bridge.

"Tarrus! Wonderful! I suggest you head to the weapons terminal and prepare the ship's weapons." Dusk said, still concentrating on flying. Without a word he started moving towards the terminal.

"Any idea why we still have life support?" Tarrus asked. Kane was still silently at work, trying to connect to the Jade. Hoping Fesh and the others are doing alright. He lost sight of the Jade when that massive laser bolt blasted through. He hoped they managed to dodge the attack Dusk was. Though Kane did hear Tarrus's question. He started to think of an answer, but Dusk beat him to it.

"Most likely Gwen is still attempting to fight the U.G.G off. Using all available processing power at this point." The Anvol explained. Which was enough for both of them. Tarrus then took a seat at the weapons terminal. Working as fast as he can to activate the few weapons the ship has. Once online, he kept a close eye on all of the stats for each of the coil guns as they automatically got to work. Firing on the closest enemy targets. Thankfully, the rather simple AI the weapons were assigned too was disconnected from Gwen. So chances of the weapons being hacked were slim. Ammunition reserves seemed to be plentiful so they should be going for a while.

"Weapons online!" Tarrus announced on the bridge, hearing the muffled sounds of the bullets firing at the incoming *U-4* fighters dashing for the ship!

Austin Patten

"I'm still unsure of our chances of reaching our objective." Dusk said, sounding a little worried as he tried to guide the ship towards U.G.G transports already flying out of the U.G.G capital ship. "The U.G.G seems to have the upper hand in this conflict." Dusk added, seeing the remains of the pirate *battleship*. Both Kane and Tarrus gasped at the sight. That huge pirate *battleship* was nothing but a handful of debris. The ships that were once close to it either joined the graveyard or were heavily damaged. Yet, one thing that Kane noticed was that not a single pirate ship was backing out of the fight. Even with the odds tipping in the enemy's favor. Each ship that jumped in or was still fighting continued to push forward. Kane spotted a couple dozen pirate fighters escorting roughly eleven bombers to the frontlines of the U.G.G *corvettes* and *destroyers*! The *destroyer* that joined Kane soon soared at full speed to join and assist the fighters! Firing it's large laser cannons at the U.G.G ship! One of the *corvettes* attempted to flank the *destroyer* but was abruptly obliterated by a direct hit from a few pirate *cruisers* exiting a jump! Then Kane looked down at the communication terminal and saw that he was being hailed by the Jade! Without a second thought he answered the call.

"Kane! You're alive!" Ryko said with a surprised smile. Seeming relaxed to get his transmission answered.

"Yes! So are you guys! I nearly thought you guys got killed out here!" Kane exclaimed, just as glad to see Ryko is alive.

"We got a new transmission from Draz! The U.G.G are doing everything in their power to keep this next wave of reinforcements protected. So instead of throwing as many ships as she can to stop them, she wants everyone to send anyone they can to help the fight on the surface. That includes you since your ship isn't exactly equipped to handle long term combat in space, plus you have the cargo she desperately needs." Ryko said, turning back to the front of the Jade to assist Fesh, who was silent as she was fully concentrating on keeping the Jade intact.

"Understood, good luck Ryko." Kane said, forcing himself to comply rather than argue. Even if Ryko wanted to say more, he knew he had to fully concentrate to help Fesh, so with nothing but a nod, he ended the transmission. Though almost immediately after another transmission was being hailed to Kane. To which he answered. This time a human pirate was being shown to him. Her face was dark and scared.

"Kane?" she asked. Kane nodded, "Yes, who am I speaking too?" The female pirate was looking down, checking one of her weapons as Kane heard a click. "Call me Salone, however this will be brief. I'll be marking a set of coordinates of where we will be landing on Jev. We'll get an escort but our window is running out. Putting it simply you got five minutes." Salone warned before abruptly ending the call. Kane then turned to Dusk,

"You got that?" The anvol nodded, already steering the ship in the direction of the given coordinates. The ship's weapons have been doing a decent job keeping fighters away from the ship. Thankfully it became easier once they reached the pirate's zone of the battle. *U-4's* that attempted to still chase Kane's ship were almost instantly shot down. So it didn't take long for the attacks to stop. From there, it was painless for Dusk to fly past allied pirate ships to reach the coordinates. As the ship drew closer, Kane spotted a large group of ships sitting by the area. As if on cue, when Kane's ship got closer they all began to light their engines and began to move towards the planet!

"Not even a warning?" Kane asked out loud. Strapping himself tightly in the seat. Tarrus only chuckled as he did the same.

"Pirates aren't too much like the folk under the U.G.G. Communication isn't our strong suit." Tarrus explained, typing the on weapons terminal. Having the ship's weapons aimed at the front of the ship till they detect another wave of enemy ships.

"I'll keep that in mind." Kane said back. Breathing carefully in his Eva, hearing the sudden hiss of oxygen suddenly leaving the ship! The Eva's would have enough oxygen to last up to ten hours. Which will be enough to last for the landing for sure. Though Kane didn't know if Gwen would come back. Or if they will need to find some other way to fix her. However, he knew he couldn't be thinking about that now. Especially when Dusk took everyone's attention.

"You should both brace yourselves. This will be a rough flyby getting past those cruisers." Dusk stated, increasing the speed of the ship to catch up with the escort. Kane however, got out of his seat and made his way to the anvol piloting his ship.

Ignition: Unknown Criminal

"Alright, Dusk, I'll get us through that blockade."
Dusk turned to Kane, who was already in front of him.
Getting up, he immediately knew Kane was their best
option.

"Understood." Dusk said, moving to the
communications terminal to take a seat. Kane then sat
down and took the controls.

A series of *destroyers* and *corvettes* already began
to open fire on the U.G.G cruisers. With the combined fire
concentrated on the closest ship, the U.G.G *cruiser* burst
into flames, crashing down to the planet below. While the
other four returned fire at the pirate ships. Enormous shells,
lasers and missiles lurched towards the escort. Who took
every shot the U.G.G ships fired. Doing everything in their
power to prevent any pirates transports from being harmed.
Even *corvettes* allowed themselves to be pummeled with
enemy firepower. To which would lead to them being
completely destroyed. Kane watched in silence as several
of the pirate *corvettes* exploded. Only gritting his teeth as
he shifted the ship to the side, wiping past other transports
to avoid the oncoming debris.

A few smaller pieces of debris managed to crash
into the cargo bay! Kane checked the monitors for a hull
breach, thankfully however, the hull was still intact. Helix
beeped behind Kane before exiting the hangar to repair and
possible damage.

Other ships weren't as prepared as chunks of debris would smash into their frail transports. Decimating them in an instant.

"We are almost past the *cruisers*!" Kane shouted, putting all of his concentration on keeping everyone alive. Tarrus heard the human, but was concentrating on the terminal showing that the weapons were now firing on *U-4's* that broke through the escort.

"Bring us closer to those fighters! We need to keep them away from the transports!" Tarrus ordered, watching as an entire squadron managed to squeeze through! "Got it." Kane replied, suddenly veering the ship towards the *U-4's*. In that moment, the ship's weapons locked on the enemy fighters and began to fire! A wave of blue and green lasers filled the sky as the fighters didn't seem to be expecting resistance once they broke through. Five *U-4's* were then abruptly destroyed by Kane's ship's lasers. Though the ones that remained switched directions, attempting to gun for Kane's ship! However, they were taken by surprise again as several pirate fighters deploying out of the *destroyers* attacked the *U-4's*!

"How are we looking, Kane?" Tarrus asked, feeling useless as he could only sit and watch. His grip tightened on his arm rest as he felt the ship rumble from a distant explosion. Kane however, stayed quite keeping everything on flying the ship. As he noticed what's left of the pirate escort ships fighting the U.G.G *cruisers*, he spotted a gap and shot the ship in that direction. Other pirate transports got a similar idea. Moving at full speed to push through not only the gap Kane spotted, but any other available openings to get to the planet surface. Kane was silent the entire time, even once they got past the blockade. Everyone knew even once they landed on Jev they were far from safe. If anything, they just reached the heart of danger.

CHAPTER NINETEEN

Fay's grip hardened on her safety straps as she felt the *Falcon* shake from a nearby explosion. The pilot had informed the soldiers aboard that pirate ships had been trying to push through the cruisers protecting them till they got to the ground. Yet, from the sounds of the laser fire outside of the walls of the ship, Fay began to get the same worry every soldier got during an invasion.

Am I even gonna make it to the ground?

It was a reasonable fear to have. Since countless have perished in transports above the world they were sent to attack. Fay had been lucky enough to be part of the defense of worlds, not the offense. Until today. To make this situation even worse, she was going against an opponent she's never faced before! Pirates, she's heard the worst from the sergeant, who was right next to her on her right. Axel was on her left. Seeming just as nervous as she was. Both hands on his straps as the *Falcon* shook again.

"Alright, we just entered the planet's orbit, luckily reinforcements were sent to keep us covered. Casualties were at a minimum." The pilot said, which made everyone sigh in relief. Though, now instead of clutching their safety straps for dear life, it was now their rifles. They all knew surviving getting shot out in space only benefited them for the moment. Once this ship landed, there were still many ways to not come back home. The Sergeant looked out the *Falcon's* window. Seeing they were now rather close to the ground.

"We are about to be at the LZ, heads up it's pretty damn hot down there." The pilot warned, bringing the ship closer to the battle on the ground. With that the sergeant was on his feet, one hand on one of the bars on the roof of the ship. The other facing his holo-watch. Awaiting the orders from the G.L. Which came in a matter of seconds.

"All teams, your adjective is to support the remaining soldiers fighting on the ground. Once a solid defense is established you'll receive further orders." Alan said briefly from his transport. Then the transmission ended. Quick and to the point. Just how every soldier needed. Especially when minutes away from landing.

——

When Alan ended the transmission, he gave the orders to his soldiers. Standing inside the *Falcon* he was on board, he took a second to look out the window before double checking his *Hize*. One of his personal favorite hand cannons. Plus, with this one in particular, he managed to modify it to his liking. Firing large bullets over lasers. A blue laser sight was added as well. Assisting his accuracy far more than in anticipated. With his upgraded, cybernetic eye, he would be able to track the laser much better than relying only on organic vision. The very metals for the weapon were custom made as well. Making the weapon much lighter and easier to use in battle. Which was perfect since Alan planned on only keeping the weapon in one hand. His human, organic one. While his cybernetic arms were used for more...specialized tasks in the front lines. Flexing his metal fingers, Alan was more than prepared to face the battle on the ground. His scout armor tightly pressed against his chest. Then one of the *shock troopers* accompanying him stepped up behind him. When Alan heard the large trooper move up, he craned his head back.

"Yes?" Alan asked, observing the *shock trooper's* armor. Which was rather intimidating, even to Alan. They shared similarities to standard marine armor. Though they had more slimmed down design, what made the biggest difference, visually anyway. Since *shock troopers* went far more advanced and vigorous training, it was that they had energy shields built into their armor. Allowing for much more protection for them in the front lines. Especially since *shock troopers* were sent into either the heart of battle or behind enemy lines. With this extra protection for the shields. It made many ballistics nearly impossible to penetrate their armor. Lasers however, were still able to prove to do a rather decent amount of damage to them.

"Captain Vale wanted to inform you that Kane Lons had managed to get his ship alongside other pirate transports past the blockade." The *shock trooper* said, offering a quick salute after. Alan pursed his lips. This had been unexpected, he didn't realize Kane would've been able to finish his task so swiftly.

Ignition: Unknown Criminal

What exactly was he doing?
Alan had no idea, but if Kane was on his way to Draz
now…
　　"Did Vale manage to track his location on the
planet?" Alan asked, holstering his *Hize*. The *shock trooper*
nodded, "The location should be on your holo-watch sir."
Alan then checked, finding the set of coordinates placed.
　　"Perfect. Inform Vale I need fighters to continue the
chase on those pirates. I'll deal with Kane personally."

——

"Hey, what's going on?" Axel asked, looking out the
Falcon's window. Fay and a few other soldiers looked in
the same direction to try and see what he was talking about.
Nearly a quarter of the reinforcements were going in a
different direction. Fay looked back at the Sergeant, who
kept quiet. Showing that he most likely had no idea what
was going on either.
　　"Keep your head on the mission." The sargeant
ordered, "Whatever the G.L has planned is over our pay
grade." Axel looked at Fay, though neither could read each
other with those helmets on.
　　Then suddenly the ship shook, followed by the
sound of muffled explosions.
　　"We're near the L.Z! You boys and girls better be
ready to get off my ship!" The pilot shouted. Bringing the
ship down. Forcing the sergeant to tighten his grip while

the others sunk into their seats. More explosions and soon gunfire was heard. Fay knew they had to be close to the ground now. With one hand gripped on her rifle, she undid her straps as she waited for those doors to open. Since everyone knew once they did it was a sprint for the nearest piece of cover. From the sounds she heard, she expected to be chaos down down there. Then with a heavy thump, a yellow light appeared by the door, indicating they landed. Then within a second, it shinned green.

"Light is green! Go! Go! Go!" The sergeant shouted. Once those orders came out, the doors came down. Allowing the charging marines to join the battle.

CHAPTER TWENTY

"We're clear of the blockade." Kane announced, keeping his ship close to the other pirates that managed to push through as well.

"How's my ship?" Kane asked, looking back as Helix came back from the cargo bay, he typed,

"Pretty good all things considered."

"We lost four out of our six coil guns. One of them is badly damaged. Moderate damage across the entire hull. Engines are ok however. Communication satellites are slightly damaged. Cargo is safe." Dusk informed him, continuing to monitor the terminals.

"And how much longer till we reach Draz?" Tarrus asked, not entirely a fan of the condition of their first line of defense. Kane was silent for a moment as he surveyed where exactly they were. Using the monitors to assist, he noticed they were over some of the mountains of Jev. However, as they continued to fly, they spotted the battle on the ground far in the distance. Though it was so distant, the only signs of battle they could actually see were the explosions. Most likely from Mechs battling it out. Possibly other ground vehicles getting in the mix as well.

"I'd say not too long if we keep at this pace." Kane replied.

Then suddenly one of the pirate ships was barraged with lasers. Exploding nearly instantly by the sheer overwhelming number of incoming fire. From then, the other ships started to scatter. Losing their close formation to force the enemy to spread out their firing. Those who were still in decent condition attempted to fire back. Kane spotted as even a few remaining pirate fighters swooped in to attack enemy *U-4's* that moved in!

"That's a lot of fighters!" Tarrus shouted, watching the one cannon on Kane's ship opened fire as well. Trying just as desperately as the other damaged pirate ships to repel the incoming U.G.G forces.

"I see U.G.G transports coming to our location as well!" Kane shouted, seeing several transports soaring closer firing their own weapons. Even with being in a better position, the pirates ships were only getting shot down. In fact, they seemed to be only getting shot down. Kane tried to keep a close eye as one of the larger pirate transports came crashing down on Jev's surface. Tarrus widened his eyes at the sight.

"We need to help them!" He yelled, pointing at the massive ship that laid in the forest. Dusk however only shook his head, "That's a bad idea, we can't risk the cargo." Tarrus glared at the anvol. "Those are our people down there!" Tarrus shouted again. Knowing Dusk was only speaking the fact, Kane could see the lykoi took offense to the reply, so he spoke up. "There's nothing we can do anyway. U.G.G transports will surely be on their way to kill the survivors." He said carefully. Especially when Tarrus turned to him. Holding that glare on his face. Though, in a second or so, he let up.

"Yeah, you're right." Kane veered the ship to the right, trying to avoid drawing the *U-4's* to their location. However, as more of the pirate ships were getting shot to the surface of the planet. There were becoming fewer ships to rely on. Kane noticed quickly and moved to a terminal to start a transmission with Draz. To which she thankfully answered almost instantly.

"I got newsssss you're on the planet." She hissed. Kane nodded,

"Yeah, but we're in trouble. The U.G.G knows that we got past their blockade and have sent ships to bring us down. Transports are then sent to deal with the survivors." He explained. Watching Draz as she thought of her options. Kane could only imagine how many intense and stressful decisions she's had to make in the few hours. She then began to speak, "What are the chancessss of you getting shot down?" She asked. After a couple seconds of concentrating his flying Kane replied,

"I'd say pretty high." Draz then sighed, seeming to be looking at another screen.

"You may be on your own for a while Kane, stick close with those that survive alongside you. They may be your only chance of survival until I can send a team to get you out of there." Kane sighed as well. Placing a hand on his *Lance*,

"Understood." Was all he could muster to reply. Draz then looked at the human one last time,

"Good luck." Then the transmission ended. Kane then turned to Tarrus and Dusk, knowing in a matter of minutes they would be his allies in the field of battle. Dusk then said,

"The others are trying to land." Tarrus looked forward, away from the weapons terminals.

"What?" He asked, stunned to see they would attempt such a move. Kane saw it two. The remaining transports moved down, towards the forest, where several other ships laid. Crashed, crippled.

"I say we join them." Kane said. "It's our best chance of survival." Kane turned the ship, no one argued. Another explosion smashed onto the side of Kane's ship again. Large enough to shake the whole interior violently. Even shot Tarrus out of his seat. Slamming his back on the cool metal floor. "Ah!" He gasped. Unprepared for the sudden fall. Kane saw *U-4's* coming in fast. Swarming Kane's large cargo ship. Pelting the hull with lasers as he tried to bring them closer to the ground.

"We're going to land now!" Kane shouted, feeling another explosion ravage his ship.

"Understood." The Anvol said, staying in his seat. Though, even with their little numbers, pirate fighters flew in to help deal with the *U-4's*. Firing their lasers at the squadrons so Kane could have more time to land. Which seemed to be plenty as Kane soon saw the trees.

Ignition: Unknown Criminal

"We are reaching the landing area. You two better have your weapons ready." Kane said, rushing the ship through the trees before spotting the pirate ships. Most already on the ground. Kane didn't waste a moment. Deploying the landing gear after slowing the ship down considerably. Then being as careful as he could, he started to touch the grassy floor of the forest. Kane gripped the ends of his armrests tightly. Feeling the ship shake and rumble roughly. Thankfully, he turned, he spotted Tarrus back on his seat. Seeming to be holding himself down just as tightly as Kane. Then, after a few more seconds of the shaking, everything was still. Quiet even, besides the muffled sounds of combat outside his ship.

"Everyone on their feet!" Tarrus shouted, immediately standing up, rifle now in hand. Kane soon followed, placing his *Lance* on his right hand. Helix was still floating beside Kane, sticking close. Lastly Dusk was up, *Vandal* now in his hands. However, when he walked over to Tarrus, he offered the weapon to him.

"You may need this." He said, displaying a digital smile. The lykoi rose a brow.

"What about you?" Taking the large shotgun with one hand.

"Well, someone has to lug that cargo." Dusk replied, walking to the cargo bay. Kane then walked up to Tarrus,

"Guess that's fair." Tarrus chuckled, "In that case, you can have this," he said, bringing the rifle to Kane.

"Thanks for letting me borrow your rifle." Holstering his *Lance* again. Kane smirked,

"No worries, let's try to not lose that while we're fighting this time." Tarrus only laughed as the two moved towards the exit of the ship.

"No promises." Tarrus then saw Kane move towards the main console. Typing quickly before a chip suddenly stuck out of the side. With a sigh, he grabbed the chip and placed it in his pocket. The lykoi tilted his head,

"You're saving your ship's A.I?" he asked, unsure if that's actually what he saw. Kane looked at him a nod,

"Of course, Gwen is part of my crew too." He replied, as if that was obvious. Tarrus returned with a short laugh.

"Got it." Once the three reached the ramp, Dusk came out of the cargo bay, holding a crate in one hand. The other was magnetically holstered to his back.

"Let's go." Dusk said. With that, Kane slammed the button to open the ramp. Which revealed the other pirates getting out of their ships. Some were carrying heavy weapons, trying to help shoot down the enemy fighters still attacking other pirate ships in the sky. As the four rushed down the ramp, moving past pirates running towards cover or an advantage point to take down enemy aircraft, Kane had spotted the majority had gathered by a large trench between several large boulders. Seeming to create excellent cover for the time being.

"That seems like our best place to meet up!" Tarrus yelled, leading the way towards the group. Helix used his plasma gun to provide some covering fire as the others ran.

Ignition: Unknown Criminal

However, Tarrus soon found himself stopping midway when a *U-4* suddenly came gunning towards a few other fleeing pirates! Firing a barrage of lasers, most of those in its sights were either sent flying or were shot down where they ran. One human crashed into a tree, dead on impact. Though Tarrus could keep on running, he cursed in his language. Seeing good fighters getting blasted so easily. Once they regrouped with the other survivors, All four moved to hear what one that seemed to be the leader was shouting.

"Our time is short! We must make a push through the forest if we have any chance of getting out of this alive alive!" A female gwarian shouted, having a union rifle strapped on her back. Her dark yellow armor made her stand out from the rest of the others, who wore mixes of armor. From shabby custom builds to stolen pieces from other factions. "Are you crazy? We need to fend ourselves here!" Someone within the crowd shouted, getting a few nods in agreement. When the human twisted her face in frustration. Another explosion made most of the crowd scream! Heavily shaking the ground as few lost their footing. Kane knew it was only a matter of time before those U.G.G transports would make their way here. He was willing to bet their numbers would effortlessly overwhelm this position. Without much thought he shouted, even surprised himself how loud he managed to get.

"She's right!" He bellowed, getting the attention of every pirate. All faces were now turned to him. The leader included. Kane had no time to think, so he just started spitting out everything he had in his head.

"We need to force our way to Draz. If not we all die here now. No help is coming. Anyone else is in the same desperate battle we are in right now. So we must push forward." He yelled, only after paying attention to the reactions of everyone. Especially the leader, who laughed.

"About time someone had some damn common sense. I'm with him! Join us, or die!" She added, her voice just as, if not more booming than his. At this moment, more people took their weapons in their hands. What first started as just murmurs soon became a roar! Every pirate, smuggler and fighter shouted at the top of their lungs. Using any built up fear they had to fuel their rage against the U.G.G.

"That's what I like to hear!" The leader shouted! Soon joining in the shouting! Even Tarrus yelled, letting his anger come over! Kane can only guess how much pain the U.G.G has done to him. After a quick breathe he looked at the crowd.

Fuck it.

Without any warning, Kane joined in the crowd, screaming at the top of his lungs. This united yelling ended after a couple seconds. Now that everyone was riled up, everyone turned back to Kane. Which took him off guard. The leader also looked at the cargo pilot, crossing her arms, she asked,

"So, what's your plan?" Kane stepped back,

"What?" The yellow armored gwarian kept her stance, "You managed to convince these meat heads to fight again. You think they are going to listen to me?" She shot at Kane, as everyone awaited for what the human was gonna say. However, after the human stopped to think and noticed something, what he said next confused everyone.

"You hear that?" All the pirates paused, listening. It was...silence.

"No...?" Someone in the crowd somewhat answered. Kane nodded,

"Exactly, the fighters were called off. That or something else caught their attention. Either way, this is our chance." He said, taking in one deep breath, to think clearly. He's by no means a tactician, but this isn't his first time trying to slip away from a predator.

"We need to stick together and push further into the forest, but when we spot union soldiers, scattering and throwing them off may be our best bet of fighting. We can't afford to be surrounded and get killed off in one strike." Kane said, keeping as much of an eye on everyone he can. Though no one objected. "Alright, then let's move." Kane ordered, feeling odd to do so but he knew they couldn't stay here any longer. Dusk then stood beside Kane.

"Allow me to lead the way. I have Draz's location marked." The anvol offered. To which Kane gratefully nodded. Since he had no idea where he would be heading. With that, everyone took their weapons and began to spread out lightly as they followed Dusk. Giving room in case the fighting began. Kane walked closely to Dusk, who still carried the cargo. The lack of noise concerned Kane greatly. Hearing the crunches of leaves and sticks under people's feet and the wildlife amongst the forest was all he could detect. Looking to his right he could see Tarrus had stepped back to stick with some of the other pirates. More specifically with the wounded. When Kane actually took a second to notice, he saw at least a quarter of those with him were hurt one way or another. As much as that harmed their odds, the fact they were still able to move on and possibly even fight still gave Kane some much needed hope. Look on his shoulder, he found Helix watching the front intently.

"Hey buddy, we may need some recon." Kane said seriously, wanting to know where those transports could have landed. Helix then launched his boosters, avoiding to burn Kane's shoulders like usual and quickly typed.

"On it." Before ascending in the sky. As the cybel rose to the sky, some of the pirates looked at Kane, seeing that the cybel came from his shoulder. Though no one actually bothered to question. They all had more important matters that required their attention. Staying alive, for example. Those that weren't injured, or not as badly as the others kept their weapons close. Waiting for the U.G.G to appear at any moment. Kane would check the sky every couple of seconds, hoping Helix would be able to give him some information soon, since, like the others behind him. The uncertainty of the situation was starting to put him on the edge. Kane didn't quite realize it, but his grip tightened on his rifle as he looked up for the sixth time. Which after that, Helix did come back down, quickly in fact. Once he was close enough to read the text on his digital screen. Kane's eyes shot wide open!

Ignition: Unknown Criminal

"They are moving to the left! The G.L is with them!!"

Without wasting a breath, Kane suddenly shouted!

"Watch your left! The U.G.G is com-!" Kane was cut off when a row of Union marines started to open fire! Tearing through the first row of pirates! Others either started to rush to the right or fire their weapons! Regardless of the choice, a brutal skirmish had started!

CHAPTER TWENTY ONE

"Watch your flank!" Axel shouted, pulling up his union rifle to blast a pirate charging behind Fay. The lifeless pirate slammed back onto the ground, dropping his crude melee weapon. Fay had just emptied her last magazine, plus she didn't even notice the brute sneaking up behind her. In the chaos of battle, it became easy to let your back become unguarded. As you would expect your fellow soldiers to be nearby. Which in this case Axel was able to spot the pirate before he could even touch Fay. Though she was extremely grateful for that, she showed it by giving a thankful nod before slamming in a fresh mag in her rifle. Fay cursed herself for allowing that to happen. Catching up with the rest of her squad, who were suppressing another group of pirates on a hill they and another platoon managed to capture. With plenty of rocks and debris from vehicles to use as cover. Axel was close by, spraying down bullets at more pirates that tried to move from their cover. The sergeant spotted the two and waved them over.

"Over here!" He shouted. The pair moved to crouch down by him, Fay spotted private Alis firing down the hill, but drooped a ear,

"Where's Erans?" She asked, to which the sergeant only replied by pulling out a pair of dog tags.

Ignition: Unknown Criminal

"He got shot minutes after exiting the drop ship." He said calmly, yet with a hint of sorrow. Losing soldiers hardly got easier. Fay sighed, knowing she can't allow herself to get sucked into her emotions. She hardly knew Erans, but he had potential.

Had. Damn.

Shaking herself out of it, Fay then looked at the sergeant,

"Orders, sir?" She asked, wanting to swap the topic quickly. Checking his holo-watch, the same orders appeared,

"We have been ordered to assist in pushing towards Drazz's location, under the command of major Howard until the G.L returns." The sergeant replied, getting ready to stand with his rifle tight in his hands. "Understood." Both Axel and Fay said.

"Until we get the orders to move, we're gonna use this position to our advantage, get to it everyone!" He barked, turning around and began firing his rifle. Axel soon joined, crouching beside the sergeant and carefully picking off more pirates that came onto the field below. Fay crouched near Axel, taking a moment to observe the battle. To her left, she saw other U.G.G infantry push alongside tanks and mechs. Down at the field, they were the main attack group. While those on the outside were meant to provide support for the push. Which is why taking this hill was currently essential. Having the high ground gave the U.G.G an advantage needed when numbers were limited.

Fay spotted a handful of groups of pirates suddenly rushing for the hill!

"To the right! Pirates pushing in!" Fay shouted as loud as she could! Not only trying to grab the attention of her squadmates. Other squads nearby managed to hear her, turning to the bottom right to spot the incoming pirates! Those squads tried to warn those that were closest. Most were able to turn and open fire! A few weren't so quick. They were swiftly shot down, plummeting to the ground. Those that were close to the pirates tried to move back! As the pirates were relentlessly charging forward! Uncaring for the ammunition being fired upon them! Fay aimed her rifle in the direction of those trying to fall back! Hoping she could at least provide some covering fire while Axel, the sergeant, and other squads kept firing below. A few other soldiers had the same idea as Fay when they spotted her aiming her rifle at the close attackers. Fay kept her finger close to the trigger as more soldiers moved back, one of them seemed to be communicating on their holo-watch. Barking orders, Fay could barely hear due to the combat. However, a sudden thump that shook the ground took her off guard. Though she kept her balance. Though the thump came again, much heavier this time! At first, Fay had worried it was a pirate mech! To which it would shred both her and most of the infantry on this hill easily! However, she soon realized it was coming from an ally *Escort*! A sudden barrage of missiles dropped onto a majority of the pirates that attempted to push! Obliterating them in seconds! The rest were sent flying, slamming into rocks, debris or simply the ground. As the dust cleared from the

Ignition: Unknown Criminal

explosion, a massive, towering robot known as the *Escort* appeared! Deploying a shield around the squads on the hill! While firing another barrage of missiles at the enemy below! Fay couldn't help but look at the enormous machine in awe! Though it's fighting capabilities were limited to either its missiles or crushing an enemy underfoot, the *Escort's* shields made it an excellent support unit. Alongside the fact the massive A.I core stored inside made the machines rather intelligent and even flexible in battle. In fact, Fay was willing to bet the *Escort* warned the U.G.G the barrage was incoming. Fay watched it's massive triangle shaped "eye" scan the battlefield. Most likely calculating the most optimal area to fire to give the most damage.

"We got new orders!" The sergeant then shouted, getting the squads attention. Fay turned to the sergeant, ready to listen. "Everyone is needed to force the current pirates to retreat, the U.G.G mechs and *Escorts* have managed to heavily weaken their defenses here and need to make use of that." The sergeant explained.

"We are pushing the moment that *Escort* moves." He ordered, "Stick to it, it may be our only chance of surviving this." Everyone nodded at that, showing they understood. "Good, for now, we keep on suppressing these bastards." The sergeant ordered again, already firing his rifle after reloading with a fresh mag. Fay and the others joined in, firing at the pirates that were heavily pinned as the main attack force had already started to move in! Tanks and mechs were up front, with infantry using them as mobile cover. A few meches were in the back however, those with longer ranged weapons or anti air. After feeling an abrupt and heavy THUD, everyone jumped over their cover as the Escort began to walk forward. The squad stood close, giving only a few feet worth of distance as they kept on firing on the pirates! Who were either trying to flee or were forced to hide in cover before being annihilated. Fay spotted a few pirate mechs becoming desperately sloppy as they attempted to hold the U.G.G forces back. Refurbished *Sentries* rushed towards the main attack force! Fring light machine guns at the advancing union forces! However, this hardly helped as the union mechs immediately opened fire at the charging machines! A series of lasers, bullets and missiles soared towards the pirates, muting out the pilots screams inside as they exploded! Sending the burnt remains scattering behind! Fay kept an eye on one mech that only lost its legs. Toppling on the ground with a thump! The pirate pilot managed to scramble out, however, by that point several squads of union marines spotted him and instantly gunned him down. From there, the other pirates ran. Firing blindly behind them as they retreated. Then, other than the squad leaders barking out orders and the sounds of U.G.G vehicles and mechs moving, it was quiet. The L.Z was secured, and they had one that fight. Though it was victorious, the U.G.G had lost many to gain this area. Medics carrying wounded soldiers rushed past Fay and her squad. Running towards a transport to bring them off planet. Fay wondered how many actually managed to only become wounded. Looking across the land, she could see many lifeless bodies scattered around. Many were U.G.G, she doubted many from the first and second wave survived. The *Escort* seemed to continue to follow the squads with Fay's as they moved towards the main attack force. At the front of that massive group of the U.G.G troops was Lieutenant Howard. He held his holo-watch up to his face as he spoke, which transmitted his voice to the other squads that would've been too far away to hear his voice.

"Excellent work everyone!" He yelled trumphly, "With our L.Z secured, we can finally start our assault on this filthy neutral world! We will be swift! We will destroy the pirate scum that threatens our people and our worlds!" He shouted, raising a fist in the air! Receiving a rage filled roar from the soldiers! "After receiving the order from our Galactic Leader, who is off fighting a company of pirate reinforcements as we speak, we are to assault the main city Draz hides herself in! Once we rip her out her defenses and eliminate her, we are to escort the G.L back to transport and leave this horrid planet for another time." He ordered, watching the soldiers collectively give him a salute.

"Good, now, prepare yourself soldiers. Take a look around you, what you see is all we have. No more is coming to join us in this upcoming battle. Those brutes won't give up easily once we march onto their doorstep. Lock and load, have each other's back and we'll make it out of here alive." The lieutenant said, reloading his pistol before turning to lead the march. Every soldier, vehicle and mech started to follow. Forming a more defensive formation as the tanks were still in the front. Mechs were either on the sides and the back of the formation. Then *Escorts* were within the middle, providing their enormous dome shields to protect the infantry. Fay and her squad were on the right of the formation, their Escort still nearby while a *Nemesis* stomped behind their squad. Creating a vibration under the ground with each of it's heavy steps. Each of its four legs were nearly twice the size of her. It was a good thing it was on her side. She could bet those Nemesis's in the rear provided plenty of assistance in taking down the pirate vehicles and mechs at the L.Z.

"How are you doing?" Axel asked from her left. She then turned to face him, their helmets still blocking any facial expressions.

"Alright. Let's save the question for when we got off this rock." She said back, checking her ammo counter on her rifle. The green LED read that her current magazine was twenty three out of forty. Which was enough for her to keep it in.

"Right." Axel said with a sigh, since the possibility of not coming home was always available in battle.

Just like for Erans.

CHAPTER TWENTY TWO

Alan braced himself when he watched a pirate toss a plasma grenade in his direction. The dark blue cylindrical ball flew towards him and his *shock troopers*! Alan used his mechanical eye to scan the grenade, checking how long he had.

8 seconds.

Without a word the G.L sprinted towards the plasma grenade.

"G.L! What are you doing?" One of the *shock troopers* shouted! Firing at a pirate that tried to jump Alan with an energy axe.

4 seconds.

Alan ignored the shouts, catching the plasma grenade and immediately tossed it back at the direction it came from. Jumping for the ground, Alan hardly heard the screams from the pirates before the grenade suddenly exploded. Shaking the ground and causing a sudden and loud ringing in the G.L's ears. Having the fact this wasn't his first time having his hearing affected from an explosion. Alan soon got back to his feet, seeing the half of a pirate laying on the ground beside him. He scoffed at the sight, taking his *Hize* as three of his *shock troopers* ran to catch up to him. Two stood on each side, firing their weapons at any pirates they spotted. While the third looked at Alan,

"Are you alright sir?" She asked, scanning him for injuries within her helmet. Which other than some scrapes and bruises, Alan was fine. Though her question was muffled from the ringing in his ears, he nodded in response, looking around the trees. Seeing union marines fight alongside the other *shock troopers* to take down the pirate scum. However, they were fast, scattering to the other end of the forest while others would cover them.

"Have we managed to spot Kane yet?" He asked, moving behind a tree as the three followed closely. The other two *shock troopers* began to reload their weapons, soon about fire again. However Alan shot a thumb behind him when he looked at the two.

"You two, move up. We'll be fine over here." He ordered. "Yes sir!" They replied, pushing up without questioning, firing their rifles to cover themselves. The third *shock trooper* then replied to Alan's question,

"Not yet sir. It seems he may be deeper behind the other pirates." She suggested. "It seems we may have to-Look out!" She shouted. Watching a pair of pirates jump out of the bush! One carried a S7 SMG and began to fire at the pair! While the other dashed forward with a homemade looking sword. The second the *shock trooper* heard the S7 firing, she jumped in front of Alan! Taking the brunt of the ammunition the pirate unloaded. The shields protecting her armor held, but she dropped her rifle in the process. Only able to make herself cover for the G.L at the moment. Alan acted quick, with both hands he crouched and fired two heavy shots into the gunners knee! Blowing off his leg, he crumpled onto the ground howling in agony! Hearing Alan's shot take the pirate down, the *shock trooper* suddenly spun around. Getting face to face with the other pirate. Who flinched at the sight of her! The *shock trooper* used this to swing an armored fist at the pirate's face! Instantly breaking his nose as blood shot out of his face! However, the pirate kept his ground, removing his hand off of his face to show the damage she's done! His nose slightly flattened and turned to the right of his face!

"You animal! I'll kill you for that!" He shouted, charging her with his sword, slashing his weapon at her. Though it would hardly damage her armor, the *shock trooper* jerked back, dodging his swings. Her helmet scanned the pirate to estimate his next attack, which was a jab to her chest. Being prepared for the strike, the *shock trooper* took hold of his arm. Stopping the attack short, she then used her fist to punch him chest. Knocking the air out of his lungs and forced him to release the sword. With a clang, it hit the hard dirt floor. Before the pirate could try to recover from the attack, the *shock trooper* swept a leg under him, tripping the pirate. After crashing on the ground, the *shock trooper* grabbed her rifle and turned to the pirates on the ground before her.

"W-wait! Ple-" The *shock trooper* lifted up her rifle and shot him in the face, silencing his begging before shooting the other. Alan moved back behind the tree, scanning the forest for his target as the *shock trooper* caught up to him. She didn't bother to ask if he was alright this time, they both knew the answer to that. "The pirates must be retreating in the direction of Draz." Alan said to himself, watching them getting farther and farther away from his current location. He then looked at the *shock trooper*, "Give the order to chase them down. We can't afford Kane to be protected under Draz. We need to keep her forces separated when the attack force arrives," He ordered. Pulling out her holo-watch she began to bark the order. Alan watched as the union forces moved into three groups, one on each side and the others chasing closely behind.

"What are you thinking?" Alan asked, pushing up with the other soldiers. The *shock trooper* was right beside him when she replied,

"I plan on having them surrounded soon enough. If not, our troops will whittle down their numbers until there's no one left but our target." She said sternly, aiming her rifle forward to shoot a fleeing pirate in the back. As the two ran, the *shock trooper* took little care when she stepped on the dead pirates hand. "Don't worry Galactic Leader, we will find him." She reassured. Alan nodded, keeping a serious expression on him.

"Let's hope you're right, if Draz manages to send reinforcements soon, I doubt our chances will be high." He said as they caught up to soldiers giving chase. The shock trooper didn't reply to his statement, instead, she was barking additional orders to the troops around her.

Ignition: Unknown Criminal

"Get down G.L!" She shouted again. Six pirates suddenly appeared from the trees. Firing auto-laser rifles. Four union marines were shot down the moment they appeared. The rest bolted for cover, returning fire right after. Alan did as he was told and jumped behind a large rock before any of the lasers could hit him. The *shock trooper* was right beside him. Using the cover to try and see where those pirates were.

"We need to flank them." She said, trying to cut the idea that it was an order, but Alan showed no signs of being offended by it. If anything, suggestions are what he needed.

"Good call," He said, pulling up his *Hize*, "Let's make it quick." He ordered, moving around the rock. With the *shock trooper* right behind him, he peeked around the corner. Seeing the pirates were distracted with his soldiers Alan motioned the *shock trooper* over. "Stay here, you can get more targets from this location." Alan said. The *shock trooper* cocked her head.

"And what are you going to do?" She asked, aiming her weapon at the pirates. The G.L then clenched his mechanical fist, with the *Hize* in his other hand. "I'm about to get a bit more personal." He replied coolly, "Begin firing now, I'll see you soon." He said, dashing across towards a set of trees left of the pirates position. The *shock trooper* didn't even have time to argue, not that she'd have a choice. Instead she did as she was ordered and fired at the pirates. Firing in bursts to help conserve her ammo. The first burst of bullets smashed into one of the pirates chest.

Obliterating his chest armor and going right through him. After a sudden shock of surprise from the two closest to their fallen ally, they both spotted the killer and began to shoot at her. Sliding behind the rock, The *shock trooper* had no choice but to wait for an opening before she could attempt to fire back.

However, within a couple seconds a silver, mechanical fist came flying towards the nearest pirate. Upon colliding with his face, the lykoi coughed. Feeling his face getting smashed into as the impact broke his jaw. The punch sent him crashing into the other pirate as they both fell to the ground. The other, a gwarian, hissed as he moved the whimpering lykoi off. Alan had already pulled out his *Hize* and fired a shot at the lykoi. The gwarian used this split second moment to lunge at him. Using his left arm and leg to boost him towards As his right hand curled into a fist. Although, Alan had already prepared for the attack. Moving back to avoid the attack as the gwarian swung to the left. Alan quickly returned with an elbow to the side of the gwarian's face! Even if it was with his organic arm, the gwarian still shifted backwards, hissing in pain. Glaring at the G.L he rose both arms to defend an incoming punch from Alan's mechanical fist! However, the brutal strike broke his left arm. The gwarian forced himself to suppress a scream. Instead, he used that pain to fuel rage, without thinking and before Alan could throw another strike, the pirate smashed into Alan's face with a headbutt. Throwing the G.L off guard, stumbling back as he was blinded for a second.

Ignition: Unknown Criminal

The *shock trooper* spotted this from a distance but another distant pirate found her and began to fire at her location. Forcing her to concentrate on taking him down. Alan hastily ducked, barely missing an incoming kick from the pirate. He then threw two solid punches at his gut. Making the gwarian cough and step back. Using this moment to go on the offensive, Alan dashed forward with his mechanical hand out. Before the gwarian could even try to dodge, his face was suddenly grabbed by Alan! Covered by his mechanical hand as the pirate's head was smashed into the nearest tree. Being greeted by a savage crack! The pirate was suddenly limp as blood ran down the tree. Releasing the dead pirate's face, Alan quickly picked up his fallen *Hize* and began to fire at the remaining two nearby pirates. Each heavy shot tore through them as they both crashed onto the ground in a heap. Soon after, the union marines pushed up beside the G.L, including the *shock trooper*.

"Impressive work sir." She complemented, taking cover behind the tree beside Alan's. Alan only nodded,

"Any response on the teams you've sent to surround the pirates?" He asked, getting irritated at the sight of them continuing to flee. "Not yet, however, I'm sure they will complete their objective soon sir." She answered. "I'll report the moment they do." She added. "That'll have to do then." Alan sighed, "Keep your soldiers pushing after them, these little attacks shouldn't be slowing us down this much." He ordered. The *shock trooper* immediately pulled out her holo-watch, giving the order to move up. Watching the soldiers do exactly as ordered, Alan moved right behind them. The *shock trooper* tried to stick close to his side this time.

CHAPTER TWENTY THREE

Dusk threw one of the packages at the soldier. At first Kane thought he imagined it, but no, the yellow crate slammed right into the union marine's face plate. Staggering him as he dropped his rifle. Dusk ran full speed into him, knocking him on the ground. Before the soldier could actually react, Tarrus moved up and shot into the soldier's chest. Dusk turned back to the lykoi after picking up the package.

"Thanks for the assist." Tarrus smirked,

"Anytime." Three additional pirates moved in the direction that squad came from.

"That was from the right." Kane pointed out, starting to run again as the gunfire from behind became louder. Helix was close by, letting his weapons cool down. Dusk and Tarrus followed as well,

"You think they are trying to surround us even though we are moving?" he asked, Kane only raised a brow, answering the lykoi's question. He then gave a short, half laugh,

"Bastards." Kane wondered how pirates there were still alive. From the sounds of the fighting, he assumed there were still quite a few. But assumed those numbers were dwindling fast. Kane didn't exactly get a number count when the U.G.G first ambushed them. Though it definitely looked like a lot. More than they had available.

"Any idea how far Draz is from us?" Kane asked, sounding desperate. His only plan was to only push towards her location and hold off the U.G.G but they had brought far more troops than he had originally anticipated. Though he didn't know exactly what to expect in the first place. This was his first time trying to plan avoiding union soldiers trying to gun him down.

"Not close." Dusk replied simply, and that was enough for Kane. "At this rate, I estimate we have twenty minutes before our survival rates plummet."

Twenty minutes.

If Kane's heart wasn't pounding out of his chest before, it definitely was now.

"If Draz wants whatever the hell is in those damn boxes so badly, she better send someone quick." Tarrus said, gritting his teeth as he kept the heavy plasma shotgun tight in his hands.

"Well, I'd like to hope those chances remain high." Kane said, turning to Dusk to only see a grim expression on his digital face.

"Alright," Kane sighed, "What if we all regrouped? Fighting until she sends help?" He asked, ignoring Tarrus's confused face. "Would that at least buy us more time?" Dusk was silent for a couple seconds before answering,

Ignition: Unknown Criminal

"Yes. That would give us approximately thirty minutes." Before Tarrus could try to reject the idea, Kane turned to him,

"Tarrus, think you can relay the message?" The lykoi nodded, not even bothering to fight since time was short.

"Yes, but where can we meet?" He asked, not finding a very defensible location. Kane darted his head in all sides. Trying to find something, anything. However, he was only seeing the same thing as Tarrus, trees, bush and a few rocks scattered. Kane then pointed ahead, where two dead trees covered each side.

"There! That's our best bet for now!" Tarrus then brought his holo-watch up to his face. Giving a small prayer to himself that this crazy idea will work. "Everyone! This is Tarrus! Come meet at our location! Running isn't working! It'll only be a matter of time until we are surrounded! We must fight and hold them off! We are by the two dead trees straight ahead! Hurry! We'll cover you!" He shouted, ending the transmission, hiding behind the tree across from Kane. Both of them peeked to face the rear, where the brunt of the U.G.G forces were coming. A few squads and remains of pirates were already nearby when Tarrus made the call. In moments they moved in and set themselves up to the best of their abilities. Kane was grateful most of those with him had ranged weapons. He thought those that charged with melee weapons were insane, yet he didn't complain. He assumed that they managed to take down a few marines during their fight.

"So this is it?" One of the pirate's asked, a gwarian, she aimed her stolen union rifle at the rear as well. "We wait for death to approach?" Kane wanted to say something either comforting or inspiring for her. Anything to reassure she could survive this. But, he had nothing. He too was terrified for what was about to come their way. Though, he refused to simply stay silent.

"Yes," He started, which he received a few gasps from that in response. "Death, the U.G.G are coming. And I won't lie, we will be fighting them. For all we know, we are already surrounded. Now, we can only hope Draz will send help. If not, die here. But I won't be easy for them. " He continued, turning to face every pirate with him, alongside those that just got there. "I may not be a fighter like you, but I'll make damn sure I'll fight and struggle until they manage to put a bullet in my head." He said bluntly, sounding far darker than he expected. But the look on the gwarian changed, she became serious, maybe even angry. Not at him, but at those charging towards them. "Sounds perfect to me." She replied, putting the sight to her eye. Ready to pop the first marine she found. The others did similar moves, in all directions they prepared themselves for a fight. A fight no one was prepared to win. Regardless of that, they were ready as they could ever be. Behind the natural cover this planet provided and with stolen, possibly modified weapons, this was their last stand. Kane turned to his brothers in arms. Helix was right beside Kane, aiming his weapons at the rear as well. The little bot's screen was red. Most likely indicating he was in an attack mode. Dusk and Tarrus who were both staring intently at the rear. Dusk placed the packages on his back, which magnetically connected. One of the pirates spotted this and pulled out his pistol. "Hey Dusk! Take this!" He yelled, tossing the hand held weapon towards the anvol. Who swiftly turned around and took it. The pistol was something very standard, at most U.G.G police would use. Dusk didn't worry, as he cocked the pistol he knew he could still take down a few marines with this. Tarrus on the other hand wiggled his fingers on the grip of his *Vandal*. A sigh came out of him as he waited. Kane, he aimed his rifle at the rear, shaking a little. There was no shame in his apparent fear. He was still very new to combat, but he still planned on giving his all. At the very least he could see the G.L face to face. See the man who'd spent so much time, resources, soldiers and blood to finally get to him.

CHAPTER TWENTY FOUR

It didn't take long for the U.G.G forces to reach the city Draz had hid in. Most of the outposts they found had been abandoned. Fay assumed they were ordered to fall back to defend the city. Once they reached it, she believed her assumptions were correct. The pirates had both infantry mechs and even fighters waiting at the front of the city. The mechs, just like before, were rather impressive to Fay. They were either stolen from other factions or a mix of stolen parts to rehash a newly working machine. The number of them however was rather staggering. It seemed they had the same number as the force she was attacking with. Plus with air support. The major however, from what she can see, didn't seem fazed at all. The U.G.G officer scanned the defenses he'd need to break. Taking note as the pirates were yelling amongst each other as most began to point at his army. A plan of attack was forming in his head. He had made the correct formation for an attack like this. With his infantry, tanks and *Escorts* in the front, they should be able to punch right through their forces. And with the mechs along the sides and rear, they will be able to provide necessary support in the battle. Now, there was only one last thing he needed to do. Pulling up his holo-watch he began to speak.

Ignition: Unknown Criminal

"Begin the assault." With him in the front, he took out his pistol as he yelled with all of his might. Charging the pirates as the *Escorts* brought down their dome shields. The soldiers with him, Fay included, also began to yell. Moving towards the pirates at full speed as those in front began to fire their weapons.

Within their quickly made trenches and deployed portable cover, the pirates began to fire their various weapons as well. Though it hardly damaged the *Escort's* heavy shields as the infantry and tanks pushed forward.

Behind Fay, she heard one of the tanks fire a blast of lasers towards the pirates in front of her. The green laser exploded on impact. Eradicating those within the explosion. Others flew across the battlefield. Within seconds, Fay watched as the pirate mechs began to fire back as well. A few even began to stomp forward. Unloading lasers and missiles into the multiple shields from the *Escorts*. The pirates' mechs closest to the U.G.G forces didn't last long as both tanks and infantry began to target them. Releasing blasts of lasers at the towering mechs.

Tanks aimed for the cockpit and chest while the infantry worked on crippling their legs. Which seemed to be a perfect tactic as the pirate mechs were being either destroyed or toppled. However, soon enough, as the attack force met the pirates defenses, pirates began to run into the shields. Able to actually fight union marines under their shield. Marines stayed behind the tanks, using them to cover themselves from the incoming bullets and lasers from those that breached their *Escort's* shield. Fay and her squad ran behind the nearest tank as well, having to share it with two other squads as all of the soldiers fired their weapons at the pirates. Standing on the right of the armored vehicle, Fay aimed her rifle as she spotted a large group of pirates charging their location. The sergeant was the first to make the order,

"FIRE AT WILL!" He yelled, firing his weapon at full-auto at incoming scum. Fay and the other soldiers didn't hesitate after that. Pulling their triggers, they began to shoot down the pirates moving closer. It seemed most of them carried melee weapons. Not much of a surprise to Fay though. She doubted most of these pirates had much in their pockets to spend on weapons. Although, some did have rifles, pistols and even heavier weapons.

Behind the many that charged with blades were a few smaller groups of armed pirates. Fay moved back when a red laser fired in her direction. The shot smashed into a soldier behind her. A few others were gunned down as well as the ranged pirates continued to open fire within the shield.

Fay was tempted to get on her holo-watch and try to order the tank crew she was hiding behind for assistance, but when she noticed that their tanks were trying to keep incoming meches from moving in, she didn't bother. Instead, she waited for an opening to fire back at those pirate's. When she looked beside her, crouched, Axel seemed to have the same idea.

Though, it wasn't long before they both got their opening. Using it, Fay whipped around the tank, with her

Ignition: Unknown Criminal

rifle in three round bursts, she pulled the trigger to send a spray of bullets towards the first pirate she got her sight on. A lykoi pirate was given the dose. Having all three bullets rip through his upper torso. He dropped on the ground as Fay continued to fire the burst at the pirates. Axel, still crouch kept his weapon on full-auto as he shot down three pirates within seconds. Due to the lack of cover they had once they crossed into the shield. It became easier for the union marines to take down the pirates. Unfortunately for them, the majority of the pirates were already killed before they could fully realize their mistake. As the last pirate within the shield was shot down, the marines were about to move up. Until a destroyed pirate mech suddenly crashed down in front of them! Smashing onto the ground hard as the entire ground shook violently. A few soldiers fell back from the heavy rumbling along the ground! A thick fog of dust wafted over everyone! Creating a lack of vision for everyone. Though, Fay and the other soldiers by their tank stayed close to it as the large vehicle began to drive forward. It was hard to tell, but Fay was able to barely see the other soldiers starting to push up as well. Having to move around the collapsed mech, Fay kept her eyes forward as the dust began to clear.

"Fay! Watch out!" Axel shouted, jumping back. Fay didn't even question and instantly used all the power in her legs to launch herself backwards, narrowly avoiding the gigantic mechanical foot stomping down on the tank. Flattening it instantly as a *Colossus* suddenly appeared. The bulky, large bipedal, mech looked down at the scattering infantry as it not only destroyed their cover but their best line of defense against enemy mech. With the tank gone, it aimed both of it's laser cannons and began to fire upon the union marines.

Axel without warning or thinking, suddenly ran towards Fay as she was trying to run. He jumped right behind her as he was shot down by a series of lasers. Crashing on the ground, he died instantly. Looking back, through her helmet her eyes widened.

"NO!" She shouted. Watching what was once her last good friend she knew in this army die before her. She was tempted to stop. Turn and fight right there and avenge her best friend. Before she could do anything that foolish. A barrage of missiles slammed into the *Colossus*. Making the massive machine step back. However, before it could aim at the *Escort* it came from, the towering robot fired a second volley at the mech. Destroying it for good as it's upper half exploded. The legs soon fell backwards afterwards with a huge THUMP! Creating another round of brutal shaking! Once the mech was destroyed, Fay dashed towards Axel's body, which was covered in large scorch marks. He was completely still. Fay guessed he was gone the second he was shot by that monstrous machine, and the pirate piloting it.

"Axel?" She asked, sounding like a soft whimper. When she got no response she kneeled down. Quickly checking his pulse. Only to feel tears roll down her face when she felt nothing. The sergeant soon ran up to catch up to her.

Ignition: Unknown Criminal

"Axel! Fay!" He shouted, stopping right beside her. Watching as she gently removed his dog tags. She turned around in silence, answering the question for him. Bringing her helmet to face his, she offered the tags to him. The sergeant only softly shook his head.

"Keep them...I'm sorry." Was all he could say to her. Fay sighed, nodded gently before placing the tags in her pocket. The other marines were already pushing forward. Fay didn't need to hear the order from the sergeant to get moving, since the moment he began to catch up, she was right beside him. She reloaded her rifle and kept watch for any pirates that dared cross her path. As the anger however, began to seep in. She began to want to find one. So she could deal with the rage for losing another loved one within the week. Following the other marines, Fay aimed her rifle forward. Hearing the continuous sounds of combat all around her. She darted her head on both sides to find any possible pirates attempting to assault her or the other marines alongside with her. From what she can tell however, the U.G.G seemed to be winning this battle.

As both sides collided into each other, she noticed that there were far fewer remaining pirate mechs then U.G.G. That barely deterred them from fighting though. If anything, she guessed those that were remaining must be their best pilots on the field. She observed a pirate *Arc Sentry* dash side to side, easily dodging incoming fire from three U.G.G mechs. Then leaping forward, the *Arc Sentry* finished charging up it's weapons and began to unleash a wave of lasers towards the two closest meches. Two standard union *Nomads*. Medium sized, three legged mechs with square like bodies armed with standard heavy machine guns and a rail gun on top. Both of them were completely shredded by the laser fire as the one of the left exploded entirely. The other lost its right leg and toppled into an *Escort*. Smashing into the huge machine as the collision caused the robot to fall as well. Crushing a tank and a few squads of union marines. After delivering the devastating blow, the *Arc Sentry* used its boosters on its legs to jump back and allow its weapons to cool off. Pirate infantry and turret defenses attempted to protect their pilot. The U.G.G forces however, showed no signs of stopping, even after the blow. Fay looked to her right, seeing a row of tanks rolling towards the *Arc Sentry* and those trying to defend it. Opening fire, they shot massive lasers in its direction. Wanting to assist as well, Fay looked around for a better weapon. The sergeant noticed this and went back to her.

"What are you doing?" He asked, as they both heard the other squad's starting to fire at another group of pirates.

"We need to take those mechs down sir!" She said, pointing at the few but powerful and fast moving mechs firing down at the union infantry and tanks. The sergeant nodded,

"Alright." Looking around as well, he spotted a down squad of heavy union marines. Their *Bison* rocket launchers looked like they were still in good condition. Problem was there were pirates opening fire by their corpses!

Ignition: Unknown Criminal

"Over there!" He shouted, dashing behind a dismembered mech leg for cover, Fay moved in beside him, ducking from the incoming bullets. "We need to get past those pirates if we want any chance of getting those weapons!" The sergeant shouted. Seeing every other squad had their own battle to win at the moment. The two were on their own.

"You have your plasma grenade?" Fay asked, pulling her own out from one of her uniforms pouches.

"What are you thinking?" He asked, taking his out as well.

"Well, here, take mine." She said, handing over the hand-held explosive. Still unsure what she was thinking, he became hesitant to take it. "I think you're a better throw than me." She added, gesturing the plasma grenade. Finally grabbing the grenade he said,

"Alright corporal." Then, with his back against the destroyed mech leg, he looked over the corner, jerking himself back as a burst of lasers flew past him.

"Might need some cover." He ordered, looking back at her. Fay didn't even wait, with a full magazine in her rifle she turned around with a crouch and held the trigger down tightly. Sending a stream of bullets in the pirates direction. One of the pirates wasn't quick enough to hide and had her chest torn apart from the attack. The sergeant then whipped around the corner, standing right behind Fay as he ignited both grenades in his hands and hurled them with all of his strength. Watching the two balls of the death fly towards them, the pirates screamed and attempted to scramble, but Fay was ready for them. With her rifle aimed at the backs of the fleeing pirates, Fay easily shot each of them down with quick and viscous spray of bullets. The sergeant was soon in a full sprint to reach the *Bison's* laying on the ground. Fay was right beside him as they both picked up the large weapons. Finding the same *Arc Sentry* from before.

"There he is!" She shouted, checking the small screen on the side of the rocket launcher, indicating there were two rockets inside. Then both of them aligned themselves as the pirate mech was distracted by a standard union *Sentry*. During its battle, the rear of the *Arc Sentry* was shown to the pair!

"Fire!" the sergeant shouted! Both triggers were pulled as four rockets went flying towards the pirate mech! The *Arc Sentry* soon fell forwards after an explosion took out it's legs. Smashing cockpit first into the ground. The sergeant soon received a transmission from the pilot from the *Sentry*.

"Thanks for the assist!"

The sergeant nodded, "Your welcome, good luck out there." He then ended the call, moving up to Fay as they both dropped the rocket launchers.

"They're falling back." She said, her breath a little shaky from the mix of emotions. As the survivors fled into the city, Fay reached into her pocket and felt Axel's dog tags. This time, she managed to force herself not to cry. Though the sudden reminder was painful. However, she shot her head up when she heard several pirate ships suddenly leaving the city. *AA Mechs* were already starting to fire. Shooting most of them down but a few managed to slip by. The sergeant spotted it too, pulling out his holo-watch to inform the major.

CHAPTER
TWENTY FIVE

It seemed that less than a quarter of the pirates that Kane started with survived. When the U.G.G forces started to fire upon their position, there had been less than fifty that managed to reach him in time. Kane could only hope that the others were forced to fight elsewhere. If not, he began to worry what their chances were about too look like. Even so, every single fighter he saw at the moment continued to fight. So he planned on doing the same. As bullets and lasers chewed through the tree he hid behind, Kane flipped his rifle over and held the trigger down as he fired blindly to his left. Firing in full-auto until the weapons needed to cool down, which didn't take long as he pulled the weapon back and pressed the button to start cooling the plasma rifle. Though he couldn't tell exactly how close the union marines were. He would assume they were only gaining ground at this point.

"Kane Lons!" A voice suddenly shouted. Kane looked around, desperately trying to find who was calling his name. Though all the pirates, including Dusk and Tarrus were occupied fighting the soldiers that surrounded their position. Then, looking to his right, a pirate was shot in the face. The gunshot was loud, and close. Looking around for the attacker, Kane held his plasma rifle closely. Then, with hardly a second to react, a mechanical fist came smashing through what was once his cover. Attached to said arm was the cyborg G.L, Alan Dokes! Kane's eyes widened at the sight of him!

"G-G.L? So it is true!" Kane shouted, aiming his rifle at Alan. He couldn't believe it! The head of the entire U.G.G came to a world like this to kill him personally, for a lie! However, before he could try anything his rifle was shot out of his hand from the cyborg's *Hize*!

"Yes." Alan said coldly. Ripping his arm out of the tree. Holstering the *Hize*, he finally faced the traitor.

"To think Admiral Scone thought so highly of you." He spat, walking closer as he scanned the other pirates. Who were all too busy with his troops to even notice.

"You were once one of the best pilots we had under our belt. Now you used this talent to help our enemies!" He shouted, slamming his mechanical fist down. Completely obliterating the rifle Kane used to block the attack. Knocking him flat on the ground at such a rapid pace it punched the air out of him. Now in a panic, Kane smashed his left leg into Alan's gut. Making the G.L groan as he took a step back. Trying to get back to his feet, Kane didn't have time to avoid the incoming punch from he G.L. Even with his organic fist, Kane felt a sharp pain throughout the whole left side of his face. Although, he had no time to fully notice the pain as he quickly dogged to the right. Barely missing that metal fist punching past him. With the few seconds he had, he pushed the G.L back. Making Alan nearly trip over a tree root. As Alan tried to regain balance, Kane attempted to go on the offensive and prepared a heavy swing to the left. Aiming for as much of the soft side of Alan's face as he could. After a loud crack. Coming from both Alan's cheek and Kane's fist, the G.L stepped back further. Slamming his back into the tree he nearly destroyed. While Kane took a few steps back himself, shaking his hand.

"Ah, damn." He hissed in pain. Having enough with this cargo pilot, the G.L quickly, but recklessly pulled up his *Hize* and fired. The large bullet flew right into Kane's right shoulder. Blowing off the entire arm. Kane screamed at the top of his lungs in agonizing pain. Dropping down as he quickly started to bleed. Once Alan was back on his feet, he didn't get the chance to fire again as a cybel came flying in and crashed into his face. Pushing him back into the tree. Helix had finally fully charged his weapons again and began to unleash his firepower. The G.L jumped to the left. Avoiding some of the hot plasma, though even on his feet and running to the side. A few shots smashed into him. Causing him to yell as he tried to fire back. Getting behind a large boulder as his *shock troopers* moved at full speed to assist once they heard he was in danger. Three popped out of the large rock and began to fire. Forcing Helix to move back. Kane layed on the ground, currently in Dusk's lap as the anvol used his hand to stop the bleeding. The human only whimpered as he looked up.

"I-is this it?" Kane croaked to the anvol. "Is this when I die?" Dusk just looked down with a solemn expression. Unsure how to answer. The probability was high but he didn't exactly want to tell Kane that. So, instead, he kept quiet and added pressure. That was, until Tarrus ran over as well. With a few pirates covering him, he used all of the bandages he had to wrap Kane's arm. Which wasn't much, and the once white dressing became red very quickly, it was better than nothing.

"This is bad. Very bad." Tarrus said, seeing up to maybe ten pirates still standing while the marines and shock troopers only got closer!

"We fight." Kane mumbled. His eyes looked weakly at the three. "We fight. W-who…" He then slowly pointed up. Which all three looked as they saw a few ships move in. Fast. Tarrus eyes widened.

"Holy smokes! One of those is Draz's ship!" He shouted. Then, it happened so fast. One second they saw the ships coming in, the next they saw the enormous gwarian giantess jump down. Dusk held Kane a little tighter as they watched the grey figure get closer and closer. Before landing in front of them with massive THROOM! Violently shaking the ground as a few unlucky marines stood where she landed. At that moment, the shooting stopped. Everyone turned to face the gigantic being before them. Even the pirates were shocked at the sight of her. She wore no armor other than the light chest piece and the belt that holstered her weapons. Alan soon stepped out from his cover. Covered in a few scorch marks, he growled at the sight of her. Knowing this just made things complicated. Ignoring the attention she drew, she turned to Dusk.

"You sssaved the package?" she asked. To which the anvol gently released Kane to pull out both of them from his back. Bringing her head forward, she pulled out her holo-watch, when she heard the sounds of the transmission being answered, which took seconds, she spoke,

"The package is secured. Time to hold your end of the deal." There was a chuckle from her massive holo-watch before a male voice replied.

"Already repaying the favor as we speak." With that, the transmission was ended. A muffled and distant explosion was then heard. Everyone cranned their heads up to see the massive explosion in the sky. Alan was shocked at the sight.

"No…" There was only one thing he knew that could create such an enormous explosion. Bringing up his holo-watch, he attempted to call the capital ship. Though there was no response. With his emotion becoming a mix of shock and rage, he screamed in all of his might. Taking everyone off guard. "Attack! Take down this scum! Fight with me, my soldiers!" With his *shock troopers* making sure to stay close this time, he charged towards the pirates. The marines soon began to fire as well. Some even tried to attack Draz. Who only grinned at their ammunition merely bounced off her thick hide.

"Foolssss." she scoffed, pulling her giant laser pistols and began to fire at the marines. Completely disintegrating them with each shot. A few marines attempted to attack from behind. Only get stomped on if they were too close or were crushed by a swing from her wrecking ball of a tail.

`Alan continued to charge towards the pirates. Blowing a hole into one of the pirate's chest as he moved towards his target, Draz. Dusk spotted the G.L and the *shock troopers* moving in. Tarrus fired a blast from his shotgun. A wave of plasma moved towards Alan and his *shock troopers*. Those in the front were shot back into a smouldering pile. Helix couldn't do much himself as his weapons were still cooling off after his last attack. Kane, with what little energy he had left, pulled out Dusk's pistol. Having no idea how much ammo was left in it, he began to fire. Weakly pulling the trigger as fast as he could. The pitiful weapon did nothing to the *shock troopers* shields as they moved up.

Before the row could open fire on Tarrus, who was the first line of the defense at the moment, a drop pod suddenly landed in front of the shock troopers. Alan was surprised by the logo that was imprinted on the pod. "The Xhell Corporation?" He said surprised. At the same moment the pod opened, more pods began to land around the battle. CORC's began to pour out of the pod. A total of six from each pod. Corporate Operated Robotic Combaninant's or CORC's were the mainline soldiers and security forces used by the mega-corporation known as The Xhell Corporation. Holding a mix of rifles and SMGs, the CORC's immediately opened fire at the *shock troopers*. At first, it seemed manageable, though as more and more pods landed, the numbers CORC's soon became the size of a small army. Alan blasted as many of the CORC's as he could. Each shot tearing through the metal soldiers. The *shock troopers* fired as well. Though as the *shock troopers* started to fall, Alan started to notice how desperate the situation was really becoming.

Looking at Draz, she was mopping up the rest of the marines. Alan assumed he had maybe minutes. Clenching his mechanical fist, he sprinted towards the CORC's. Even if he lost this battle he still planned on taking Kane out. Flailing that metal fist of his, he sent the robotic soldiers flying back as he ran at maximum speed. His *Hize* was in his other hand. Tarrus watched in horror as the CORC's were being bulldozed by the G.L. Raising his *Vandal* up he braced himself for Alan to appear from the wall of robots. Then, to his left, a row of CORC's crumpled on the ground as the cyborg leaped towards Tarrus. The Lykoi yelled, trying to aim the shotgun up but the G.L was already coming down. Tarrus fell on his back, dropping the weapon.

Alan however, ignored the surprised lykoi, jumping past the pirate as he moved towards the distracted gwarian giantess. Dashing towards the rear, Alan dogged the incoming firepower from the pirates. Clenching his fist, he used all of his might to punch Draz's heel. She hissed in pain as a sudden shooting pain erupted from her heel. Turning around, she looked down to spot Alan aim his *Hize* at her face. Using the blue laser sight, Alan quickly aimed for her right eye before firing. Draz protected her face by swiftly bringing her hand to her face. Hissing, she removed her hand to spot the G.L jumping from her foot to her other legs knee. Thanks to that mechanical leg. To create additional pain for the giantess, Alan used all of his might to stomp down on her knee. Feeling a crack as she hissed again. Draz stepped back with her good leg as she dropped her massive laser pistols. Alan then aimed himself to make another jump. Although, he paused when Helix flew right in front of him. Alan's eyes widened when he spotted the fully charged EMP being fired at him.

"Ahh!" He screamed, feeling his mechanical parts seize. Losing balance, Alan fell back. A giant hand then reached down and grabbed the entire upper half of the G.L. A thumb crushed his cybernetic arm, Alan gave a muffled cry of pain. His legs bucked and kicked as Draz lifted her fist up. With Alan being crushed inside. Tarrus swallowed down hard, watching Alan being pulled up. His muffled screams became more faint. Draz ignored him as she looked around hearing silence, finally.

All of the U.G.G soldiers laid along the ground, dead. Looking behind her, the other ships landed to get the wounded, including Kane as Tarrus and Dusk carefully walked him over to one of the ships. With a sigh, seeing so little survivors, Draz was a little amazed how close she was to losing everything. Feeling the struggling within her hand, Draz was reminded of the little G.L she had. Looking down at her fist. Draz wanted to personally enjoy this moment. Make the man that almost took everything away from her suffer. But she couldn't, it will take weeks, possibly months to get everything back in order. So, with sudden pressure added within her grip, she felt Alan quickly crunch in her hand. His legs became limp as she felt the wiggling fade. Red blood oozed between her fingers. Taking a deep breathe she tossed the broken corpse on the ground.

"Finally." She muttered, wiping her hands on the grass before turning around to walk to her ship as the transports began to head back to the city. Her holo-watch went off. When Draz answered she was greeted with a holographic image of outside the city walls. The entire U.G.G attack force was destroyed. From the infantry to the mechs. Everything. All that stood was the Xhell Corporation mechs and CORC's which there seemed to be thousands.

"There you are." The same voice said, "Our deal is complete." Draz was impressed with the work,

"The same is within orbit? And outside of the planet?" She asked, wanting to make sure there was zero trace of the U.G.G still alive.

"All of the union forces have been eradicated. Just as promised." He replied calmly, yet slightly irritated he needed to assure her.

"Good. Enjoy your precious package then." She said, hanging up. Even though Xhell Corp's help was needed in the end, Draz was quite pissed off they managed to obtain the cargo she originally wanted to steal.

AI's like those could've been so useful.

Ignition: Unknown Criminal

Hissing under her breath, she got inside her ship, booted up the engines and began to make her way to the city.

CHAPTER TWENTY SIX

Kane woke up feeling light headed. Even with his head pounding he forced his sore eyes open. Helix beeped softly when he saw Kane. Typing,

"You're awake!"

Kane gave a tired chuckle as he looked at the hospital room he was laying in.

"Ah, you're awake." A doctor said, seeming a little cheerful. A male lykoi walked up to Kane, checking his vitals on several screens. "You seem to be recovering wonderfully. If all goes well you'll be out of here within a couple days." He said, soon going back to his data pad. "Oh, you have a couple people who'd like to see you." He added, opening the door with his free hand. Kale, Fesh, Ryko, Dusk and Tarrus walked in.

"Hey you're ok!" Kale shouted. Running over giving a soft and gentle hug. Which made Kane smile, after the day he had, the affection was more than needed. Fesh smiled, crossing her arms.

"Not bad, I was told you kicked some ass out there." She chuckled.

"That he did." Tarrus added, "After reviewing the footage from Helix, you handled yourself pretty well for being a cargo pilot." Ryko was silent, but he nodded with a serious smile on his face. Kane guessed everything he was gonna say was taken. Dusk brought his hand, showing that same digital smile on his face.

"I'd like to offer a high five for our fantastic job!" He said gleefully, well, as gleeful as a robot can get. Kane couldn't help but chuckle as he slapped his hand on Dusk's, receiving a surprisingly crisp high five.

"Thanks guys, I'm glad to see you all made it. Things got pretty intense back there." Before anyone could try to talk to their injured friend, a human walked in. Kane just barely noticed him. He looked like one of those servants for Draz.

"I'm sorry to interrupt everyone, but Draz has requested to meet with Mr. Lons as soon as possible." No one dared protest, for the obvious reason. So, saying their goodbyes, they left the room. When Kane sat up, he noticed the bandage covering the stump where his arm used to be.

Getting on his feet, he quickly placed the shoes that were given to him and followed the man to Draz. Helix was right beside Kane the entire time. Resting on his good shoulder as they moved within the city and the club. Then, once the massive doors opened, he saw her, Draz. Sitting in the same throne he saw her in before. When she spotted Kane walking in she placed the large data pad down and waved the servant to leave. After a bow, he did so immediately.

"Good to sssee you again Kane." She said with a smirk. "Ssorry about the arm. Those hand cannonsss pack quite a punch." Kane shrugged,

"It's alright." He said. The gwarian giantess only nodded. She then shifted her position as she leaned forward.

"Now, it'sss time to discussss a more permanent position for you." She started, beginning to think where to start before Kane began to talk,

"Well, I was thinking. Since you destroyed the man that forged the lie of me being a criminal and all. I was hoping to know what'll take to go ba-" Drazz interrupted him as she bellowed a deep chuckle.

"You really think the U.G.G will take you back? After all of thisss??" She asked, clearly showing sarcasm. Kane gulped, but tried to stand his ground.

"Yes...I mean-" Drazz was quick to get annoyed with him as she bluntly said,

"NO." Kane was taken back by how serious that sounded. He even found himself taking a few steps back as Draz stood up, her shadow looming over the little cargo pilot.

"After everything they lost today, you would be more than just some criminal Kane. You're a dead man. Heh, I mean, you helped kill the G.L!" She hissed. "Sssso, no, you won't be going back. Starting today, I own you Kane." She said, stepping closer. Kane gulped as the ground shook the step, the advisor prevented him from moving further back as Draz grinned.

Ignition: Unknown Criminal

"You made a wonderful day for me, in return I'll assign you with Nightwave. I expect great thingsss from you in the future." With that, the servants, alongside Helix, escorted Kane back to hospital, where he can think about everything during his adjustment.

Once the doors were closed and Draz was sure Kane was gone, she picked up her data pad again. A smirk came onto her face as she began to type a message:

Austin Patten

To: Eng Wares

From: Draz

Subject: Kane Arrangement

Date: 09/06/2466

To put things shortly, Kane had successfully joined me. Finally. Your space credits will be sent within the hour.

Draz

P.S.- I'm sorry for your losses on Gwars, if your people ever need refuge they are more than welcome on Jev.

Ignition: Unknown Criminal